ELYSIUM

GARDEN OF EVIL SERIES

EDEN – BOOK 1
EXODUS – BOOK 2
GENESIS – BOOK 3
ELYSIUM – BOOK 4

Shade Owens & Ash S-J
www.shadeowens.com

Edited by Nikki Busch
www.nikkibuschediting.co

RED RAVEN PUBLISHING

ISBN: 978-1-990271-09-0

PROLOGUE

With my head held high, I walk through the prayer room as countless women grovel at my feet. Some reach for my hands, while others crawl on their bellies and reach for my heels. Every few steps, I take a moment to touch a woman's face, reminding her of who I am.

They all behave the same when I touch them—fluttering eyelids, parted lips, and trembling hands. One woman with short red hair climbs over several bodies, her elbows digging into people's backs, simply to touch my pant leg.

As my heels tick throughout the cathedral space, I feel whole.

Ahead of me is my new throne—a chair custom made by my women. As I draw in nearer, I'm able to appreciate every inch of its magnificence—red velvet cushions with matching tufted buttons, a smooth hand-carved golden frame that glistens beneath the overhead lights, and a backrest so tall it makes me feel like royalty.

I climb up the marble stairs and step onto the pedestal platform, feeling like the queen that I am. The chair's wooden structure feels like silk against the tips of my fingers.

When I turn around, glassy eyes and dreamy grins greet me. They're prepared to do anything I ask of them... anything at all.

Slowly, I lower myself onto my new throne, lean my back against its velvet cushions, and cross my legs.

Finally, everything is as it should be.

CHAPTER 1 – LUCY

I storm through Elysium's Hub with warm tears streaming down my face.

If I don't do something about this now, I might lose my mind. How can I let her get away with what she's done? Eve killed my mom. She deserves to die. I walk fast, the steak knife I stole from the kitchen tucked inside my back pocket. I can feel its serrated blade scraping the back of my thigh with each step, but I don't care. All I imagine is how it's going to feel for Eve when I kill her the way she killed my mom.

I know I'm being stupid, and I'm definitely not acting like myself. To take a life? This isn't me. I would never want to hurt anyone. But I'm so overtaken with rage that I can't stop myself. All I see is red. Eve isn't my godmother. She's a monster. Killing her wouldn't be murder... Murder is when a human being kills another. Eve isn't human. She's evil, and she doesn't have a soul.

As the thoughts race through my mind, the rational side of me argues that I'll never get away with this. And even if I do get close enough to Eve... will I be able to put a knife in her? Will I be able to penetrate her skin and allow warm blood to soak my hand?

Suddenly, I think of the video footage projecting from my H-Cap. I see my mom's face as Eve slits her throat, and I'm filled with a blinding rage.

You're dead, Eve.

Word has it that Eve spends most of her time in her Monarch Suite on the twelfth floor, so that's where I'm going. I've been mulling this over for days, trying to convince myself that hurting Eve isn't the answer. But every night, I'm drawn back to my H-Cap, and for some sick reason, I feel the need to watch the video clip again—the one in which she kills my mom. Eve has no idea that I know about it. She's been so caught up trying to run Elysium that she hasn't paid any attention to me. That means she'll open the door for me. She won't suspect a thing.

As I storm through Elysium, I glance up at the cameras that are positioned throughout and wonder if anyone is watching. Will anyone see me enter Eve's room, only to leave covered in blood? Part of me hopes they will. Everyone deserves to know the kind of monster she is. Fury consumes me and I can't think straight. Once this is done, and once I've calmed down, my life will change forever. I'll probably spend the rest of it behind bars somewhere in Elysium. Either that, or Eve's crazy followers will kill me. But I don't care. I don't give a shit. After what she's done, she has to pay. It doesn't matter what happens to me. It'll be worth it.

This is for you, Mom.

For a split second, I imagine Mom telling me to stop. What would she say if she saw me like this? If she saw me scowling so hard that I barely resemble myself? Maybe she's here with me, trying to convince me that revenge isn't the answer. My rational mind tells me she's right; I'm not a murderer. I can't even crush insects. But it isn't my rational mind that's guiding me to Eve's room. It's my anger—a red, fiery ball of fury.

That's all I have left.

The elevator doors glide open as I walk toward them, and Nola steps out.

I don't even notice it's her until she says, "Honey, is everything all right?"

She must be referring to the hateful look on my face.

No, everything is not okay, and if you had been here for me these last few days, you'd know about it, you bitch.

I don't mean the last part. That's my rage talking. I still love Nola, even if Eve has managed to get inside her head.

"I'm fine," I lie, brushing past her.

She reaches for my shoulder, but I pull away violently.

"Sweetheart—" she tries, but I close the elevator doors.

From behind the glass doors, she watches me, petrified. Nola has never seen me this upset before. Admittedly, I flipped out on her when Emily was sick and I thought she might die, but this is different. There's a coldness in me I can't describe, and Nola must sense it.

Manually, I enter the twelfth floor on the

elevator's command panel. I don't bother using my Luminous Sphere to make the command. I turned it off. Something about it gives me the heebie-jeebies. I mean, with how advanced Elysium's technology is, couldn't our spheres be used to watch us? Sure, it's my key to everything in Elysium, but with how psychotic Eve is, she probably monitors us through them. Like how the government used to track and collect everyone's personal data through their smart devices before the war. It's the perfect monitoring system if you think about it.

So for now, I'll keep my sphere turned off and tucked away unless I need to get into my room. That's if I even make it back to my room after this. Maybe I'll be dead. Who knows? It doesn't matter. What matters is that no one figures out what I'm doing until *after* it's done. And if I can get away with it without anyone ever finding out, even better.

As the elevator floats up smoothly, Nola shrinks in size. She's always been like a mother to me, and to see me this enraged must have her worried. If I don't hurry, she might spill the news to Eve and tell her that I'm behaving peculiarly.

Don't worry, Nola. Eve won't be alive much longer to hear any of your status reports. And when she's dead, I'll forgive you for taking her side.

I feel a bit crazy having these thoughts, but I can't help it.

The elevator takes me up to the twelfth floor and the doors open in a whoosh, inviting me to exit. With clenched fists, I step out, my sneakers landing on solid marble.

I'm so close that I can smell Eve's perfume. Although it's likely all in my head, it's like I can smell her. I envision her face—smooth pale skin and piercing blue eyes—and wonder what she'll look like when all the life has left her body.

What's wrong with me? How could I think something so... evil?

And is this really happening? Am I going through with this? My heartbeat quickens and my palms get clammy. I can't back out now. I can't. I'm so close.

Fighting to steady my breath, I walk down the left corridor and take a right turn. It feels like the walls are caving and expanding with every breath I take. Adrenaline courses through me, and nothing feels real anymore.

I continue toward the Monarch Suite at the far back of the twelfth floor. No wonder Eve wanted this room—it's the most private space in Elysium. She's always been big on privacy, and now that I know what a monster she is, it all makes sense.

Who else has she killed?

Suddenly, the image of Vrin in her military attire flashes in my mind, and I'm taken back to a few nights ago, when Eve came barreling down Elysium, accusing Gabriel of having slain Vrin.

I breathe in so sharply my lungs ache. Could she have been the one responsible?

I shoot a glance at the overhead cameras, wondering if anyone is watching me. For a moment, I consider smiling. Is this what it feels like to *break*? To feel as though someone else has hijacked your body? Because that's exactly what it feels like... Like I'm not even me anymore.

If you are watching, I think, *try to stop me. You'll never catch me in time.*

Glaring at Eve's gold-encased nameplate on her door, I march straight ahead and raise a fist, prepared to knock. But a small blue light flashes in the corner of my eye, distracting me. It's the door's access panel—the same technology I have on the outside of my room that allows my Luminous Sphere to open the door. But why is it blue? It's never blue. It's either red when locked, or green when open.

Ignoring the light, I knock on Eve's door. It doesn't matter what color her access panel is—it's not like I plan on trying to break into her room. When Eve realizes I'm the one standing outside her bedroom, she'll welcome me inside with open arms.

With a trembling fist, I knock again, only louder this time.

Suddenly, footsteps echo from behind Eve's door. *Click. Click. Click.*

Any moment now, she'll open the door and be elated to see me. What she won't know is that I'll be waiting for her with a knife in my hand. I picture the knife in my pocket, and it feels hot against my leg.

As the clicking grows louder, I reach behind my back and pull the steak knife out of my pocket. I keep it hidden behind my back, its serrated teeth facing upward.

This isn't you, Lucy. You're acting like Eve.

This last thought only makes me more furious.

I'm nothing like Eve.

I regrip the knife behind my back when my palms

become sweaty. Eve's footsteps draw nearer to the door, and suddenly, the access panel flashes red.

Red? I swallow hard. Why is it red?

I've never seen it do that before.

I wait with clamped teeth and a pounding heart. Sweat drips down my forehead and my legs begin to tremble. Any second now, Eve will appear in the crack of her doorway, and I'll do what I came here for.

"What the fuck—" comes Eve's voice. "Lucy? Sweetheart, is that you? The door won't open."

She must be looking at me on her door camera.

Act *normal*, Lucy.

It takes everything in me to force a smile, making me feel even more psychotic, like Eve.

"Oh, that's weird," I say.

The door rattles as Eve slams her fists into it. "For fuck's sake. I'll have to call someone. Could we speak later?" she says. "I'd love nothing more than to spend some time with you."

Spend some time with me? Do you want to kill me, too? The way you did my mom? And the way you probably did Vrin? You psychotic bitch.

I clench my teeth, wanting to smash the door's access panel with the handle of my knife. How is this happening? I was so fucking close. I'm standing inches away from Eve, separated by a sheet of metal. Through flared nostrils, I sigh. "Um, yeah, that's fine. We can talk later."

My tone comes out a bit cold, but I can't help it. Although I can hide my anger, I'm not as talented as Eve.

"Okay, I'll talk to you later, Lucy. I look forward to

it.”

Rather than responding, I turn away and storm down the corridor, muttering to myself.

“This is bullshit. I was right fucking there.”

As I turn the corner, frigid arms tighten around my waist. I’m about to scream when a hand covers my mouth and someone whispers into my ear, “Shhh.”

CHAPTER 2 – EVE

I pace back and forth, wanting to tear my hair out.

If there's one thing I hate more than incompetence, it's feeling trapped. Not once has my door ever failed me, which leads me to believe human error is to blame. I'm the leader of Elysium. To be trapped like a prisoner is unacceptable.

I kick my couch, its leather sinking but not tearing. Clenching a fist, I say, "Call Trinity."

My Luminous Sphere floats up near my face, beeping wildly as if excited by being given a command. A digital trickling sound escapes its mini speakers until finally, Trinity's voice comes through.

"Trinity," she says.

"Trinity," I say, swallowing my rage, "I'm locked in my room—"

"What happened?" she asks.

The fright in her voice confirms to me that this is an isolated case, which means it was no accident. Trinity has been around for quite a long time. She was Vrin's right hand, after all, which means she's privy to information others are not.

I want to say, "How should I fucking know? The door won't open and it's your job to figure out why!"

but I don't. I must uphold a certain level of professionalism around Trinity. If I am to gain her loyalty the way Vrin did, she needs to feel valued and respected. Criticizing her won't help me in the long run.

"I don't know," I say. "The access panel is lighting up red."

"Sounds like an override," she says. She fidgets with something in the background, almost as if flipping through a paper notebook.

I'm about to question her on what she means by *override* when she adds, "Hang tight. I'm on it."

Hang tight? How does she expect me to *hang tight* when I'm forbidden from leaving my room? I inhale another deep breath, reminding myself that while I may not yet feel for Trinity the way I felt for Freyda, she shows promise. Perhaps with time, I'll learn to admire and appreciate her for who she is—not who I *wish* she were.

The fact that she worked alongside Vrin for so long means she's more than capable of maintaining control in Elysium. Some days, I consider reaching out to Freyda. Perhaps if I beg her to return by my side, she'll come back to me. But there's no use. I've lost her. She's fallen for the one man I despise more than anything—the man I condemned to a life behind bars to exonerate myself from Vrin's murder.

Someone had to take the blame, and he happened to be the most suitable candidate.

Now, all I have is Trinity, which means I need to be careful with her. If she's permitted to see my true colors, she may launch an investigation into Vrin's death.

Trinity ends the call and my Luminous Sphere descends back down onto my glass coffee table. I breathe in through my nostrils, feeling my lungs expand.

It calms me, but only briefly.

How long will I remain trapped inside this room?

"Fucking bullshit," I mutter to myself.

Surely, Trinity will have this sorted out momentarily, and whoever is responsible will be reprimanded for their ineptitude. I get back up, walking about mindlessly across my enormous room for what feels like hours until finally, Trinity's voice seeps through the cracks of my door.

"Eve?" she says.

"Trinity?" I say, rushing to the door. I place an ear against the cold metal. "Open door!"

Unfortunately, my command doesn't work. The light atop the switch lights up red and flickers the same way it did when Lucy stood on the other side. Does this mean my access is denied? Is this what Trinity meant by an override? Has someone revoked my access?

"Eve," she calls out again. "There appears to have been an error in the access system. Lucas Green is looking into the matter."

"Lucas," I mutter. I don't trust that boy at all. He's been spotted everywhere in Elysium with Lucy by his side. The two have grown seemingly... close.

"I'm sorry, what was that?" Trinity calls out.

I clear my throat loudly. "Nothing. Is the issue localized?"

She pauses, almost as if afraid to answer my question.

"Yes," she says at last. "There have been no other reports of access issues today."

I smirk, though not out of amusement, but out of anger. How convenient that only my door would lock. Who did this? And why would they want to keep me confined to my room? To distract me from a larger issue? I think of Zander, Elysium's second-in-command, who fought for power after Vrin's death. He may have been imprisoned, but surely, he has followers.

Is he the one behind this? Are they planning a coup?

This is precisely why I ordered that all male soldiers be stripped of their weapons. They can't be trusted. I knew Zander would try something. Maybe imprisonment was too lenient. I should have had him hung.

I catch myself hyperventilating at the thought and calm my breathing. Once I find the person responsible, I will punish them to the fullest extent.

"How long will this take?" I shout through the door.

"It shouldn't be long," she says. "He assured me he's on his way now. But Eve—"

She pauses, and I sense something is wrong. What could be worse than what's happening right now?

"We have a situation," she says.

You mean other than this nightmare?

This is precisely why they locked me up, isn't it? So that whoever is orchestrating this *situation* can do so without my involvement.

I press my face even harder against the metal until it hurts and the pain soothes me. "What is it?" I shout.

Trinity mumbles something so faintly that I squint, wondering if the pressure against my face has caused me to lose some hearing.

"I can't hear you!" I shout.

She raises her voice again. "Eve, I would much rather discuss this with you privately."

"Call Trinity," I command, and my Luminous Sphere comes zooming through the air before parking itself midair next to my face. It hovers silently, and its lights flicker as it makes contact with Trinity's sphere.

"I'm here," she says, her voice much clearer now. "But Eve, this isn't something I want to discuss through our spheres, or out here in the corridor. It's about Lucy, and it's urgent."

Lucy? Is she all right? Has she gotten herself into danger? But then, another thought crosses my mind. Maybe she's behind all of this... maybe she's the one to blame. I grind my teeth and pound a fist against my locked door. When Trinity doesn't react to my outburst, I say, "Trinity... I beg of you. Get me out of here, now."

"I'm sorry, Eve," she says. "But all we can do now is wait. I tried to remove the block myself, but I'm no engineer. Something is jammed on a deeper level of coding, and Lucas knows the system in and out."

Of course he does.

I pinch the bridge of my nose and breathe out slowly. "Tell me, Trinity... Is Lucy safe?"

Trinity hesitates, which leads me to believe that whatever information she's holding back isn't good.

Finally, she lets out a steady sigh. "It isn't Lucy I'm worried about, my queen."

I roll sideways until my back is flush against the door and smile up at the ceiling.

Queen.

Now that's something I could get used to.

"If Lucy is safe," I say, "then what could be so urgent?"

Trinity clears her throat next to her sphere, creating static on my end. "You might be in grave danger."

CHAPTER 3 – GABRIEL

The guard rattles her baton along the prison cell glass, smiling in the process. I can't say I'm surprised to know there's an entire prison down here. I couldn't say for sure where it's located, but it's somewhere in the basement.

No sunlight.

No fresh air.

Plain gray walls with high-tech cells that look like a bunch of glass houses.

It's so advanced that there isn't any need for guards, but I think this woman likes being here. Her hair, short and spiky, looks like it's standing up to give her a few more inches of height.

Every time she walks by someone's cell, she pulls her shoulders back as far as she can. It's like she's trying to look tough in front of the male prisoners.

I mean, it works. The woman's built like an ox. Her calves are the size of my arms and although I can't hear her steps through the glass, I'd be willing to bet they make a loud smacking sound every time they hit the concrete floor.

She goes around every hour, making sure we all remember who we are and why we're here. I say we, but I don't even know how many other prisoners are down here. Straight ahead is a row of about twenty cells, and there are more beside me. But something tells me this place is way bigger than it looks. I also can't help but wonder... is it all men in here?

I guess I shouldn't make assumptions. There could easily be women in here, too. But everything's soundproof. It's not like I can hear anyone. The guy straight in front of me looks like he's making a lot of noise, but all I see are his fists banging against the thick glass. His mouth, a gaping hole, keeps opening and closing in the middle of a dark face.

Now and again, I reach for my ear, thinking I've gone deaf. It's so damn quiet it's starting to freak me out. How long will I be in here? Is Freyda working on proving that I'm innocent? Because I sure as hell can't do it. I'm stuck. Helpless.

Eve can't get away with this.

Sitting down on my thin foam bed, I drop my head into my hands. I haven't slept since they locked me up. My eyes are dry and irritated and my nose is running. It's like they keep the temperature in here cold enough to make you uncomfortable.

Thankfully, I'm usually hotter than I am cold, so I'm doing okay. One guy straight ahead, though, looks like he's going through hell. He doesn't have a blanket, either. He shivers on his bed, his legs up against his chest, and keeps mouthing something like he's praying.

Although this is the first time I see Area 82's prison, I've heard about it numerous times before. This place is where they kept foreign criminals and terrorists... prisoners no one knew about. There's a torture chamber down here, too. Apparently, all the torturing down here is how the United States stopped a major terrorist attack from wiping out half our population.

Everyone called the torture chamber the OT... that's short for Operation Tank. I hated hearing about it from the guys. It turns out that the Tank is where some of the biggest international secrets were told... through torture.

Guys getting their balls shaved off with a cheese grater.

Prisoners being forced to stay alert with high doses of medication while their organs were carved out.

It's disgusting. But the list goes on... and on and on. It makes me sick to my stomach to think that human beings could be so cruel to one another, so I'd rather not think about it.

Vrin wouldn't have used the Tank, would she? She never looked the type. Besides, who would they be keeping prisoner down here, other than a few bad seeds? Being an asshole or breaking the law doesn't warrant torture. Staring at the two men across from me, I can't help but wonder what they did to get in here.

The dark-skinned one paces back and forth, his naked chest standing out from that pearl-white wall behind him. He's scrawny, too, but it doesn't look natural. Have they been starving him? Will they starve me?

The man pounds his fists again, causing the

slightest vibration to run along the glass. Does he seriously think he's going to convince anyone to let him out? Or is he simply blowing off steam?

The spiky-haired guard walks right past him without a care in the world. Clearly, she's used to his outbursts. But when she briefly glances his way, his features harden and he points at her. With his other hand, he slides a finger across his throat.

Shit. He shouldn't have done that.

With her back stiff as always, the woman reaches for something on her belt. The man seems to know what's coming. He raises his hands in submission and his face distorts. What the fuck was he thinking? That she, the prison guard, wouldn't do anything? You can tell by her body language that all she wants is to *do something*.

He steps backward and waves his hands in front of him. It's a gesture that says, No, *please don't do it*.

But it happens too fast for him to prepare himself. Without warning, his hair shoots straight up at the top of his head, and his entire body contracts. His pecs pop out like little balloons being blown into, and his veins surface across his entire body. His eyes, wild and hollow, stare at the ceiling as he convulses.

The guy's being electrocuted.

But from where?

Fuck.

Suddenly, the metal floor feels cold against my feet. I step backward and pull them up onto the bed with me.

The woman eventually lets go of whatever button it is she's pressing and the man falls to his knees, depleted. She throws her head back and forms a tiny hole with her mouth. I can't hear her, but I think she's whistling.

I glance around my cell, hoping to uncover what other booby traps might be hiding in here. And that's when I realize something... There are no cameras. Anywhere.

This is great.

Fucking great.

It doesn't even matter what Vrin believed in, or what Eve believes in now. They aren't down here. They don't control what happens. And the fact that there are no cameras to watch us, well... that only means whoever's running this place doesn't want anyone knowing they're watching us.

CHAPTER 4 – LUCY

I slap him in the chest over and over again.

"Why would you do this?" I cry.

Lucas flattens a hand over my mouth for the fourth time and bulges his honey-brown eyes at me, warning me that if I don't keep quiet, he will continue being forceful.

I breathe out hard through my nostrils, hot air bouncing off his fingers and back up into my face. He removes his hand and allows it to hover inches away from my mouth, prepared to slap it on again if I start reaming him out.

"If anyone finds us in here, we're done for," he whispers.

By *in here*, he's referring to the broom closet he so kindly forced me into.

"I almost had her," I hiss. I ball a fist, prepared to take another swing at him when he raises his palms in defense.

"I know," he says. "But I had to stop you, Lucy. This isn't you. And trust me when I say that as much as you want to hurt Eve, you would have regretted this for the rest of your life."

My throat swells, and all I want to do is hurt him.

I was so close to avenging my mom. How could he do this? As much as I want to stay angry with him, I can't. I've been angry for so long that I can no longer contain the hurt. I part my lips to say something, but nothing comes out. Instead, tears stream down my face and snot spills out of my nose.

"I-I-I was right there," I blubber.

He pulls me tight against his chest, and I don't resist. "It's okay," he breathes. "Lucy, I'm so sorry you're going through this. I can't even imagine what she's done to you. I'm also sorry to have been the one who got in your way, but I couldn't let you make the biggest mistake of your life."

I want to say, "It wasn't your choice to make," but I'm crying too hard to say anything. All I keep picturing is Eve's demonic face and my mom's angelic smile. I want my mom back. That's all I want.

I burst into another fit of tears again, slobber soaking his clean white shirt.

He doesn't seem bothered by it. With his hand, he cups my head and holds me tightly. "Shhh, it's okay."

If I weren't so upset, I'd be embarrassed by my emotional outburst. I don't like to cry in front of anyone, and now this guy I like is holding me in his arms as giant balls of snot come sliding out of my nostrils. I want to stop bawling, but I can't. Every time I try to talk, my throat hurts and more tears come spilling out.

He lets me cry it out until I come up for air, then tenderly cups my chin with his warm fingers. I blink away the moisture in my eyes as he elevates my face and makes eye contact with me.

For a moment, I feel a little bit less alone. I feel safe, understood, and most of all, cared for.

He's cautious. He's clearly afraid to say the wrong thing and have me break down again.

I stare at him without saying a word.

With his thumb, he wipes the tears away from underneath my eyes. "What you almost did could have cost you your life."

Suddenly, all of my hurt and sadness disappears, and I pull away, prepared to lash out at him again.

"My *life*?" I say. "What do you care about my life? My own godmother—"

I seal my lips before I get too angry again. How can I trust Lucas? I've just discovered that my godmother killed my mother. How can I be certain that Lucas isn't working with Eve? I'm not certain of anything anymore, and it's driving me crazy.

And then, something hits me.

How did Lucas know what I was *about* to do? I pull away and scowl at him. "Are you working with her?"

He pulls his face back and arches a brow. "With who? Lucy, you look exhausted—"

"Eve!" I shout.

He raises his palms again as if to say, *Hey, take it easy.*

"Lucy, what are you talking about?"

I'm an idiot. How did I not see this? Lucas was following me. That's how he knew what I was about to do. I can't believe I didn't recognize it. How could someone possibly care about me? Eve doesn't, and she'd do anything to keep an eye on me. What better way than to send a charming young guy my way?

That bitch.

Lucas suddenly grabs me by the wrists, shaking me from my neurotic trance. "Lucy, listen to me."

I tug hard, but he doesn't let go. He scowls at me, almost as if upset by my thoughts. How does he know what I was thinking?

"I don't know anything about your relationship with Eve," he says. "All I know is that she hurt you and you want revenge. I'm not working against you in any way, if that's what you think. I have a brain of my own, you know. I'm not anyone's puppet."

The last words come out sounding accusatory, and I immediately feel bad for making him out to be a bad guy.

"I get that you have trust issues," he says. "But I promise you that I'm on your side. I wasn't following you or keeping an eye on you. I like you, okay? Sometimes when I'm in the monitoring room, I like to see what you're up to. Only because I like you and I like to see your face, okay? If that bothers you, I won't do it anymore."

I stop trying to pull out of his grip, and when he senses my tension release, he lets me go.

"I like to know that you're safe," he says. "And happy."

I stare into his big brown eyes and find warmth. It's hard to imagine Lucas as a villain. He's done nothing but help me. Besides, what would he get out of following Eve's orders?

"You saw me in the cameras," I respond matter-of-factly.

He nods. "You seemed upset. I didn't mean to

watch you, Lucy. I needed to know you were okay."

A shy smile tugs at his lips.

I'm not sure whether to believe him or not.

He must sense my doubt; he reaches for my hand and gives me a warm embrace. "I never monitor the cameras in your room. I promise. This happened to be a fluke, and am I ever glad I was in the monitoring room this morning."

"Why do you even go in there?" I ask.

He stares at me like I'm missing the big picture. "Lucy, I still have a job to do. I control most of Elysium's electrical and HVAC systems. I was the one Vrin trusted to keep an eye on Elysium to ensure systems continue to function as intended and to make sure everyone remains safe. When issues occur, I write up incident reports."

"Do you get paid to do this?"

"Paid?" he says as if the idea of currency is something of the past.

"Yeah," I say. "Why do you do it? For fun?"

I realize I'm coming across as an interrogator, but I need answers. I need to know I can trust him.

"Well, yeah," he says. "That's how things work around here. You get a job and you contribute. It isn't money like in the old days, but it's a digital currency that gets uploaded into our spheres. Haven't you ever wondered why some people have nicer rooms than others? Or where all the children's toys come from?"

He's making sense and answering everything right, but I can't help my reluctance.

"Lucy, if I were plotting against you, do you honestly think I'd be sitting in a broom closet with you, risking my neck? I have one of the best-paying jobs in Elysium, and the authorities trust me. Why would I put that at risk if I didn't care about you?"

If he's trying to come across as a gentleman, it's working.

"So you jammed Eve's door to stop me from doing something stupid," I say.

"Yeah," he says. "I saw you pull a knife behind your back—I had to do something. I mean, you've been acting funny for days... I should have talked to you sooner, but you looked like you wanted to be left alone."

He's perceptive. I did want to be left alone, especially since I spent most nights watching the video footage, fantasizing about ways to get my revenge.

"But when I saw you pull that knife out, Lucy—" He doesn't finish the rest; he doesn't have to.

I know exactly what he's thinking, and I'm ashamed of what I've done. I feel even worse knowing that Lucas is the one who caught me doing it.

"I'm sure you have every reason to want her dead," he says. "I don't trust that woman either. But killing her wouldn't have solved anything. I did this for you, and if anyone ever finds out, I could lose everything. Especially since I'm supposed to be down there right now, fixing what I did."

"But I was so close," I say. "You shouldn't have interfered."

"Maybe one day, you'll thank me." He repositions himself, causing a cardboard box full of paper towels to topple over. "Until then, you can hate me all you like. If it means I stopped you from ruining your life, then I accept that."

Why is he being so nice? I want to be angry with him, but it's getting harder and harder.

"You know what?" I say. "I didn't need your help then, and I don't need your help now, either. I have my H-Cap. I have proof. All I have to do is show the people of Elysium what their oh-so-perfect leader is capable of."

He releases a long, calculated breath. "Can I tell you something?"

I'm getting tired of all the talking. All I want is to take Eve down. But there's a warmth in his eyes that makes it impossible for me to argue.

"When I was twelve, the military came barging into our home, demanding that my father join them. My dad wasn't the fighting type. He was a gentle giant. Sure, he could knock heads together to protect his family, but he didn't even like to crush insects and refused to set mousetraps. When he said no... they shot him in the face, right in front of me and my mom."

He turns away, clearly distraught by the memory. Overhead, the small light bulb sways from side to side, causing shadows to dance across his cheeks.

I reach for his shoulder. "I-I had no idea—"

"And when my mom ran to help him, they shot her, too."

I swallow hard, not knowing how to respond. Do I hold his hand? Hug him? For a moment, I forget my anger. I forget that he's the one responsible for getting in the way of my revenge.

"Lucas, I'm... I'm so sorry."

He shakes his head. "It's okay. I'm not telling you this for pity. I want you to know that... Well, I know what it's like. The anger you have. Eve hurt you. She hurt someone you love. I can see it in your eyes."

I clear my throat. "How did you manage your anger?"

He shrugs nonchalantly, his slobber-stained shirt moving up with his shoulders. "I spent years working toward my revenge."

Is this supposed to be a motivational pep talk? I thought he was trying to steer me away from avenging my mother, but now, I'm not so sure.

"How?" I ask.

"Slowly," he says. "I signed up to join the Black Marines' tech team. I learned everything I could from the inside."

How was *helping* the military a form of revenge?

He smirks, lost in his memories. "I screwed with them big-time. Fucked with their equipment and erased all traces of my involvement. Cut the power supplies to military towers. Jammed weapons midwar."

"What did that do?" I ask.

He slants his brows and stares at the wooden panels between us under his shoes. "People died. A lot of people. I thought it would make me feel better, but it didn't, because I never caught the people who killed my parents. And even if I had... I'm not sure it would have done anything."

"Why are you telling me this?" I ask. "How does this help me?"

He sighs. "Revenge won't make you feel any better, Lucy. It'll only make you feel awful once the storm settles. What you should chase after is justice. Killing Eve is revenge. Once it's done, you'll feel like a monster and she'll be out of her misery. I don't want that for you, Lucy. I don't want you to feel like a monster... to feel like me."

How could someone as amazing as Lucas feel like a monster? I want to tell him he's the most amazing person I've ever met, but I can't bring myself to say anything.

He raises his head, shadows disappearing from his cheeks. "Taking her down and exposing her for what she is... that's justice."

"And how am I supposed to do that?" I ask.

He leans forward, wrapping his arms around his folded legs. "You said you have proof on your H-Cap."

I pull my knees close against my chest and nod.

"Can I ask what happened?" he asks.

I'm afraid if I talk about it, I'll burst out crying again. But Lucas needs to know. Everyone does.

"She... she killed my mom."

Saying nothing, he slides across the dust-covered floor and positions himself next to me. His warmth radiates against my side, and he wraps a strong arm around my shoulders. Although I want to hate him and accuse him of being a bad guy, I can't. Deep down, I know one thing's for sure: Lucas is the only person I can trust.

I close my eyes, inhaling the crisp scent of his body wash the best I can through my stuffy nose.

"You have this proof on video?" he asks.

I nod, my forehead slippery against his stubbled chin.

"Then I have an idea."

I pull away to look at him. "What is it?"

He offers me a smug grin—one that has me wanting to reach for his face and kiss his lips.

"We broadcast your video across all of Elysium."

CHAPTER 5 – EVE

What's taking her so long? I dig my fingers into the leather of my sofa as my anxiety worsens. I've waited long enough, trapped inside this room. If Trinity doesn't get me out soon, I don't know what I'll do with myself. I thought Lucas was fixing this. How complicated is it to unlock a fucking door?

He doesn't want to unlock it, Eve. He wants you trapped so he can have Lucy all to himself.

From across the room, I spot my reflection—rounded shoulders, messy blond hair, and a scowl so prominent it looks as though someone glued prosthetics to my face. If anyone were monitoring me, one would easily think I'm arguing with someone else from across the room.

Eve, get a hold of yourself!

Closing my eyes, I suck in an overly long breath, my back cracking as my lungs expand. I feel calm, or at least, calmer than I did only seconds ago. I'm about to take another breath when a faint knock echoes throughout my room.

I immediately lunge over the coffee table and hurry to my door. "Trinity, is that you?"

"Yes," she says loudly. "The error has been fixed.

Go ahead and try to—"

"Open door," I command.

My Luminous Sphere hums faintly as it hovers through the air, and without delay, the control's light flashes a vivid green. A soft tick escapes the latch and my bedroom door creaks open.

Trinity stands before me, her black hair looking wet as it always does in that tight bun of hers. Her jaw, chiseled and square, gives her a menacing look that most children fear. She stares at me from behind dark, almost coal-black eyes, waiting for a command.

Trinity is a hardened version of Freyda. While Freyda may have served time on the police force, Trinity comes from a military background, and it's noticeable in the way she carries herself—straight back, swift movements, calm demeanor.

Across her black military vest is a blue and red badge I've seen before. It represents a division within the Black Marines. I'm surprised to see her still wearing her military uniform, considering women were banished from the military during the war.

Yet, she wears it proudly, as if the Black Marines were once the only home she ever knew. Although I can't say for certain, I imagine Trinity spent some time in Elysium *before* it became Elysium. It would explain her knowledge of this place.

She comes across as a strong silent type, *strong* being the key word. Several months ago, she tackled three grown men to the ground after they became verbally abusive toward Vrin. She uses her height and muscular build to her advantage, and they serve her well. What I love most about Trinity is that she never hesitates to take action during a time of crisis.

I sigh loudly, and it's as though a thousand pounds have been lifted off my chest. I want to throw my arms around Trinity and thank her for rescuing me, but I immediately remind myself that emotions are for the weak. She doesn't need to know to what extent this has affected me. It would be preferable that no one ever discover how badly I suffer from claustrophobia. Should someone ever get a hold of this information, they could easily use it against me.

"Thank you," I say, matter-of-factly. "Did you figure out what caused it?"

She runs a hand over her slick black hair and plants two veiny hands on her hips. "Unfortunately not."

Unfortunately not? How difficult is it to diagnose a system issue? Wasn't she trained for this? I know she's familiar with Elysium's infrastructure. Trinity often works in the basement. I'd get Nayma involved, but Nayma pegs me as the peacekeeping type. When I stripped Zander—along with every other man in Elysium—of their weapons, she didn't seem pleased. She stared at me with slanted brows and rigid lips, a look that told me she didn't approve of my methods. If she finds out that someone tried to hold me captive in my room, she might try to remind me that I've brought this upon myself, which may catapult me into a fit of rage.

Right now, all I have is Trinity.

"I want answers," I say coldly.

Averting her gaze to my white floor, she reminds me of a disobedient dog. She wants to please me despite not having the means to do so.

"Lucas says there was a short in the main control unit," she says.

I scoff. "A short? That's his explanation?"

She tries to mirror my expression. "Yeah, it doesn't make much sense." Crossing her arms over her padded chest, she blows air out of her tight lips. "I-I can try to run some tests myself if you'd like..."

"Yes," I cut her off. "I refuse to believe the system did this on its own. Find out who is responsible for this and bring them to me."

She clasps her hands together and bows her head, something I could get used to.

"You wanted to speak with me," I say, softening my voice. "Earlier, behind the door. You said—"

She looks behind her as if scouting the corridor for nearby spies.

"Come in," I order.

She walks in with long strides and her head held high despite my authoritative voice—confidence I admire. The second she's inside, I flick a finger toward my Luminous Sphere and say, "Close door."

My double doors click shut behind her, and I invite her to join me in the living room. She walks behind me, her military boots clacking against the floor, and sits on the white leather sofa opposite to me. Sighing, she leans forward, her back round and her elbows digging into her knees. When she bites her thin bottom lip, it becomes clear to me that whatever information she has, it isn't good.

"Is Lucy safe?" I ask.

She fidgets with her fingers, clearly

uncomfortable with this newly acquired information. I want to tell her to spit it out, but I remind myself to be kind to Trinity. She needs to feel safe, needs to trust me the way she trusted Vrin—with her life.

Slowly, I get up and sit next to her.

"Lucy's safe," she says.

I rest a hand on her knee. "Then what could possibly be the problem?" I offer her the sweetest smile I can conjure. "Whatever it is, we can find a solution."

Her dark eyes dart sideways and she sits up straight. "Lucy has information that could ultimately lead to the end of your rulership."

I rip my hand away and scowl at her. What is she talking about? How is that possible?

Slowly, she turns her head to the side and watches me carefully. "A video, Eve. One in which you murder someone."

I involuntarily gasp and press the tips of my fingers over my parted lips. How? And which murder is she referring to?

Calm down, Eve. This might be a trap.

Is she waiting to see how I react? Perhaps she's made this all up, and she's hoping to get a confession out of me. It would make sense, after all. She loved Vrin. Maybe this is her way of avenging her.

If I don't compose myself, Trinity might sense that I'm panicking on the inside, which would be an admission of guilt.

"What?" I say, playing coy. "I don't understand. Murder? That's preposterous."

"She has the video footage on an H-Cap," she says.

"Something she keeps in her room. I did as you asked, Eve. I've been monitoring Lucy closely, and this morning, when I reviewed last night's footage, I saw her watching the video."

"What video?" I sneer.

"It was in the White House," she says. "You slit some woman's throat. I assume Lucy—"

"And you're only telling me this now?"

She crinkles her nose at me. "I came up as soon as I saw the footage."

I suck in a sharp breath and stare straight ahead, my eyes so wide I feel as though I may never be able to close them again. I want to tear my skin off my body. I want to rip my hair out. I'm beyond infuriated. How could Lucy possibly have this information?

I'm too preoccupied with thoughts of losing everything I've worked for to even consider how Trinity might be perceiving all of this. Has she come here to arrest me? To make me pay for what I've done?

She wouldn't have told you privately if she wanted you punished.

Does this mean she wants to help me? Or, has she simply come to warn me before announcing my crime to the people of Elysium? I consider lashing out at her, but I need her on my side now more than ever.

So rather than release my anger, I allow tears to come streaming down my face. "I never meant to. It was an accident. Ophelia... She was my best friend."

I drop my face into my hands and bounce my shoulders to give off the impression of uncontrollable crying.

The moment Trinity touches my back, I open my eyes inside my palms. I've got her right where I want her.

"May I make a suggestion, Eve?"

Before removing my hands, I crinkle my eyes.

"If you would allow me, I can retrieve the H-Cap and dispose of it without anyone knowing."

I straighten my posture and stare at her. Is she offering to help me bury my secret? Why? What does she have to gain from this? She must sense my distrust. This time, she's the one to reach for my knee. I don't pull away. On the contrary, I appreciate the warm touch—a touch Freyda no longer offers me.

"I may have served Vrin," she says, "but I've always believed in you. Anything you've done... you've done for your women, and no matter what, I will always stand by your side."

I cup her face with my palm. "You are incredible."

Her cheeks darken to a rosy pink and she smiles as if being touched by a celebrity.

"I have access to all of Elysium, except for your room, of course. This means I can gain access to Lucy's room to retrieve her H-Cap. Once I have the item in my possession, I will destroy all evidence. I've already deleted the video footage from last night... The one in which she plays the footage."

I'm so elated I could kiss her.

"I could not ask for a better right hand," I say. "If you could do precisely that, I would be forever grateful."

She gets up in a hurry, but I reach for her hand and kiss it. "Thank you, Trinity."

She nods like a soldier. "Anything for you, my queen."

A sense of relief washes over me as she makes her way to my suite's door. But before she exits, I call her name out and she turns her head to the side.

"One last thing," I say. "The boy... Lucas. Has he been spending a lot of time with Lucy?"

"Yes," she says. "Every day."

I rub my chin, lost in thought. I can't separate them—that would only aggravate Lucy. Now that I know she's seen the video, I must approach this situation delicately.

When I remain silent, she says, "Is there something else you'd like me to do?"

My eyes shoot up at her. "As a matter of fact, yes. I want him reassigned to a different position. Having him work in the control room is far too dangerous."

A sly smirk tugs at the corner of her lips—one that tells me Trinity and I share the same ideals. "Consider it done, my queen."

CHAPTER 6 – FREYDA

Defying Eve is a stupid idea. Doing it behind her back might be even dumber. But what choice do I have? The man I love—

I clear my throat at the thoughts resonating in my mind. *Love?* Do I, in fact, love the guy? I barely know him. But when I think of Gabriel's face—his soft brown eyes, his thick and nicely shaped brows, and the stubble on his face that gives him a sexy, rugged look—I feel at home.

No matter the cost, I need to get him out. And the only way I can do that is by impersonating a guard. Is it risky? Extremely. But I sense that Gabriel is part of the key to taking Eve down. I don't know how to explain it. It's a gut feeling, and as an ex-cop, I always trust my gut.

There's a reason she put him behind bars. Is he a threat to her rulership?

If Eve finds out I'm behind this, she'll want me dead. I know her better than anyone, and I know what she's capable of. Having her in power will tear this place apart. Granted she's been through a lot, and I get why she hates men after everything that's happened. But her anger is misplaced. In her mind, all men are evil and deserve to die.

If I don't get Gabriel out... If we don't stand together against Eve's maniacal ways, I'm afraid of what this place will become. Men and women are already at each other's throats. Ever since Eve took over as leader of Elysium, women who once refrained from speaking their minds have been insulting men left and right. And on the other end of the spectrum, men are growing tired of being verbally abused. I don't blame them.

Eve spreads hatred like a deadly virus. Sometimes, part of me wonders if she does it on purpose, or if she's so caught up in her hatred that she doesn't realize the effect she has on people. Her views are those of an extremist, and although I tried my best to stand by her when she ruled over Eden, I never agreed with her views. I tried to help guide her, but it was no use. Eve's hatred will never go away.

People need to stand up to her, and for that to happen, we need Gabriel. We need to prove to the people of Elysium that Gabriel didn't kill Vrin, and their leader is the one responsible for her death. I don't yet have proof, but I know it in my heart.

The prison's main entry point beeps and the guard slips out. Immediately I lower my baseball cap and turn away to hide my face. This guard—a woman with short hair and a masculine way about her—comes out every day at precisely 12:05 to break for lunch.

Unlike other locked entry points in Elysium, the prison can't be accessed with a Luminous Sphere. The door opens with the scan of a good old access card, a system that was probably implemented by Vrin to ensure that if all system accesses were compromised, the prison wouldn't also be affected. It's smart, but it has its flaws.

Now, all I have to do is get my hands on her access card. Admittedly, I haven't exactly figured that part out yet, but I'm working on it.

I've spent the last few days scouting the place, learning the ins and outs. I've worked out every guard's schedule, and I've even drawn up a schedule outlining when they leave for their lunch breaks. The main guard—this short-haired woman who looks like she enjoys torturing people—runs the prison during the day. At night, a scrawny woman—with flat eyelids and a dull demeanor that makes her look like she hates her job more than she hates life—guards the prison. Although I can't see inside, I imagine the night guard spends most of her time reading a book. With those flat eyelids of hers, it wouldn't surprise me.

The good news is that only one guard at a time watches the prison. Why? This place has top-notch security. If anything, they're more of a deterrent. Elysium's technology does most of the work. I'm even willing to bet that if a cell is opened, someone gets notified regardless of whether the action was authorized by the guard. So getting inside the main prison is one thing, and I have no idea what to expect after that. I'll do my best to go unseen by the cameras, but Gabriel, well, he'll have to leave Elysium for good.

But I have a plan for that, too. As it turns out, Elysium's underground infrastructure is huge. I've managed to locate an entry point several miles from here, past the military vehicles. I may or may not have stolen restricted blueprints from Nayma's office last night.

So now, all I need to do is get that access card.

But how?

I have a few options: I can bump into her in a crowded space and pick her pocket—a skill I mastered in my younger days; I can corner her when she's alone and take it by force; or I can forget the card altogether and threaten the guard to release Gabriel.

The guard strolls past me, whistling a creepy tune that sounds like it's intended for a horror movie. All she's missing is a knife in her hand. If she had one, she'd likely play with it by throwing it into the air and catching it by the handle.

With my head bowed, I stare at her wide hips where the access card bounces around as she walks. Atop the card, a silver chip reflects a ray of light, and I suspect that if the card ends up at a certain distance away from its carrier, an alarm will go off. No one would be stupid enough to give a guard a physical access card without some backup security system. That means I'll have to act fast.

She's headed to the lunchroom, which is where she goes every day at this time.

Think, Freyda, think.

If she's going to the lunchroom, she'll be surrounded by countless bodies, and I might stand a chance of plucking the access card without getting caught. If I do get caught, it's game over, so I'd better get this right.

With a swing of my upper body, I launch myself

away from the cold wall and follow the prison guard.

CHAPTER 7 – LUCY

"I don't understand," I say, wanting to punch a hole in my bedroom wall. "It was right here."

I whip my arm toward my bed, and Lucas watches me with his puppy eyes. "Lucy, are you sure?"

Does he think I'm stupid? I wouldn't misplace something as important as my H-Cap. That thing means the world to me. I placed it under my pillow last night after watching the video as I've been doing every night for the last few days.

"Yes, I'm sure!" I say. "Someone must have come in here and stolen it."

He knits his brows and rubs his chin in thought. Without speaking, he inches closer to me, bends forward, and sits back on the edge of my bed. It makes a soft creaking sound, but this doesn't seem to distract him from his train of thought.

"If what you're saying is true—"

"I'm not a liar!" My abrupt voice makes him lean back a bit.

I'm ashamed of the way I'm behaving, but I can't help it. I'm freaking out. My H-Cap is the only thing I have that could take Eve down once and for all, and it's missing. Worse, all of my pictures are on there.

Pictures of my mom, pictures of me as a kid... Everything. My whole life. Maybe I'm the idiot for having left it in my room. I should have carried it on me at all times.

But I thought it would be safe in here. In Elysium, we're responsible for keeping our rooms clean. No one should be entering anyone else's room without permission. It's impossible. We all have specific accesses assigned to our spheres, which means I can't go opening up other people's doors, same as they can't open mine.

So what else am I supposed to think? The only plausible explanation is that someone broke into my room and stole it. And if they did, why would they do that? Why would they take my most prized possession from me?

My throat swells, but I fight back the tears until it feels like someone has me by the throat. It's painful and it wants to come out, but I refuse to start bawling again. Instead, I drop onto my bed next to Lucas. "Who has full access in Elysium? Eve? Maybe she came looking for me after I knocked on her door."

He doesn't seem convinced. "What would Eve want with your H-Cap? I can see her coming in here, but I can't see her taking your H-Cap from you. Unless—"

"Unless she turned it on and saw the video," I finish.

"Yeah." He nods. "Maybe. But she would have had to be snooping, and what reason would she have for that?"

He glares intently at the gray wall as if trying to

locate microscopic bugs on the paint. "I don't know Eve the way you do, but I know she's a smart woman. After all, she managed to make her way to the top. That means we have to assume we're dealing with someone extremely cautious. Sneaking into someone's room isn't exactly cautious."

Out of nowhere, he stops talking and aims his gaze at the ceiling. "We shouldn't be talking about this here."

I follow his eyes to a small black camera at the corner of my room.

He's right. If Eve is watching us, she could be listening in on our conversation. And if she doesn't know about the video, we'll give it away.

"Give me a hug," he says.

My mouth goes dry. A hug? When I don't move, he inches closer to me and pulls me in. I don't fight it. My entire body loosens, and I rest my head on his neck. For a moment, I'm calm and at ease.

In my ear, he whispers, "I saw you turn off your sphere after we entered your room. Keep doing that, okay? Mine's been off since this morning. Also, Elysium's cameras are all over the place, which means if Eve, or someone else, saw you *watching* your H-Cap, they know about the evidence. But we can't talk about it aloud anymore, okay? Not until we find a safe location."

Still mush in his arms, I say, "You told me you have access to the monitoring room. Did you see anyone else go in there?"

"Actually, yeah," he says. "I bumped into Trinity this morning, right before I ran up to stop you. Don't get me wrong, I'm not accusing anyone. I like Trinity a lot, but she's sort of like a loyal dog. She'll do anything for her master."

My heart pounds hard against his chest. "Maybe she's the one. She works for Eve now that Vrin's gone, so maybe she's doing her dirty work. Is there a way to look at past footage? Could we see who entered my room?"

To anyone watching, we must look like we've lost our minds. We hold on tight to each other, whispering.

"I can run an access scan downstairs. It'll give me a list of names along with a time stamp of everyone who accessed your room in the last twenty-four hours. But Lucy, it's okay. I also made—"

I pull away from his stubbly face. "Let's do that. I want to know who did this."

Without giving him the time to talk about this any more than necessary, I rush out of my room. Lucas follows me from behind with long strides as I rush across the Hub and toward the elevators. I realize I need him to get into the basement, but I know he'll keep up.

Around us, men and women go about their day, entirely oblivious that their precious leader is a cold-blooded murderer. But that's okay. The moment I get my H-Cap back, I'll expose Eve, along with whoever else is doing her evil bidding.

As we walk quickly, I imagine bumping into Eve. What would I say to her? Would I be able to control myself? Could I pretend that nothing is wrong and that all I want to do is spend time with her? Or would

I lunge straight for her throat? My heart races at the thought, and a tingling sensation extends down my arms and into my fingertips.

Anxiety. I hate this feeling. It descends into the pit of my stomach and I swallow hard to keep from throwing up.

"Lucy!" Lucas hisses.

I swing my head around to find him gawking at me with enormous eyes. He walks with tight fists swinging at his sides like he's upset that I'm making him jog. What's his problem? Why is he trying to slow me down?

Without saying a word, he stares upward with an exaggerated look on his face. He doesn't need to vocalize his thoughts for me to understand exactly what he's saying—I'm drawing unnecessary attention to us. What better way to alert Eve than to have me and Lucas running across the Hub? And running toward the basement, on top of it.

Wiping hair away from my sticky forehead, I slow my pace. It's hard, and it feels like I'm wasting time, but I have to act normal. Marching furiously toward the basement like my life depends on it isn't exactly normal.

Lucas catches up to me and walks at my side.

"How long will this scan take?" I ask.

I have to go about this with the assumption that Eve is onto us. And if my assumption is correct, that means we don't have much time. It's important I get my H-Cap back before Eve, or whoever else is responsible, deletes the footage.

Lucas walks up to the elevator glass doors as they

gracefully part. "Not long."

When a young girl with golden pigtails steps out, he steps aside like a gentleman. She smiles up at him, as does her mother, and Lucas smiles back. How does he do it? Even in a time of crisis, he remains polite and respectful. When the mother glances my way, I catch myself frowning, but I can't reverse it.

Likely sensing my rage, the mother instinctively wraps a protective arm around her little girl and leads her away from me. We step inside. He presses *Basement* on the control panel and enters a PIN on the flashing screen.

I've never seen him do that before. It must have something to do with him not wanting to use his sphere.

"How are you always so calm?" I ask.

Without looking at me, he shrugs a shoulder. "I wasn't always like this. But I had to learn to mask my emotions when I joined the military."

His gaze shifts to the floor. Lucas may not express his pain or hurt, but it's obvious that his past is still haunting him. And why wouldn't it be? He witnessed both of his parents' murders. I reach for his hand, and a weak smile tugs at his lips.

With his hand in mine, I feel like anything is possible. He makes me feel warm, safe, and strong all at the same time. The elevator descends swiftly into the basement, the Hub's natural light disappearing as we go deeper. I suck in a deep breath and slowly blow it out through my mouth, trying to mimic his calm demeanor.

We can do this.

I'm not exactly worried about being able to do it—Lucas is a mastermind when it comes to technology. What has me freaking out on the inside is whether we'll figure this all out without getting caught in the process. If Eve finds out what I'm up to—if she doesn't already know—she'll want me dead. Eve hates when anyone defies her. I can only imagine the kind of freak-out she'll have when she finds out her goddaughter is trying to expose her.

Maybe it'll feel a bit like finding out your godmother killed your mom.

I clench my teeth at the thought, my anxiety fading. Instead, anger builds inside me.

One way or another, Eve, I'll expose you for the monster you are.

The air is still and quiet as we enter the dimly lit basement. Up ahead, blue lights flicker and a static noise runs down the corridor. Above us, air vents blow out a cool breeze, tickling the top of my head.

"Lead the way," I whisper.

With his fingers still wrapped around mine, Lucas walks down the corridor and past the first room full of computers, wires, and gadgets. The room emits a blue hue, making it look like it leads into another dimension. He turns right, but the moment we round the corner, he stops abruptly and I bump into his back.

In front of Lucas stands a dark figure looming over us.

"Hi, Lucas."

A cold blue light flickers above her head, revealing a woman with slick black hair and features so sharp and pronounced she looks like a vampire.

"Um, Trinity," he says.

Trinity. Eve's guard dog.

She looks even scarier than I imagined. Unlike Freyda, this woman doesn't give off a warm, caring vibe. She appears heartless and robotic—the kind of woman who would kill anyone without question if requested by her master.

"We need repairs in the East Wing," she says. "You're being reassigned positions."

"Oh," Lucas says. He scratches the back of his head like he's caught trying to decide between arguing and running away. "I'll head over there in a few minutes. I have—"

"You'll head over there now," Trinity orders.

She crosses her arms over her black uniform, looking even more domineering than before. How are we supposed to get out of this one? The woman's a giant, first of all, and she looks like the kind of woman who'd break someone's arm if they tried to take a swing at her.

"But—" Lucas tries.

"Your access to the basement main control center is suspended until further notice," she says. The light flickers again, and it almost looks like she's smiling. It doesn't last, though, so I figure I'm imagining things. "You know how security protocol works in Elysium. You can't bring a civilian into a space like this."

Her eyes shift to me and my stomach sinks.

"What were you thinking?" she adds.

"She wasn't going to touch anything," Lucas says. "I had to grab—"

"The fact that you brought an unauthorized civilian into Elysium's control area proves to me that you aren't responsible enough to have this access. Now, get to the East Wing before I change my mind and strip you of that access, too."

Lucas smiles up at Trinity, and he looks so genuine that it freaks me out. "Of course," he says calmly. His tight grip around my hand, however, says otherwise. He squeezes so hard that I have to pry my fingers out of his clammy palms.

He turns and leads us back toward the elevators.

Behind us, Trinity takes a few steps around the corner, and although I don't look back at her, I can sense her watching us. I want to turn to Lucas, but I don't. We move in silence, and Lucas clenches his fists—an indistinct chafing sound followed by knuckles cracking.

The moment we enter the elevator, he hits the control panel and breathes in so deeply it's a wonder his ribs don't crack. The doors close with a swoosh and we ascend to the main floor. As we go up, natural light illuminates the top of his hair, his tight forehead, his knitted brows, and his pursed lips.

"You okay?" I ask.

But he doesn't respond. For the first time, Lucas looks angry, which means we're in deep trouble.

CHAPTER 8 – EVE

"I did as you requested," Trinity says, greeting me at the basement elevator. "I've destroyed the girl's H-Cap and reassigned Lucas to another position."

Girl? She makes Lucy sound like a stranger when, in reality, she's family.

"Lucy," I correct.

How dare she refer to my godchild as *the girl*?

Trinity is on your side, Eve.

Slowly, I unclench my fists and bow my head to express gratitude. "That is wonderful news, Trinity. I cannot thank you enough."

She nods briefly before turning away and leading me down the dimly lit corridor. Her leather boots clack against the concrete floor as she leads me toward the monitoring room. I've been down here a few times before, and although I know where the room is located, I much prefer being guided.

Without turning around, she says, "I believe assigning Lucas to another position was a smart move."

"What do you mean?" I ask.

She stops halfway down the corridor, turns slightly, and plants her hands on her hips. "Lucas came down here earlier with Lucy."

"He brought her down *here*?" I say. "He isn't allowed to do that—"

"I know," Trinity says. "Which is why I think the two of them are working together. I could be mistaken, but I'm willing to bet they've discovered that the H-Cap is missing. They likely came down here looking for it."

I stare at the intolerable blue light flickering above Trinity's head, wishing it would stop. "Did they say anything to you?"

Trinity shakes her head. "No. Lucas tried to go into the monitoring room, but I forbade it. I told him he'd lost his basement privileges for having brought a civilian into the control unit."

Smart woman.

"He was looking for something," she continues. "And when I refused to let him pass, this seemed to anger him. If you knew Lucas as well as I do, you'd know that Lucas never shows anger."

I'm torn between wanting to smile for being one step ahead of the weasel and wanting to rip his throat out for plotting against me.

"If you would allow me to find evidence," Trinity says, "we could have them both locked away for—"

"Not Lucy," I cut her off. "I don't want her harmed."

Trinity pulls her face back as if I've informed her that time travel is possible. She must think I'm lacking brain cells for wanting to protect someone who is clearly looking to take me down. But what she fails to understand is that Lucy and I share a relationship like no other. I cared for that child, and even though she's a teenager now, she will always be my little goddaughter.

As angry as I am with her for playing games behind my back, Lucy is all I have. And after what I've done to her mother, I can understand her anger.

I swallow hard at the thought, wishing I could wipe that horrid memory from my mind. It doesn't serve me, and the more I dwell on it, the more I lose focus of what truly matters—providing a haven for all of the women of Elysium. Ever since I've gained power, rumors of my extremist views have spread throughout Elysium like a plague.

These rumors, I assume, originate from the men. They're angry with me. They're infuriated that I stripped them all of their weapons, deeming them too dangerous to carry such things. They want revenge, which is why it's so important for me to prove to all of the women of Elysium that we are better off without men once and for all. This will take time, but I'm a patient woman so long as I get what I want.

"Lucy is my godchild," I say, "and she's easily persuaded. This boy is the one responsible for everything. He's planting ideas in her head and making me out to be a villain. I want you to do everything in your power to get rid of him."

Without saying a word, Trinity turns on her heels and leads me into the monitoring room—a room filled with screens of various sizes mounted to the back wall. She rolls a dusty leather chair out from underneath a table covered in empty cardboard boxes, metallic gadgets, and loose wires.

As much as I appreciate the usefulness of Elysium's monitoring room, I wish it were cleaner. As I pull the chair toward me, a wire falls to the floor and I recoil as if it were a snake.

"After they left," Trinity says, "I deleted the original footage of Lucy watching the video on her H-Cap. It would appear she's been analyzing the footage for several days. Regardless, the evidence is all gone, my queen."

Smiling, I lower myself into the chair. It feels filthy against my palms, and I squirm and wipe my palms on my pants. It's enough to make me want to peel my skin off.

"So Lucy knows what happened," I say, matter-of-factly.

Trinity doesn't say anything—she doesn't have to. Everything makes perfect sense now. Lucy knows I killed her mother, which is likely why she came to my door. But what was she planning? Did she want to confront me? Or, was she planning an attack? I've never pegged Lucy as the vengeful type, but grief makes one capable of doing many things.

"How did she remain so calm this morning?" I ask. "I spoke with her through the door—"

Trinity must be reading my thoughts. She spins around so fast a cool breeze sweeps through the dimly lit monitoring room. With a hunched posture, she types something on an illuminated screen. "What time did you say it was when Lucy came to your door?"

I hesitate, not wanting to incriminate Lucy. But I need to know if she was plotting something that might pose a risk to my well-being. What if she and Lucas were plotting against me? What if she came up to get revenge for her mother?

I don't want to believe it, but I have to consider every possibility. Lucy has always been a highly intelligent child. I remember catching her listening in on conversations between her mother and me, and not once did her mother notice.

If Lucy wants something, she knows how to pursue it.

"1:53," I say.

Trinity turns to her computer and swipes her fingers back and forth through the air, navigating the files. I haven't the slightest clue what she's doing, but she moves as if she's been working with computers for years. As she searches, I turn my attention to the monitoring screens on the back wall and watch my people through the eyes of Elysium's cameras. Masses of women stroll through the halls of Elysium, some mindlessly wandering and others walking briskly. They disappear from one view, only to reappear in another. For the most part, the halls and corridors are clear of children, which I am happy to see. Vrin may have encouraged my people to take additional time before integrating into Elysium's education system, but I never believed this was the best approach for a young child's mind. Our society requires educated individuals, and education cannot be overlooked.

"This doesn't make any sense," Trinity mutters.

I turn away from the cameras, my chair rolling slightly across the hard gray floor. With my chin resting between my thumb and index finger, I glare in

Trinity's general direction. "What doesn't?"

"That time slot," she says. She fidgets with something again, her head furiously moving from side to side as she inspects every inch of her screen. "There's nothing there. Are you sure that was the right time?"

"I'm certain of it," I say.

Trinity mumbles something and scratches the back of her head. "The file is missing entirely for an approximate duration of six minutes. Across several cameras, too."

I jump up and my chair rolls away behind me. "What are you saying, Trinity? Where is the footage?"

Steadily, she straightens her rounded back and turns to me. "Lucas must have deleted the footage of Lucy going to your room."

People only delete footage when there's something worth hiding—it doesn't take a genius to know that.

"Is there a backup?"

She shakes her head. "He wiped it clean. The kid knows what he's doing."

Son of a bitch.

"What was Lucy planning?" I ask, more so to myself than to Trinity.

"It's obvious, isn't it?" Trinity says. "She must have been coming to confront you about it. Either that, or—"

"To hurt me," I say.

Although I don't want to admit it aloud, I must. Trinity needs to be aware that my life might be in danger. She doesn't respond and instead watches me as I grit my teeth and move toward the screens, searching them frantically to find Lucy.

"There she is," I breathe.

She's walking down a hallway with Lucas by her side. She seems upset—they both do. "I want eyes on Lucy and the boy at all times."

"I'll do my best," Trinity says.

What is that supposed to mean? Her best? When I demand something, I expect it to be completed without error. To do one's best insinuates there is room for error, which I will not tolerate.

She must sense my anger. Immediately, she bows her head and adds, "It will prove slightly difficult to watch them at all times, Eve. Both the boy and the girl have turned off their Luminous Spheres."

Luminous Spheres? What does this have to do with monitoring them? My thoughts must be all over my face. She steps toward me and clears her throat.

"The technology is primarily used for accessing certain points within Elysium," she says. "It records all traces of any access or action, such as the use of the elevators and room entries." She rubs her chin in thought. "Lucy and Lucas only seem to turn theirs on to access their rooms. There's no trace of them using the elevators, which means they must know about its monitoring functionality."

"Monitoring?" I ask. "Are you telling me there are cameras in these things?"

I swat at my floating Luminous Sphere, at once feeling watched. It buzzes a few times before returning to my side. No one bothered to tell me that as long as I allow my Luminous Sphere to follow me, I have no privacy? My stomach sinks.

Vrin.

Her murder.

I had my Luminous Sphere on me at the time. Does this mean proof of the murder exists?

"Are you all right, Eve?"

I force a sweet smile as a droplet of sweat drips down between my eyebrows. "How does it work, exactly? Is everything recorded?"

"Not quite," she says, and I can breathe again. "You have to hijack into the Sphere's programming. This allows you to access the Luminous Sphere's sensors—which are small cameras—as well as its microphone. I tried to get eyes and ears on the children this morning, and that's when I realized I had no access... That they'd turned them off."

I move closer to the monitoring screens, watching Lucy and Lucas move from one screen to another. Where are they going? What are they planning? I tap my finger on my chin, lost in thought. "Trinity, is there a way to disable the power button on these spheres?"

She seems intrigued by my question, almost as if it's something she's considered before but never received the approval to look into it.

"Anything is possible," she says. "I could isolate Lucy's software and change her programming."

"Will she notice?" I ask.

"Not if I do this right," Trinity says. She whistles, her Luminous Sphere appearing at her side like an obedient fairy. With her thumb and index finger, she grabs the small silver ball and holds it in front of her.

"The only indication of power is its blue lights. Theoretically, I could program her sphere to turn off the power light when she attempts to turn off her sphere. In other words, it will never truly be powered down. Instead, all she'll be doing is turning off the light."

Theoretically?

"Can you do this or not, Trinity?"

She interlocks her fingers in front of her belly. "Yes."

Smiling, I turn to the monitors. "We'll have eyes and ears on her at all times, and she'll have no idea she's being watched." I hold back an excited laugh. "Do it."

CHAPTER 9 – GABRIEL

The guard bends forward with an evil twinkle in her eye. Honestly, you'd think she specifically asked for this position. She wants to be down here, working with prisoners and getting some sick pleasure out of it.

"Rice and breadcrumbs," she says, her maniacal grin making her look like the Cheshire cat.

She pushes the plate of mushy food through the small window of my cell.

I don't want the food, but I know if I don't reach for it, she'll do something awful to me. She always does when I don't obey or do what's expected of me. I stare into her dark beady eyes, wondering if she even has a soul. Part of me thinks she's *hoping* I don't reach for the plate. Because then she'll get to do whatever she wants to me.

Reluctantly, I stand up and make my way over to the small window. She watches me like a spider waiting for a fly to land in its web. When I reach for the plate, that wicked smile of hers gets even wider, splitting her face in half.

What the hell did she do this time? Yesterday, she gave me a slice of bread with a dead fly on it. And she does this to every prisoner in here. She puts shit in our food and watches us eat it. The woman's fucking sick in the head, maybe even sicker than Eve.

Since I've been here, which has only been a few days, I've probably lost about five pounds. She's only giving me one meal per day. I don't know her name, so I call her Medusa. Her salt-and-pepper hair, short and spiky, might not look like snakes, but it suits her evil persona. And the reason I chose Medusa over any other villain is that every time she looks inside a prisoner's cell, they freeze. Why wouldn't they? She always has some sick punishment up her sleeve. Everyone's terrified of her.

As I pull the plate up to my nose, I sense her watching me. With one eye closed, I peek at the plate in my palms, suddenly losing my appetite. White rice lies messily across the plate. There's no seasoning, salt, or anything, and on top of the biggest pile are little globs of snot.

My eyes dart up at her, and she lets out a sadistic laugh that sounds more like the grunt of a cavewoman. Her grunting amounts to full-blown laughter, and she holds her belly as if trying to keep it from imploding. The small window clicks shut as she straightens her posture, and the sound of her laughter disappears instantaneously. When I don't take a bite, it's obvious she's infuriated. She watches me like an animal on the verge of pouncing. Then, she wraps a fist around an invisible spoon and starts scooping air into her mouth.

That's a translation for *Eat up, buttercup*.

I'd rather get a beating than eat this shit.

Yesterday, when I refused to eat the fly on the bread, she electrocuted me through the floor. More than once, too.

Today, I decide to be proactive. I rush to my bed and hop on, removing my feet from the metal floor under me. But the second I do, her sharp, overplucked eyebrows come close together as if I've insulted her.

Oh, God.

If she can't electrocute me, what the hell else is she planning? Gagging, I reach for my spoon and scoop up some rice. She's waiting. At the center of the spoon is a small glob of mucus with a string of blood clinging on for dear life.

I gag again.

Fuck.

I can't do this.

Fuck this.

I'd rather be electrocuted, cut, or beaten.

Knowing she's about to torture me, I toss the bowl across my cell and straight into the toilet. It makes a loud clanging sound throughout my room as grains of rice fly all over the place.

Later, after she's had her fun with me, she'll make me clean my cell by collecting every individual grain with a pair of plastic tweezers. But I don't give a shit.

Suddenly, an explosive sound fills my room. It's like a siren, only constant and so loud that I slap my hands over my ears, feeling like my head might burst into a thousand pieces. But even that isn't enough to block it out.

I push harder on each ear as pain radiates into my

head. The sound is so loud that its vibrations travel into my goddamn teeth.

Fuck, this hurts.

I squeeze my head until my arms go numb. Baring my teeth, I desperately look through the glass in search of Medusa. How long will she keep this going? She has to stop. She has to.

With her bulbous nose pointed upward, she leers down at me. In her hand is a metal gadget and at the center, a big red button. She keeps her white thumb pressed down hard on it.

Please, make it stop.

But she doesn't stop.

"Stop!" I shout. "Just stop it!"

I can't even hear my voice. Instead, my vocal cords become raw the more I scream.

Medusa throws her head back and laughs. Behind her, other prisoners bash their fists on the glass of their cells, trying to get her to let go of the button. I get the feeling they've gone through this before and wouldn't wish it on anyone else.

"Stop!" I shout again.

But the sound doesn't stop.

Raising her chin into the air, she walks away, her head held so high the spikes of her hair point backward.

I try to yell out again, but a sharp pain radiates in the back of my throat and I fall back onto my bed.

* * * * *

I can't tell if I'm asleep or dead.

I blink hard, trying to regain focus on my surroundings. Something warm suddenly trickles down my jawline. I reach for it, the wet fluid coating the tips of my fingers.

What is that? Blood?

I pull my fingers away to find them covered in a red liquid.

That bitch perforated my fucking eardrums.

Instinctively, I reach for the other side. There's no blood, but I can't even hear my fingers rubbing against the skin on my face or my beard. Why can't I hear anything? I snap my fingers in the air.

Nothing.

I'm about to freak out when I spot something in the corner of my eye.

At the end of my bed is a woman dressed in black with a ball cap shadowing her face.

I jump backward, my head hitting the wall behind me. "What the fuck?" I say, though I can't hear my own words.

Her mouth moves, but I can't catch what she's saying. Who is this woman and how did she get inside my cell? I peer behind her to spot my prison mates smashing their fists against their Plexiglass barriers.

Does this mean I'm not imagining things? Is there someone standing in my cell?

I rub my eyes and stretch my jaw, hoping something might pop and cause my hearing to return. But nothing happens. I squint, trying to make sense of what I'm seeing, when the woman raises her chin until the shadows on her face disappear.

Freyda?

No, it can't be.

What the hell is she doing here? I'm hallucinating.

I blink so hard this time that it hurts the back of my eyes. What did Medusa give me? She must have drugged me after the siren. Or... did she poison me? I wouldn't put it past her. I wave a hand in front of my face, expecting it to look green, or deformed, or something... but it doesn't.

It's just my hand. I'm still me. I'm not hallucinating. Aside from being deaf, everything else feels normal.

What the fuck is going on here?

"Freyda?" I shout.

My voice sounds faint, almost like I'm wearing noise-canceling headphones. She scowls at me and slaps a finger over her mouth, warning me to keep it down.

"What are you doing here?" I say.

She takes a step forward and reaches for my hand.

I hesitate. What if this is a trap? What if Medusa has a way of creating projections? With how advanced technology is around here, it wouldn't surprise me.

She says something again, but I can't hear a word. She looks panicked, like she's trying to get me to hurry up. That's when I notice something. Behind her, my cell's glass door is wide open.

If she's real, does this mean she's breaking me out of prison?

I frown at the thought, holding back anger. Why would she do something so stupid? She'll either get herself locked up or banished from Elysium. And for what? To save me? Why?

When I don't move, she marches straight for me, grabs me firmly around the wrist, and starts walking toward the open door. But I don't budge, which causes her to stumble backward. Her perfectly shaped brows meet in the middle of her forehead and her lips open and close. With a stiff finger in my face, she mouths something else, and although I can't hear her, I know she's saying something along the lines of, "You'd better get your ass up now."

Yep. That's Freyda all right.

Holy shit. If this is real, it means we don't have much time before Medusa or the night guard returns. I have no idea whether it's day or night at this point.

"Why would you do this?" I say, trying to control the volume of my voice.

She answers me, but I can't make out what she's saying. By the frustrated look on her face, I assume she's finding all sorts of ways to call me an idiot. She says something else, this time articulating every vowel and syllable, and I somehow make it out: "We have to go, now."

I stand up to follow her, and right before we exit my cell, she pulls from her pocket a crumpled black ball cap similar to hers and hands it to me. I unfold it and slip it over my head.

Is this happening? Am I seriously breaking out of Elysium's prison? We jog through the large prison toward the back door. As I run past other prisoners, I can't help but feel sorry for them. Some stand close to the glass with their palms flat against their glass barriers while others pound their fists, spewing words that will never leave their cells.

With my head held low, I stay close to Freyda.

"I don't get it," I whisper. "How did you get in

here? Security couldn't have been easy."

She gives me a sly look that says, *Are you doubting me?*

She mouths something for a while this time, likely explaining to me every detail of her plan, but I can't understand any of it. Whatever it is, I'm sure she's thought it out.

She then turns away and blasts through the back door. I follow her out, natural light flooding the dark prison as we step onto lush green grass.

CHAPTER 10 – LUCY

This doesn't make any sense.

Why would Trinity reassign Lucas? She knows something, doesn't she? And if Trinity knows something, does that mean Eve is on to me? On to us? For her to punish Lucas must mean she knows we've been spending time together. Either that, or she doesn't want Lucas having access to the monitoring room. If she knows that I know about my mom's murder, she'll take every precaution necessary, and that starts by ensuring we have zero power.

Inconspicuously, I glance up at Elysium's cameras, wondering if Eve is watching me this very second.

"This is bullshit," Lucas says.

I'm too stupefied by his anger to respond.

"Listen, Lucy, I'm sorry about this. I hoped that if I got down there, I could—"

Abigail suddenly appears in front of me with bright red ears, rosy freckled cheeks, and parted lips. It's a look that tells me she has a lot to say—even more than usual. Before I can tell her to calm down and tell me what's going on, she shouts, "It's Tommy!"

Who's Tommy?

She makes some exaggerated hand gestures in the air. "I didn't know where else to go. I can't find Mrs. Moretti anywhere. They won't stop, Lucy. I tried to tell them to leave him alone. He didn't even do anything. They started—"

"Abigail, slow down," I say.

Two days ago, Abigail insisted she start school before it became compulsory for us Eden kids. Something about not wanting her brain to turn to mush. And now there's already trouble stirring. Maybe this was why Vrin didn't want us integrating with the Elysium kids right away.

She keeps going on about how *he didn't do anything*, and every time she says that she throws her arms in the air and nearly hits Lucas in the face. So I grip her firmly by the shoulders and give her a good shake. Emily comes running toward us, panting to catch her breath.

"What's going on?" Emily says. "I heard kids screaming—"

"It's Tommy!" Abigail says, her voice jumping an octave.

"Abigail," I say, squeezing her shoulders, "you need to tell me what's going on. Calm down and tell us, okay?"

She nods so fast her freckles seem to blend together. "The girls in the class next to mine are hurting Tommy. Mrs. Moretti left for a few minutes—"

"Who's Tommy?" Emily asks.

I swing around and shoot her a glare—a look that says, *Does that matter right now?*

Then, I refocus my attention on Abigail. "Take us there."

I give Lucas an apologetic look, but all he does is smirk and shake a hand as if to say, *It's no trouble at all. Do what you gotta do and I'll catch up with you later.*

Abigail turns on her heels and darts down the hall, her shoes squeaking against the tiled floor. Her hair, a big orange fuzzball that resembles a kid's craft project, bounces as she races across the Hub and toward school. Or, as the people of Elysium call it, the NWE Institution. It stands for New World Education.

It's located in the South Wing of Elysium and has well over twenty classrooms all on the same floor. No bell ever rings from the school, which I like—instead, kids are taught for four hours per day and that's it. Instead of a lunch break, they have short breaks in between each forty-five-minute class.

Mrs. String, the principal—or as Vrin used to call her, the chief of education—comes from a place where their education system followed the Diogo Method. I'd heard about the method in Eden when I was old enough to understand that our education system was the result of adults gathering and simply deciding how kids should learn. As a kid, I never thought about it. School was just... school and something we had to do.

The Diogo Method suggests that kids learn better when they aren't forced to sit around all day. Not only that, but it encourages school time to be much shorter so the kids don't feel overwhelmed with new knowledge. It's been proven to help kids learn. I wish

I'd grown up in a system like that.

"Here!" Abigail says, squeaking as she makes a sudden stop in front of a closed classroom door.

The sign next to it reads, "Mathematics," but I don't pay much attention to it; I'm too distracted by the yelling coming from inside.

Abigail blasts the door open, and the first thing I notice is all the empty seats. There aren't old wooden desks or even the fancy thick plastic ones I used to sit in. They're sleek white tables with cushioned seats and they match the polished, shiny floor.

The windows, two giant squares without any sort of blinds or curtains, bring in massive strips of yellow light that spread across the whiteness of the room and bring along with it a comforting heat.

"Stop it!"

"He's a pig!"

"Dirty!"

"Ow, please!"

"He shouldn't even be in here with us!"

What the hell is going on? In the back, students of all ages gather so close together it's hard to tell how many there are. A few of the older kids, no doubt the young teenagers from Abigail's class, try to pry the attackers off of Tommy.

"Enough!"

"Stop it!"

Some of the teenage guys restrain a few of the girls, but all that does is worsen things.

One of the teenage girls pushes back hard. "Keep your fucking hands off her!"

"Get your man hands out of here!"

What happened here? It's like ever since Eve took charge, which was only a few days ago, hatred is spreading across Elysium like a coronavirus. How can one person have so much influence?

Watching the disaster unfold, I grind my teeth and ball my fists.

Don't lose your cool. Don't lose your cool.

I'm going to lose my cool. No one's getting a handle on the situation and it's only getting worse. Suddenly, three chairs fly across the room and one girl throws herself on the tallest guy in the group. She wraps her long legs around his waist and starts slapping him across the head. He flinches as his hair flies in every direction, and he spins in circles, trying to shake her off. The kid doesn't even look pissed off—he's confused, eyes narrowed, and arms held up to shield his face. "What... What're you... Stop that."

"You think just because"—she slaps him again—"you're the biggest guy"—another slap—"around here"—smack—"you can put your hands on us?"

"Anebelia, get off of him!" shouts a young girl with huge puppy eyes.

Without giving it any thought, I fill my lungs with as much air as I can. "Enough!"

My voice comes out raw and tired, reverberating off every wall in the room. Everyone freezes, including Anebelia, whose cheeks glisten a bright red. She watches me with an open palm raised next to the teenage boy's face.

"What the hell is wrong with all of you?" I shout. "You, get off now!" I grab Anebelia by the wrist—she's bigger than me, but I don't care—and pull as hard as I can, sending her flying into one of the sleek metal desks.

"And all of you—" I don't even have to finish my sentence. The young girls who were heckling the little boy scatter as if they were threatened with losing their new movie night privileges.

"Don't you realize what you look like?" My chest heaves as I fight to catch my breath. My legs are trembling, but I ignore them. I can handle a burst of adrenaline. "You're acting like your parents, all of you!"

They seem taken aback by this—some bow their heads in shame and others glare at me, no doubt wanting to punch me in the face for speaking ill of their dead parents.

Emily stands at the back of the crowd, looking heartbroken. I hope she knows I wasn't referring to her father, who she's described as a saint.

"Some of you might be too young to remember the war, but most of you aren't. And you can't possibly be dumb enough to let history repeat itself."

My voice carries across the brightly lit classroom, and no one says a word. At the same time, Mrs. Moretti enters the class with a cheerful grin—the famous smile that led students to start calling her Mrs. Cupid. Every time she runs into Mr. Wallace—the only male teacher in all of Elysium—she spends the next hour beaming, even if all she's doing is correcting homework.

But the moment she catches us crowded at the back, her goofy smile vanishes as quickly as a leaf caught in the middle of a hurricane.

"What's going on here?" she says.

Anebelia, now regaining her footing, brushes her long brown hair back, clears her throat, and says, "Nothing, Mrs. Moretti. We heard that Tommy fell and hurt himself. We were only checking on him."

Mrs. Moretti doesn't look convinced, but she doesn't have time to do anything about it. One by one, the older kids make their way out of the classroom with their gazes shamefully aimed at the floor.

Emily and Abigail stand still near the exit as everyone brushes past them, staring at me in disbelief as if seeing me for the first time.

CHAPTER 11 – EVE

I'm at a loss for words.

The women have gathered around me as the children used to do in our garden, Eden. They watch me as I speak—my lips, my expressions, my every gesture.

They truly admire me.

Of course, there are still women who believe my role as leader of Elysium will bring about hatred and chaos, but they are few and far between. Only those with husbands, brothers, or close male relatives fear I may get in the way of their relationships.

What they fail to realize, however, is that despite disarming the male soldiers of Elysium, not once have I asked that the men and women be separated—at least not yet.

I cannot waltz in here and make such bold demands.

To get what I want—to ensure Elysium is safe for all women—I must be patient.

"Yeah, you should've seen her," Mary-Anne says. She nearly nudges me in the ribs as a friend might do to another, but stops midair when she catches my sour gaze.

She should know by now that I hate being touched.

"They were all stunned," she continued. "Of course Zander didn't want to give up his weapons, but he didn't have a choice. Eve's the queen around here now."

Queen.

I like that.

Women grin from ear to ear as if watching the entire story play out on a live feed in front of them. Those who were there to witness my election continue to describe the event: the dramatic announcement of Vrin's murder, General Zander's attempt at gaining power, and my speech, which led me straight into Vrin's previous position as ruler of Elysium.

If only they knew I was the one who murdered their precious leader.

But no one will ever know—the cameras were out, and my story adds up perfectly. Before I entered Vrin's office, Gabriel was there. I cannot imagine a more perfect setup.

"I heard the bastard's locked up in some cell," one young woman says.

Days ago, someone of her age and stature would have undoubtedly found Gabriel to be an attractive young man. Today, however, she speaks of him as if he were some vile creature unworthy of breathing air inside Elysium.

I smile, imagining him curled up on a thin, sheetless bed. It serves him right—he participated in the war as a Black Marine, so no matter how much we owe Elysium's discovery to him, he's still nothing but a dangerous man. Eventually, I'll make my way over to his holding cell to gloat.

"I heard they torture him every day," someone else says.

Immediately, I cut her off. "No one's being tortured."

The woman sitting next to her slaps her on the forearm. "What the hell, Elise? Where'd you hear something stupid like that?" She scoffs. "Tortured..."

The last thing I want is to have such rumors floating around. Unnecessary suffering leads to feelings of empathy and a need to seek out justice. Gabriel may be a murderous bastard in their eyes, but I cannot allow them to live in a world where torture is even a possibility.

I will give the women justice for what they believe Gabriel has done, but only when they are ready.

"Here, Eve, you can have mine," Mary-Anne says, placing a caramelized apple slice onto my plate.

Fighting the urge to vomit, I squint lovingly and thank her for her gratitude. Sharing food in Elysium is a symbol of utmost respect.

"Oh, mine too!" says another woman, reaching her hand out and dropping the shiny piece of fruit overtop Mary-Ann's. Then, three more women follow suit.

Smiling, I place my fork down and sit back in my chair. I rest a hand across my chest—a way of expressing how grateful I feel to have such wonderful women around me—and release a quivering sigh. "Oh, you are all so wonderful. But you'll have to forgive me.

After the virus that spread among us in Eden—" I make eye contact with a few of my Eden women; the rest of them originate from Elysium.

"Oh, of course!" Mary-Anne says, stabbing her fork into the apple slice and plucking it out of my plate. "S-s-sorry, Eve. We should have thought of that."

I'm about to touch her arm and assure her that her action meant the world to me, when suddenly, we're interrupted by heavy footsteps echoing from behind me.

"Eve," comes a man's authoritative voice.

Cringing, I slowly turn around, as does every head in the eating lounge.

The man, likely a bit older than me, stands tall with thick suede boots, loosely fitted cotton pants, and an old jean jacket over his plain blue shirt. The jacket looks like he's worn it a thousand times—a faded blue with poor stitching around the wrists and elbows. Since arriving at Elysium, I have not seen many individuals wear clothing from the old world.

Obviously, this man doesn't understand the concept of conformity and has something to prove.

"Could I have a word?" he asks, his dark eyes shifting toward the women around me.

I rest an arm on the back of my chair and stare up at him, waiting.

"In private," he adds.

I nearly scoff at him but keep my cool. Who the fuck does he think he is? After what's happened to Vrin, does he honestly think that I, ruler of Eden, would allow him to speak with me privately in a confined space?

Mary-Anne must sense my frustration. She taps the arm of my white overcoat and leans in. "I can come with you, if that makes you more comfortable."

"No need," I say loudly, wanting everyone to hear me. "We're a community. A family. Surely, whatever you have to say to me can be said to my women as well."

The women whisper among themselves, seemingly pleased that I consider them family. I highly doubt Vrin ever spoke to them in such a manner. In no time, I will have them wrapped around my finger.

The man rubs the dark scruff on his face and combs his fingers through his greasy locks. "My son was attacked in one of your classrooms," he says.

My classroom? I tilt my head, fully understanding where this conversation is about to go. This man is already on edge, and regardless of what happened to his son, he wants to ensure I understand that as leader of Elysium, I'm responsible.

"Eve," comes Nayma's voice. She quicksteps her way from the seventh floor's elevator and rushes toward me, her light brown skin glistening with sweat. "It's Mrs. Moretti's class. Something about a boy getting bullied."

The man jabs a finger into his chest. "Yeah, my son!"

Slowly, I screech my chair back and look up at him. He's much taller than me, which is even more pronounced because I'm sitting. Glaring down at me, he plants his palms on his waist. It's a dominant stance intended to diminish my authority.

Like father, like son, I think.

Surely, this boy had a reason to be bullied.

"Mr...." I start, waiting for him to introduce himself.

"Avery," he growls.

I cock an eyebrow, my gaze never leaving his. Does he want to piss me off? Does he not realize where he's standing? Amid dozens upon dozens of women prepared to follow any command I give them? He's entirely outnumbered, yet he's acting like he should be in charge of everyone on this floor.

"Mr. Avery," I say sweetly. "If I could ask you to calm—"

"Calm down?" he snaps, and the women around me flinch.

I, on the other hand, don't even blink. I will not allow a man to attempt to intimidate or humiliate me.

In any other situation, I might wonder, *How dare he speak to me like this?*

But right now, I'm ecstatic.

The brainless baboon has no idea that he's fallen directly into my trap. If I can push his buttons, the women will see how easy it is for a man to lose his temper. The more they realize how frighteningly right I am about men, the farther they will follow me.

Even the small group of women at the back—five middle-aged ladies who refused to sit next to me— observe with curious eyes.

"I can assure you, Mr. Avery, that I will—" I reach for his arm and he pulls it back hard, his closed fist missing Nayma's shiny, blue-rimmed glasses by a few inches.

"Don't you touch me!" he shouts.

Generally, people don't like being touched when they're upset. The move was a gamble, but it worked.

"You've been in power for a few fuckin' days," he says, "and my boy's already been hurt. He has bruises on his arm!"

While I'm not happy to hear someone hurt a child, the situation is playing in my favor.

Mary-Anne stands up with arms crossed over her chest, as do ten other women around my table.

The man scoffs. "Is this supposed to intimidate me? I'm not trying to be a dick here—"

Yet that's precisely what you're being. I smile up at him.

"But this is my kid we're talking about."

Suddenly, the only other man in the room makes his way over. He's slender, wears glasses, and has a slouch—the kind of man who probably used to work in some IT department. "Um, sir..." His voice sounds nasal. "I think we can agree that what happened wasn't okay. And it sounds like Eve is doing everything she can—"

"Everything she can?" Mr. Avery raises his voice. His eyes bulge out at the IT guy like he's ready to knock him out, and part of me feels bad for the other man. All he's trying to do is help me, of all people.

"Do you have any idea how fucking hard it is to be a guy around here these days?" Mr. Avery continues. "You're acting like all of this is normal. Can't you see they're turning on us? Making us men out to be monsters? Grow a goddamn pair, man!"

"Oh, boo-fucking-hoo!" says a woman standing behind Mary-Anne. Her face, plump and crimson red, makes me think that if she doesn't calm down, her organs will erupt out of her mouth and splatter all over the table. "You want to talk about gender discrimination? How about being vulnerable to fucking rape, abuse, and inequalities for fucking centuries, you misogynistic piece of fucking shit!"

If her face were any redder, it would probably blow up in flames. Dark veins pop out from her temples and make their way across her forehead.

"Yeah!" shouts one woman, followed by another and another.

I bite my tongue to keep from smiling. At the same time, four women carrying batons and rifles come rushing out of the elevators. Nayma presses her ear and nods, then glances up at me as if to say, *It's okay, I've got this under control.*

CHAPTER 12 – GABRIEL

I want to scold her. Tell her she's gone completely insane. But I can barely hear anything, and I'm worried that if I try to speak, I'll speak too loudly and give us away.

What the fuck was she thinking? I inspect her brown eye, then her blue, trying to figure out what's going through that thick skull of hers. I'm not pissed off that she saved my ass. I'm furious with her for having fucked up her entire life. She could have had a good thing here in Elysium. Sure, Eve's a bit crazy, but she loves Freyda. She would have protected her.

Freyda suddenly cups my face with her warm palms, and it calms me. It's like she can read my mind. She holds me tight and doesn't say a word. It's a look that says, *Everything will be fine. You have to trust me.*

I do trust Freyda. With all of me. But that's not what I'm worried about. I don't want her getting in harm's way trying to protect me. Why would she do that?

You'd do the same for her, comes a little voice inside my head.

Yeah, I would. In a heartbeat. I'd do anything for this woman.

What's our plan? I want to ask her. But I can't hear shit. All I can do is follow Freyda to wherever it is she plans to take me and hope we don't get caught.

She smacks my ball cap even lower on my face and gestures for me to keep my head down. I'm not sure what good that'll do. The system isn't stupid. It knows exactly which prisoner got out of their cell, and at what time. It's not like they won't figure out I'm the one missing, which means hiding from the cameras won't protect my identity.

I'm about to get lost in my head again when she grabs my hand and runs along a chain-link fence. I fight the urge to gaze up toward the sky. Cameras are everywhere, even outside. Is anyone watching us now? Will we be followed? I don't care if they know I escaped, but I do care if they know where to find us. Because that'll mean they'll catch Freyda and punish her for her crime.

But by the way Freyda's moving, it's obvious she's spent the last few days figuring out exactly where every camera is located. Every few minutes, she stops against an outdoor building, ducks, and changes her course.

She has this all figured out.

Finally, we reach an old black brick building that looks like it's been abandoned. Bits of stone crumble into the grass when Freyda leans against it. What is this place? A bunker? It sits several miles away from Elysium, though it's still within its perimeter. I never see anyone come out this way, and I suspect Vrin didn't want her people venturing this far. After all, her entire life's purpose was to keep everyone safe, and the safest place for anyone to be is inside the main center. Inside Elysium.

Near the black brick building are combat planes and military rovers that look like no one has used them in years. Tall grass wraps around the wheels of the rovers, and a thick layer of brown dirt covers their windshields entirely.

Where the hell is Freyda taking me? Before I can ask, she starts stomping the ground with one foot. Has she lost her mind? What's she doing, dancing? I want to touch her arm and ask her what's going on, but I let her do her thing.

Finally, she mouths something and drops to her knees. With her body bent forward, she searches through the tall grass blades like she's hunting for Pokémon.

She must have found what she's looking for; she digs deeper, pulling out tufts of grass along with crumbling patches of dirt.

Okay, she's lost her mind.

Crossing my arms, I lean my back against the brick behind me, wondering how long the digging will last. I'm about to make a joke about finding the perfect potty area when something shiny glints under the sun. It's so bright that I'm forced to squint.

What is that? A handle?

She reaches for it and pulls.

Suddenly, something shifts under my feet, little vibrations tickling the soles of my bare feet.

Beaming, she looks back at me. She seems excited by what she found, which means she wasn't certain she'd find it.

Talk about a gamble.

The soil in front of her splits open, revealing a dark hole in the ground. It looks like a manhole you'd see at a construction site. What is this? An entry point into Elysium's underground infrastructure?

Still smiling, she raises her ball cap slightly, allowing the evening sun to hit her face.

"You coming?" she mouths.

But before I can answer, she hops sideways and drops her feet into the hole. She grabs onto the ladder, winks at me, and descends into the darkness.

CHAPTER 13 – LUCY

"That was something," Emily says, hopping to keep up with my long strides. "You handled the situation, Lucy. Since when are you so brave?"

I don't say anything. Instead, I turn to Abigail. "What the hell happened in there?"

She pulls her face back like a turtle retreating inside its shell, making it clear to me that she has no idea how it started. "Mrs. Moretti left the class to go get something, and the next thing we know, kids in the class next to ours are yelling. I guess their teacher left, too. A few of us rushed in to see, and that's when I saw girls pushing Tommy around."

It's infuriating to imagine anyone bullying Tommy—he's one of the most docile kids I've ever met. He grew up in Elysium, and he always smiles at anyone he crosses paths with.

"It's probably because of Eve," Emily grumbles.

She plays with her long brown braid and glances innocently at the ceiling. Most people in Elysium don't dare speak about Eve unless they're praising her. So what's up with Emily? What's changed?

When she catches us watching her, she shrugs. "What? I can't be the only one who's noticed an energy shift since Eve took over. And the murder? I mean, that's a lot to take in. Why would the guy who brought us here go after the leader?"

Abigail cocks a brow. "Oh, I don't know, maybe to become the leader himself."

Emily doesn't seem convinced. She crosses her arms over her flat chest and gives Abigail a look that translates to *Whose side are you on?*

"Guys, I have something I need to tell you, but I can't do it here."

They lean in, intrigued by the secrecy.

"Is it about Eve?" Emily asks, her little pointed nose inching closer to mine.

I nod.

Abigail props her freckled hands on her hips like she's about to give me a lecture. "Lucy, are you sure you aren't upset with Eve because she isn't giving you the attention that you need?"

What the hell is that supposed to mean? It takes everything in me not to strangle her for saying something so thoughtless. She has no clue what I'm going through.

Emily must sense my anger. She wraps an arm around my shoulders and sticks her nose out at Abigail. "Don't you have to get back to class or something?"

Abigail exhales hard through her nostrils, and I can't help but picture smoke coming out.

"Yeah, whatever. At least I'm getting an education. And how will you spend *your* day? Sharing conspiracy theories?"

Emily tilts her head and smiles. "What's it to you?"

The two of them have never clicked, probably because all they do is fight for my attention.

"Listen, Abigail, I'll catch up with you later, okay?" I say, hoping she'll catch the hint and take off.

She purses her lips but doesn't say anything, then spins around and marches her way back to class.

"Twat," Emily says.

I nudge her in the ribs. "What's your deal?"

I get that Abigail can be difficult to be around—especially with how much she likes to talk—but she's a good person and she means well. I'd much prefer it if we all got along.

"I don't trust that girl," Emily says. "Why is she defending Eve?"

I narrow my gaze on her. "Why *aren't* you defending Eve? Everyone else does."

She shakes her head. "There's something off about that woman. Do you know how many times I've caught her smiling at someone, only to then make a face the second she turns away? People don't seem to notice it, but I do. She reminds me of my evil aunt back in the real world. Clarisse. That woman had severe mental problems and used to lash out at people for no reason. Dad would tell me to stop using the word *evil* because it was disrespectful. He'd say that all she needs is a bit of extra care. She'd sometimes flip out and slap Dad in the face, and I hated her for that. Then two seconds later, she'd be smiling and asking him to bake her muffins. But he was always nice about it, and he'd forgive her every time." She bites her pink bottom lip, likely fighting back tears.

Poor Emily. She's been struggling for a while about her father, always wondering whether or not he's still alive. I hope she finds him one day. Deep down, I don't think she ever will, but I can't tell her that.

She clears her throat. "Anyways, Eve reminds me of Clarisse. So no, I don't trust her. And I don't trust Abigail, either. She's too desperate, you know?"

I can't help but laugh. "What do you mean, desperate?"

"She tries too hard," Emily says. "And desperate people are easily persuaded.

"Are you saying she'd turn on us?"

"Nola did," she says.

I swallow hard. As much as I want to argue with her and tell her she's wrong, I can't. Eve somehow slithered her way into Nola's mind and made her believe I was the one who needed monitoring.

Maybe Emily's right. Maybe I can't trust Abigail with the information that I have on Eve. For all I know, she'll go running to Eve the second she's offered something valuable. I feel awful for even thinking that way about my friend, but at this point, I can't trust anyone.

"Fine," I say. "I'll be careful around Abigail for now. But you need to hear this."

She seems genuinely concerned. I've known Emily for a while now, so when something is wrong with either of us, the other senses it. It's a bond we share that I'm certain is another reason why Abigail gets so jealous.

"What's going on?" she asks. "Is everything okay?"

I fight back another outburst of tears. I've cried enough for one day, and I don't feel like making a fool of myself again. So instead, I force a smile, trying to convince my brain not to be sad. "Um, no," I say. "Everything isn't okay. Things are bad, but Lucas and I are working on fixing it."

"What can I do? You say the word—"

"Ladies," comes Lucas's smooth voice.

Emily seals her lips and smiles at me, no doubt holding back a wink.

"Lucas," I say. "Where'd you come from?"

"Just came back from a repair," he says. "It was easy, so I don't get why they would have stripped me of my basement access."

"Yeah, me neither." I cross my arms. "Lucas, is there some private place we could all talk?"

He straightens up. "Actually, that's why I came here. I'm certain they know, Lucy. We need to get you someplace safe as soon as possible. And there's something else I need to tell you, too. Come on, I know just the place."

CHAPTER 14 – EVE

The place looks as filthy as it did when I was last in here. I shift my focus to the tiled floor, where her body lay only a few days ago.

At least someone's cleaned the blood up. It's as if Vrin never existed to begin with. I move through her office with caution, inspecting every inch. It's a nice office—a large open-design concept with gigantic bay windows behind her wooden desk.

Personally, I would have preferred to never set foot in this room again, but Trinity mentioned something about important documentation that she recommended I sift through. I move toward the desk, repulsed by the layer of dust that's accumulated since my last visit.

For a moment, I consider calling someone in to clean this place from top to bottom before I so much as set a finger down on something, but Trinity seemed adamant about having me go through Vrin's files. It's best that I don't waste any time.

I approach Vrin's desk, careful not to touch the surface, and reach for the drawer. Unsurprisingly, it's locked, which must be why Trinity handed me a key this morning. I pull out the small golden key from my pocket and insert it into the keyhole. It slips in with no difficulty, and a soft clicking noise resonates as I turn it sideways. The drawer cracks open and I take a step back as if dozens of bats are about to come flying out.

When nothing jumps out at me, I use the tip of the key to pull the drawer open.

Inside is a large orange plastic binder. It's thick, easily filled with hundreds of papers and held together by a large rubber band. It isn't fancy whatsoever and it doesn't scream top secret to me.

Perhaps this is why Vrin hid her files in such a manner. It isn't obvious, like a black suitcase with a combination lock. The binder sits innocently in her drawer as if it were nothing more than financial scripts or old receipts.

Wincing, I reach inside but immediately yank my hand away and squeal when a spiderweb grazes my wrist.

I fucking hate spiders.

Instinctively I glance around at the empty room to reassure myself that no one witnessed my moment of weakness. With the small key held firmly between my fingers, I destroy the web and reach for the binder.

The filth makes it feel gritty against my fingertips.

Binder in hand, I move toward Vrin's oversized leather office chair. Before sitting, I sweep away a few fine particles of dust. I lower myself into the chair and pry the binder apart. Most of the information is written in military speak, causing my temples to pulsate. I sweep the pages aside one at a time, my eyes scanning large headers and hovering over black-and-white images.

What's so important about this document that Vrin had to lock it up?

When I reach halfway through the binder, something jumps out at me. The font isn't large, but I manage to catch it:

Western bases

Bases.

Vrin always referred to Elysium as a base, seeing as it was once a military base. Why is there mention of a western base? I glide my finger across the creamy, cardstock-like paper until it lands on another small header:

Eastern bases

My heart skips a beat.

Are there other active bases? Other survivors? Or are these still being used as military bases? The room begins to spin around me, and for a second, I feel watched. I imagine Vrin's ghost standing several feet away from me, watching me as I freak out on the inside.

Did she know about these bases?

Something else jumps out at me:

Area 82

Area 82? Are we not Area 82? What the hell is going on here? Why didn't Vrin mention the other bases? Did she intend to keep them a secret? Was she communicating with them? As much as I want to believe that the words on this page are ancient—that they predate the war—I get the feeling there's a lot going on around Elysium that I'm unaware of.

I scan through the other pages until I land on something even more frightening:

July 26, 2071

Connection established with General Torres. She has confirmed a total population of 794 within the base.

February 12, 2072

Area 81 compromised. Relocation requested by General Torres.

September 23, 2072

Migration of surviving population to be discussed.

What the fuck is going on? September 23… I glare at the ceiling, trying to recall the date. Time has never mattered to me, and the only reason I allowed some women in Elysium to keep track of the dates was for historical purposes.

I don't follow dates, but I do know we're entering the fall season, which means September 23 isn't all that far behind us. When was this discussion held? A few weeks ago? Before Vrin's death? Was she planning on immigrating new people here?

The tips of my fingers tingle as adrenaline courses through me.

This can't be happening.

We cannot have outsiders migrate to Elysium—outsiders we don't even know.

If they are military, which is quite plausible, they may attempt to destroy all that I've worked for. I haven't yet established my leadership. It's too soon.

How was Vrin communicating with them? Perhaps Trinity knows. If I can cut communication altogether, maybe I can put a stop to all of this.

As I slam the binder closed, a soft knock echoes

from behind Vrin's office door.

Clearing my throat, I slip the binder back into the drawer and say, "Come in."

Trinity's head appears before the rest of her body as if she's too afraid to step inside without being given a second command.

"Yes, Trinity, come in," I say, impatient.

"Is everything all right?"

Why is she questioning me on my well-being when she's the one who interrupted me?

"S-sorry, Eve. I meant you look flustered."

I am flustered. I'm beyond mortified at the thought of outsiders migrating to Elysium. There's no telling who these people might be, or what they might want.

"What is it, Trinity?"

She clasps her hands together the way she always does when she's prepared to give me bad news, as if I need any more of that today.

"There's been an incident," she says.

An incident? I fight the urge to reach for Vrin's dust-encrusted pen holder and throw it at Trinity. Why are there so many incidents occurring under my watch? Why isn't Trinity handling this on her own?

"What is it?" I say, forcing my voice to come out smoothly.

"The man accused of murdering Vrin—" she says, and my heart pounds hard against my ribs. "He's escaped."

My sense of calm vanishes instantly and I slam a fist on Vrin's desk, little bits of dust blowing in every direction. "Escaped?" I sneer. "How the fuck did he escape? Isn't Elysium's prison supposed to be"—I twirl a finger in the air—"advanced security or something?"

If I don't unclench my jaw, I may shatter some of my teeth. So I lean my head back against the chair's headrest and allow my jaw to go slack. "Trinity—" I say through calculated breaths; otherwise I might react foolishly and push her away from me. "What happened, exactly? Did someone help him? Or did he act alone? Where is he now?"

"I have someone looking into the matter," she says. "He's skilled like Lucas and is going through every second of every nearby camera to obtain more details."

He? I want to say, but I don't. If the only technical help we can receive right now comes from a male, I will tolerate it.

She lowers her head as if this will somehow prevent my anger from rising. "If you'd like, you're welcome to take a look at the footage—"

I stand up so quickly that my chair rolls back and hits the wall. "Yes, show it to me."

CHAPTER 15 – GABRIEL

"Explain to me again what you were thinking," I say.

Freyda ignores me, and not because she can't hear me. I'm probably still shouting. But she's so caught up in her own head that it's like I'm not even here. She paces around the room, rummaging through steel pipes and old paperwork.

"Freyda," I try again.

When her body stiffens over a pile of plastic storage boxes, I know she's found something useful. She twirls on her heels, a steel flashlight in her fist. With her thumb, she presses the power button and a bright yellow light shoots up toward the high ceiling, lighting up the metal ladder we came down from, along with the rusty circular hatch door overhead.

Aside from Freyda's flashlight and a flickering motion light positioned near the entryway, the entire space is dark, making it nearly impossible to see anything. Cobwebs fill the corners of the room and attach themselves to old, purple-cushioned chairs and piles of boxes so high they nearly reach the ceiling. It's like whoever ran this place was planning on emptying it of its contents. Either that, or they were moving it. I'm not exactly sure.

The space is small and tight, and I'm thankful I'm not claustrophobic. It reminds me a bit of an underground bunker, though I'm well aware that it's Elysium's underground infrastructure. This means it probably spreads for miles.

If I had it my way, I'd drop Eve in here and throw away the key.

She seems like the type of person who would be bothered by tight spaces. That, and filth.

Freyda flashes her light across the metallic walls until she lands on an ominous black metal door. She turns to me, half her face a blinding yellow, and shouts, "This way."

Her voice is faint, but it reverberates off the walls and I can make it out.

I want to ask her if she has any idea where she's going, but there's no use. She won't answer me, or she'll shout at me again, telling me that I have to trust her. No way has Freyda been down here before. I can tell by the way she's scouring the place. She's inspected the blueprints, but that's it. And there's no telling what version of the blueprints she saw.

She throws the weight of her body against the door and bounces back, nearly tumbling over. She tries a few more times, but the thing won't budge. She leans forward, grips her knees, and pants like she ran a marathon.

"Let me try," I say.

She steps aside, so I grab the handle, turn it, and smash my shoulder into the metal. Something shifts and the door begins to open. It's probably creaking, but I can't tell.

Freyda smirks at me—a look that says, *Show off*, and steps into the darkness with her brilliant light aimed ahead. In my peripheral, rodents scurry across the floor. They're fast, and I can't make out what they are, but if I were to guess, I'd say rats.

Thankfully, rodents don't bother me. Besides, rats have a bad rap. People think they're these devilish creatures. I recall reading an article about how scientists claimed that rats weren't actually to blame for the spread of the Black Death. Humans were.

I think back to my childhood, or more specifically, of Titus, my pet rat. Fancy rat, to be exact. He was beige and white, unlike the brown rodents racing across the metal floor near my feet. Every night, I would take Titus out of his cage and hold him in my arms, snuggling. If I brought him up to my face, he'd sniff me, his little whiskers tickling my chin, and kiss my lip with a little lick. I remember crying when I found out that our next-door neighbor killed two rats with a shovel. Mama spent several hours that night consoling me, telling me that people simply didn't understand these intelligent little creatures and often mistreated them because of it.

I smile at the thought of Titus and follow Freyda through the narrow tunnel. I'm careful not to touch the walls or reach overhead. Though I'm not a squirmy kind of guy, and insects don't typically bother me, I'd rather not touch some giant bug I can't even see.

When we reach the end of the tunnel, she steps aside again and aims her light at another door. She wiggles her flashlight, which I know is her way of saying, *Go ahead, tough guy.*

I love her sense of humor. No matter how shitty our situation might be, she always finds a way to lighten the situation.

I reach for the handle, turn it, and slam my body against the door. It opens up with ease, and Freyda continues down her path. When the tunnel splits in two—one opening on the right, and another on the left—Freyda doesn't hesitate. She turns right and keeps walking with her shoulders drawn back.

She must recognize this area from the blueprints.

We walk for what feels like over an hour until at last, we approach a door that doesn't quite look like the others. Next to it is an electrical panel with flashing buttons. Using her index finger, she punches in a keycode and the panel lights up green.

How the fuck did she pull that off? Did she use a PIN she found in the blueprints? If so, that was a huge risk. That PIN could've easily been changed many times over. This woman's nuts. I love it.

Before entering, she turns her head sideways and smirks at me.

"Who's the show off now?" I say.

She winks back at me, steps into the room, and hits a light switch.

Everything suddenly lights up a bright white. The space is industrial-looking with metal pipes running across the ceiling, wooden wall panels, a seamless metal floor, and large stainless steel cylinders that look like they're used to store important supplies.

Food, maybe.

On the right wall is a small kitchenette with a

stainless steel fridge, a banged-up microwave, and a double sink.

What is this place? A lunchroom? A break room? It reminds me of a teacher's staff lounge.

Next to the fridge is an open door that leads into a small room. Although I can't see everything in there, I do spot the end of a small single bed. A resting area? Is this supposed to be our new home?

I move to the kitchenette and turn the tap on. To my relief, cold water comes pouring out.

I perk my head up, searching for the bathroom, when Freyda points at a closed wooden door near a beige sofa. Beside this door is a shelf with dusty, hardcover books.

"That's the bathroom," she says. "Hopefully, we have hot water."

I'd love hot water, but I won't complain about a cold water shower if that's my only option.

"What about food?" I ask.

She moves toward the large cylinder tanks, rubs her arm against its foggy glass, and peeks inside. "We have enough here for several months." She moves onto the next cylinder. "Soap, shampoo, medical supplies—"

It sounds like she's whispering, but I can tell by the veins bulging from her neck that she's shouting at the top of her lungs.

"How did you know this would all be here?" I say.

She bites her plush bottom lip, which tells me she didn't know.

"You risked everything to get me out?"

She moves toward me, her hips swaying like those

of a feline, and reaches for my face. Her touch feels soft against my overgrown beard.

I hold her firmly by the small of her back and pull her tight against me. "You're crazy, you know that? This whole thing could have easily gone sideways."

She purses her lips and playfully rolls her eyes toward the ceiling. "Maybe. But you're worth it."

There's so much I want to say to her, but I can't bring myself to do it. Instead, I grab her tenderly behind the neck and lower my lips onto hers.

If I'm going to spend the next few months living underground, there's no one else I'd rather be with than Freyda.

CHAPTER 16 – LUCY

I pry a sticky cobweb off my shoulder and scowl into the darkness. "Do you seriously expect us to go in there?"

Lucas offers me a smug look that makes me want to kiss him. His confidence—subtle yet obvious—is extremely attractive, making it nearly impossible not to do what he asks.

"Do you want to discuss in private, or not?" he says.

I glance sideways at Emily, who appears as spooked as I am.

"Is there any light in there?" she asks.

"In some places," Lucas says. He reaches into his back pocket and pulls out a small, travel-sized flashlight. "That's why I have this."

Emily grabs her waist with her pale bony hands and scoffs with so much attitude you'd think she was still going through puberty. "Those had better be new batteries in there, Lucas, because I swear—"

He smiles crookedly at Emily. "Whoa, relax." He spins the flashlight around as if doing so will give us answers. "No batteries in here, see?"

Emily throws her hands into the air, nearly hitting

me in the face. "Right. That makes me feel a whole lot better!"

As much as Emily's freaking out, I can't help but smile. I'm happy to have her by my side in this. Out of the two of us, she's the adventurous one—the outgoing girl who tends to get other people in trouble.

I think back to the first day she convinced me to spy on Eve through a hole in the wall.

Emily is a force to be reckoned with, but she's also terrified of the dark. It's hard not to poke fun at her.

"It's lithium, PPMA coated," Lucas says.

She scrunches her nose and looks at me as if to say, *Is he speaking in English?*

Lucas laughs. "The battery is built in." He presses something, and a bright green bar appears near the flashlight's rubber handle. "See that? It means the battery is full. And a battery in one of these bad boys lasts about six months. That's if you were using it twenty-four hours per day. And PPMA stands for polymethyl methacrylate. Most lithium batteries now use this to coat the little nanowires inside—"

Emily throws a palm in front of Lucas's face, shutting him up instantly. "Dude. I don't need to hear all the random science technobabble. If you promise me we won't lose any light, then I'm in."

"I promise," Lucas says. "Now, place your spheres in the small box over there."

He points at a damaged cardboard box sitting next to a partially painted hot water tank.

"Why?" Emily asks.

"Because we can't trust them," Lucas says. "They

can be hacked. Mine has been off for the last few hours, and Lucy—"

"Also off," I say.

"Great," Lucas says. "Emily?"

She reaches into her pocket and pulls out her small silver sphere. With a press of a button, the lights disappear.

"Good," Lucas says. "But to be safe, I'd much rather we leave them here."

"But if they're off—" Emily tries.

Lucas shakes his head. "Don't you remember our parents' time? How they talked about their phones being tracked even when they were off? Having something powered off doesn't necessarily cut the GPS signal. Trust me, I would know."

He aims his nose at the box again, and both Emily and I drop our spheres next to his. Lucas knows technology inside and out, so if he says they pose a risk, I believe him.

"So you bring us into some—" Emily's eyes scan the cracked wooden ceiling, the seamless metal floor, and the web-infested walls. "What is this place?"

Behind us are massive water tanks the size of small houses. They make a soft humming sound, likely due to the heating elements being powered.

"They call these machine rooms," Lucas says. "As you can see, it's where the hot water tanks are stored. These aren't connected to much, but they're still in use. Most of Elysium was converted to hot water-on-demand systems. But we maintain a few electrical boxes in here, too. Every floor has one. A machine room, I mean. And as luck would have it, I still have access."

"Why wouldn't you have access?" Emily says. "I thought you were the one in charge of—"

"Trinity took his access this morning," I say.

Emily pops a brow. "Who's Trinity?"

I sigh. "We have a lot to fill you in on, but I think it's best we do it wherever Lucas thinks it's safest."

I turn to face the dark opening up ahead. While I don't want to go in there, we can't trust that we aren't being monitored every second of every day while inside Elysium. Wherever Lucas plans to take us, we'll be safe and out of Eve's line of sight.

"Okay," Emily says, "so where does *that* take us?" She points into the dark tunnel that seems to extend into oblivion.

Lucas flashes his unlit flashlight at our box of spheres and plants a finger over his lips. He then goes on to point downward.

It takes a few seconds for me to realize what he's trying to communicate, but then it hits me.

He's taking us underground.

With a click of a button, he turns on his flashlight and aims it at the dark tunnel. Inside, everything appears to be constructed of old, decaying metal.

We step inside, our footsteps echoing throughout the entire space as if we're walking inside a gymnasium. Lucas brushes past me, reaches for the door we came through, and slams it shut.

I'd be lying if I said I wasn't a little freaked. If he were to turn off his light, we'd see nothing at all.

"It's okay," he says, likely sensing our discomfort. "Come on, follow me."

We follow him down the tunnel for several minutes until we reach another door. It takes him a few tries to open it—he pushes it, kicks it, and throws the weight of his body into it—but he manages to get us through.

"No one's been down here in years," he says. "Might be a bit tricky getting through the doors at first, but they'll ease up."

"Well, that's reassuring," Emily says.

We step inside a small room that appears no larger than a walk-in closet. Lucas reaches for something overhead, and a light bulb suddenly lights up. It sways from side to side above us.

Emily beams. "Let there be light!" She dramatically reaches for the bulb.

"If we keep going a bit farther, we'll make it into the tunnels outside of Elysium. We could chat here, but I'd much rather be as far away as possible. Especially if they're onto us. It's only a matter of time before Trinity comes looking."

I nod. Lucas is right. There's no telling how much Eve or Trinity knows, or how far they're willing to go to stop us. Now that I know the truth about Eve, I'm a threat to her reign. That means if she finds me, I'm done for.

"I wish we could live down here for a while," I say.

A heavy silence weighs on us until Emily says, "Why would you want to leave Elysium? They provide us food, shelter, medical—"

"I don't want to, Emily, but I don't have a choice."

Lucas flashes his light at our torn sneakers so we can all see each other. The shadows on her face make her look like she's scowling, which she probably is. Emily's right—who in their right mind would want to leave the comfort of Elysium?

"What other option do I have?" I say. "I'm a threat to Eve now, and she'll do anything to get rid of me."

"A threat?" Emily says. "How could you possibly be a threat?"

I wanted to save the explanation for later, once we reached somewhere a little more comfortable, but Emily needs to know what happened.

CHAPTER 17 – EVE

The boy spins around in his chair the moment we enter.

He watches me with eyes that look twice their normal size behind those hideous glasses of his.

"E-E-Eve," he says. "I mean, Mrs., um... Your Highness."

"Eve, this is Quinton," Trinity says. "He's very knowledgeable about Elysium's infrastructure and electrical system."

"Trained by Nayma herself," the boy says proudly.

He reminds me of the boys I went to school with back in my day—the ones who spent several years transitioning through an awkward phase before fully growing into their facial features. Quinton smiles a set of crooked teeth at me and pushes his glasses up the bridge of his nose. Small dimples sink into his cheeks as he smiles, making him look young and innocent. Unlike Lucas, he looks like the sort of boy who would do anything asked of him.

Perhaps this arrangement isn't so bad, after all.

I wiggle a finger in the air as a way of greeting him. "Show me what you found."

He twirls around so fast in his chair that he's

forced to grab the table in front of him to stop himself from going too far. "Y-yes, of course." He inputs something into the computer and swipes his finger in the air. "This person's pretty smart. Managed to avoid most of the cameras and kept her face hidden—"

"Her?" I say. "What makes you think a woman helped the man escape prison?"

Quinton turns toward me. "Um, I can just tell, ma'am. The body type, the mannerisms—"

I flick another finger and he stops talking.

He leans forward, his back a rounded hump, and scans through a series of documents.

"Here it is," he says.

He presses something, and suddenly, the monitoring screens change view. Rather than a live stream, it's a recorded video with a timestamp of earlier today. I narrow my gaze as a figure with a black ball cap moves about swiftly through Elysium's corridors. She's difficult to keep up with. Every few seconds, she disappears from one screen, only to reappear on a different one.

I understand now what Quinton meant about knowing it's a woman.

She's thin, has a pleasant body shape, and moves about with such care and grace that it's impossible to confuse her for a man. Every few seconds, she sneaks past a camera and I lean forward, trying to make out her features.

But it simply isn't possible.

This woman, whoever she is, must have been planning her jailbreak for days. She seems to know where the cameras are and which hallways to cross without being detected for too long. I watch her as she follows a short woman with spikey hair into the lunchroom.

"What is she doing?" I ask.

"Getting the access card," Quinton says, sounding more intrigued than anything. "That's the prison guard."

He points at the woman with the spikey hair. "She knew where she'd be, and at what time. If I were to guess, I'd say she waited to do this in a public space to go undetected."

His eyes twinkle as he watches the screen. It's almost as if he admires this unknown woman for her meticulous planning.

The woman bumps into the prison guard and apologizes with hand gestures and shoulder touches. She then turns around, her ball cap still too low for anyone to identify her, and heads back toward the prison.

How did no one see this coming?

"What kind of security system do we have?" I bark. "How did one woman manage to steal a prison guard's access card? And why the fuck are we using access cards when we have an abundance of advanced technology here in Elysium?"

Trinity clears her throat. "With all due respect, Eve, Vrin wasn't big on using the prison system to begin with. She believed more in rehabilitation, so she never—"

"She should have made the women of Elysium her priority," I cut her off.

Trinity doesn't respond.

"This is outrageous. I want this woman found. I want her brought to me. I want—"

Just then, I catch something.

"Wait, go back," I say.

Quintin looks at me sideways as if I wasn't clear in my instructions.

"Go back!" I shout. "A few seconds earlier."

He inputs something into his computer and the recording rewinds to approximately ten seconds earlier, where we can see the woman standing next to the prison's entrance. She turns her shadowed face to the side, likely to ensure that no one is watching, and swipes the access card into the access panel. When it beeps and unlocks, she reaches for the handle, turns her body to face the door, and steps inside.

"Go back," I say. "Two seconds."

Quinton does as told.

"Right there!"

He pauses the video footage.

I walk toward the monitoring screens, my heels filling the room with a soft ticking sound, and stare at the back of the woman's figure. "Can you zoom in?"

Quinton shifts in his chair, so I point up at the monitor. "Right there," I say. "On her neck. Can you zoom in?"

"Of course," he says, and the footage expands tenfold.

"Is that a tattoo?" Trinity asks.

I stare at the small black tattoo of a star, feeling as though my heart might explode.

"Do you recognize it?"

Trinity's voice sounds faint and distant like the sound of a car radio behind closed doors.

I blink hard as adrenaline courses through me. This isn't possible. How could she do this to me? How could she betray me, of all people?

I clench my fists so hard my fingers go numb.

Freyda will pay for this.

CHAPTER 18 – GABRIEL

Freyda smiles up at me, her ballooned cheeks tickling my bare chest.

"That was… amazing," she says, drawing circles on my skin.

That was *beyond* amazing. How is this woman even real? She's the dream I've been waiting for my entire life.

"So, is this the plan?" I ask.

I don't have to verbalize my train of thought for her to know what I'm talking about.

"Sex every day? Just me and you?" she says. "I have no complaints."

I didn't miss that one. My hearing is coming back.

I kiss her forehead and brush her dark hair behind her ear. "No complaints on my end, either."

She lets out a cute laugh that makes me want to squeeze her even tighter. But before I can, she smacks my chest playfully. "Now I'm hungry," she says. "What about you?"

With a swing of her upper body, she gets up and climbs out of bed, her naked figure making me feel like I'm on drugs.

"Fuck, you're a goddess," I say, admiring every

inch of her curves.

She winks at me. "You aren't so bad yourself. Grilled cheese?"

I smile. "How are you so perfect?"

She slips into her pants and fastens her bra behind her back. "I'll take that as a yes. Pretty sure I saw some grated cheese in the freezer."

"Won't it taste awful?" I ask. "I mean... how long has food been stored down here?"

"Airtight bags," she says. "I'm sure it'll be fine."

She gets up and leaves the small bedroom. With those sexy hips of hers, it's hard to not want to chase after her and tug her back into bed. In the distance, she clangs pots and rummages through stuff. I still can't believe she busted me out of prison.

She must care about me to do something like that.

I stare at the metal ceiling, smiling at the thought. How much time will we spend down here, anyway? And I'm all for hiding out and laying low for a while, but we need a game plan. Are we leaving Elysium altogether? Are we waiting for Eve's reign to blow over? There's no guarantee that'll happen. For all we know, it could get worse. That woman's like the plague. Her hatred spreads everywhere, and there's no stopping it.

I lie quietly for a while, going over different scenarios in my head.

Leaving Elysium, so far, seems like the best idea. There's only one problem: I spent years out in the wild and know exactly how dangerous it can be. At least in here, we're safe. But we won't always have food. Eventually, we'll run out. I'm surprised the freezers were even loaded. Maybe the base was preparing to hide underground. Then with all the shit that went down, soldiers were deployed left and right to put an end to the war.

The thing that doesn't make sense to me is where all those soldiers went. Sure, the EMPs may have wiped out the electrical grid, along with countless weapons, but the military doesn't back down that easily. Were they ordered to retreat? To hide out until the storm settled? Because there's no way we're the only survivors in all of America. Or the rest of the world, for that matter.

I imagine leaving Elysium and going back into the wastelands. What would we eat? Where would we sleep? How could we protect ourselves from lone wanderers? Or worse, clans? There has to be another way.

The smell of hot butter and melted cheese suddenly fills my nostrils, and I forget all about trying to leave Elysium. I roll out of bed—a double-sized mattress on a metal frame—and search the closet for a pair of plain pants and a T-shirt. It's mostly all men's clothes down here, but I don't think Freyda minds. Plus, anything looks sexy on her.

I enter the small kitchen to find her poking at two grilled cheese sandwiches inside a cast iron frying pan.

"See?" she says. "Told you it would be fine."

I move closer to her and wrap my arms around her waist from behind. She seems to like this. She leans her head back into my neck, and I hold her tighter.

"Thank you," I whisper into her ear.

"It's not that big of a deal, Gabriel. It's a few slices of bread—"

"For breaking me out," I say. "I still can't believe you did that."

She smiles, her cheeks pushing against mine. "Oh, that was nothing." She laughs. "Honestly, I can't believe I got away with it. I'm not sure what I was thinking. I don't think I was. If Eve ever finds out I'm the one who got you out, she'll blow a gasket."

I can't help but chuckle. "I wouldn't want to see that. She'd probably burst blood vessels in her eyes."

Freyda bursts out laughing so hard that I release my grip around her. She laughs for a few seconds before calming down again and turning to look at me. "Is this happening?"

"Let me guess," I say. "Your adrenaline is gone, and you realize exactly what you did."

She nods slowly. "I mean, yeah. I knew what I was doing, but it all felt surreal, you know? Not because of what I did—I'm a cop. I'm used to high-stress situations. It's the fact that I went behind Eve's back and let out the one person she pinned Vrin's murder on. Can you imagine what that's going to cause inside of Elysium? People will freak."

"Maybe they'll turn on her," I say. "You know, for not keeping everyone safe like she promised."

I don't believe my own words, but a guy can dream.

"Doubt it," she says. "They worship her like a goddess. Or haven't you noticed?"

"Yeah," I say. "It's fucked up."

"You think?"

"So, what's our plan?" I ask. "I have a few ideas, but—"

She plants a warm finger over my lips. "You've been through a lot these last few days. Today, we forget everything—Elysium, Eve, you being a wanted fugitive, me aiding and abetting..."

A cute smile tugs at the corner of her lips.

"Fine," I say.

She scrapes the grilled cheese sandwiches out of the frying pan and places them on small ceramic plates. "If you want it cut up like a little princess, do it yourself."

I grab my plate and grin at her. "This is perfect, thank you."

She jerks her head sideways and leads me to the small, circular dining table. It's made of yellow oak and appears to be several hundred years old. The varnish that once protected its surface has worn off, only to be replaced by a matte finish full of scratches.

Not that I care.

"Sit tight," she says. "I found a deck of cards somewhere over there." Standing, she moves to the kitchen drawers and starts digging around. When she resurfaces, she throws an arm in the air, her fist wrapped around a small rectangular deck of cards. "Got it."

I can't even remember the last time I played cards.

She sits back down and starts shuffling the deck. Every few seconds, she sets it aside to take a bite of her greasy sandwich.

"You're gonna get the cards all greasy."

"What are you, the underground police?" she says, licking her fingers.

I hold back a laugh.

She opens her mouth wide to take another bite but stops midair, the piece of cheesy bread floating between her lips. Melted cheese dangles from both sides, but she doesn't move.

"What's wrong?" I ask.

She drops her sandwich and waves a hand impatiently as if to say, *Shut up.*

When her brows come close together, I know something's wrong. She turns her head slightly to the side and glares at me. She heard something. What did she hear? I can't hear it.

I bulge my eyes out at her, but she doesn't give me anything. Instead, she points at the door, then walks her fingers across the table.

It doesn't take a genius to understand that one.

Someone's coming this way. I'm about to point at the weapons vault, but Freyda's already on it. It's a large wooden crate filled with pistols, knives, and two semiautomatic rifles. Underneath the weapons are boxes upon boxes of ammunition.

She grabs two pistols and hands me one.

I cock my gun and aim it at the door. The last thing I want to do is fire a shot inside an all-metal underground bunker. A bullet hole through the metal walls could compromise our safety. It could penetrate the air's filtration system or allow dangerous gases to come inside.

I'm hoping that whoever's coming this way will freeze at the sight of two guns aimed at them.

Suddenly, a round green light flickers next to the door. I'm sure some beeping sound accompanies it, but I can't hear it. Instead, I stare down the barrel of my gun as the door slowly opens.

CHAPTER 19 — LUCY

The moment the door opens, white light floods the dark tunnel and Lucas takes a step back. I don't realize what's going on until he raises both hands, pointing his flashlight at the ceiling.

"Whoa, easy," he says.

"Hands on your head!" shouts a man.

My heart pounds hard, pulsating in my throat.

Shit.

Someone lives here. What the hell was Lucas thinking?

"On your knees!" comes that same voice.

"Hey, easy, okay?" Lucas says. He drops to one knee, and at the same time, a familiar voice echoes from inside the room.

"Lucas?"

Is that...?

"Freyda?" Lucas says.

"Gabriel, stand down," Freyda says.

Gabriel? As in the man who led us to Elysium? The man Eve framed for Vrin's murder? What the hell is going on here? I step beside Lucas to see inside the room. The man—Gabriel—immediately tucks his pistol into the belt of his pants and turns to Freyda for instructions.

"It's okay," she says. "I know these kids."

Why is she yelling in his face like that?

Lucas scoffs. "Kids, huh?"

Freyda smiles at him. "Get inside, all of you. L-Lucy? Is that you? And Emily?"

I wave a hand awkwardly. "Hey, Freyda."

She urges us in and closes the door behind us. "What the fuck is going on here?"

My focus shifts between Freyda and Gabriel. He looks the same as I remember—dark curly hair, light brown skin, and an unkempt beard, though it's obvious he hasn't trimmed it in a while. He doesn't smile at us, but there's a tenderness to him that comforts me.

"What are you guys doing down here?" I ask. "I thought he was in prison—"

"He was," Freyda says. She holds her gun next to her side as if preparing to use it at a moment's notice. It makes me uncomfortable. Does she think we're the enemy?

When she catches me staring at it, she says, "Who sent you?"

I arch a brow, slightly irritated by her accusation, when Lucas steps in. "No one sent us, Freyda. We're on the run, like you."

"On the run from what?" she says.

She looks like a cop right now, with her slits for eyes and deep folds in her forehead. She's looking for cues, trying to determine whether we're being honest.

"Eve," I say.

Freyda raises her chin and, like Gabriel, tucks away her gun. "Explain."

I sigh. Does she seriously want me to go into every detail about Eve, my H-Cap, and my mom? Judging from the look on her face, it's obvious she does. Until she's certain that I hate Eve with every fiber of my being, she can't trust me and I don't blame her. If it wasn't for Gabriel standing next to her, I wouldn't trust her, either. But the fact that she's standing next to a fugitive tells me she cut ties with Eve.

So I start pacing around the room, explaining the video footage that I saw and how my H-Cap went missing.

"Lucy—" Emily tries, but I wave a hand dismissively. The last thing I want right now is pity.

"We're screwed," I say finally. "Not only do I not have my H-Cap, but now Eve knows that I know, which means I can't go anywhere near her."

"No, you can't," Freyda says. "She'll lock you up the way she did Gabriel, or worse…"

By worse, she means *kill* me. I wouldn't put it past Eve. If she can kill her own best friend, she won't hesitate to kill her goddaughter if it means protecting her reign over Elysium.

"I don't know what to do," I say.

Freyda pulls a chair out from underneath a table that looks old enough to have belonged to my great grandparents. "Go on, sit."

We each grab a chair and sit at the table. I rest my elbows on the wood and drop my face into my palms. This is one hell of a nightmarish situation. I want to take Eve down, but now I can't set foot inside of

Elysium. Not only that, but I've implicated Lucas and Emily.

"We have enough food down here to last us a few months," Gabriel says. "You're welcome to stay here."

He talks loudly like he has earplugs jammed inside his ears.

I force a smile at him. While I appreciate the offer, it makes me feel like a burden. Both he and Freyda were planning on hiding out here for a while. By adding three new mouths to feed to their plan, we're limiting how long they can hide out down here.

"Well, I think it's time we start planning," Gabriel says, giving Freyda a playful look.

They must have been talking about creating a plan before we got here.

Freyda sighs and crosses her arms over her puffed chest, looking like a cop again. "Eve's gotta go."

Everyone lets out a breath at the same time—something that might easily be mistaken for a chuckle if it weren't for our awful predicament.

"That's easier said than done," Emily says.

Freyda stares at her a bit longer than necessary.

"She's with me," I say. "I trust her with my life."

Freyda nods. "Then we need to find a way to take her out, and by the sounds of it, your H-Cap has the evidence we need."

"They took it," I say.

Freyda's gaze drifts toward something in the distance. "It's got to be somewhere. If we can find a way—"

"Well," Lucas says, but Gabriel cuts in. "Eve isn't stupid. There's no way she's holding on to the H-Cap if she has it. She probably smashed it to pieces already."

The thought of that causes a hot pain to expand in my chest.

All of my pictures, my memories...

"We don't know that for sure," Freyda says.

"You willing to risk your life to chase after such a small chance?" Gabriel says.

Freyda slaps the air. "At this point, yeah. What other option do we have? That crazy bitch will be responsible for a fucking genocide."

"A male genocide," Gabriel adds.

"Guys—" Lucas says.

"What about her?" Freyda says, pointing at Emily. "Do you have any sort of special access in Elysium?"

Emily shakes her head and Freyda lets out a hard, impatient breath.

"And now you're implicated"—she points at Lucas—"which means you can't go up, either. Honestly, maybe the best thing for us to do is lay low for a while and let nature take its course."

Gabriel grabs the edge of the table and leans forward. "We could, but after what's happened... You busting me out of prison and Lucy finding out the truth about her mother, that's a huge gamble. I'm willing to bet that Eve's about to have a total meltdown."

"Can I—" Lucas tries.

"Is that such a bad thing?" Freyda says. "Let her show her true colors. She'll end up being her own demise."

"Guys!" Lucas shouts, and everyone stops talking.

He clears his throat, seemingly embarrassed now that all the attention is on him. "There's another option."

When no one responds, he adds, "I made a copy of Lucy's H-Cap—"

"What the fuck?" Freyda says loudly. "Why didn't you lead with that?"

"I tried," Lucas says. His eyes dart my way. "Several times."

"You copied my data?" I say. I'm not sure whether to be relieved that my information is stored somewhere secure, or upset with him for having breached my privacy like that.

"Y-yeah," he says. "I didn't look at any of it, Lucy. I'm a tech guy, and after your H-Cap broke the first time, I wanted to make sure you had a backup."

I can't be mad at him. "That was smart," I say.

He smiles, but his lips tighten the moment Freyda slams a fist on the table. "This is fucking awesome. All we have to do is get a hold of that data—" She taps her fingers wildly on the table, lost in thought. "Hey, kid, you any good at hacking?"

Lucas nods. "Very."

"You." She throws her chin out at Emily. "If you go back up, you think you could sneak a computer down here?"

Emily nods, and Freyda smacks her hands together. "That's it, then. That's our plan. If Lucas can break his way into Elysium's computer network, he could theoretically broadcast the footage on every floor."

Freyda's right. The plan is perfect. I turn to Lucas. "Can you do that?"

He beams. "Absolutely."

Emily doesn't appear as confident as Lucas. She knows that the weight of the world is on her shoulders right now. If she screws up and gets caught, we're back to square one. "What about you?" I ask. "Think you can do this?"

"Yeah, I mean, I think so," Emily says.

Freyda leans forward, her chest pressing against the table ledge. "Hey, look at me."

Emily hones in on her.

"It's not as bad as it looks. All you have to do is get inside one of the tech classes and take a laptop. There's no rush, either, okay? You can even register to take the class and spend a few days warming up to the teacher. You can do this, kid."

Freyda looks like a completely different person now that she isn't Eve's guard dog. For years, I've always known Freyda to be cold and calculated. But for the first time, I see her as a person and not as Eve's minion. She's calm, collected, and knows how to take charge of a situation.

She's exactly what we need.

Emily nods fast.

"All right," Freyda says. "Let's take this bitch down."

CHAPTER 20 – EVE

I stare at the ceiling, envisioning Freyda's face as it swirls into a jumbled mess. Her hideous mismatched eyes move close together before exploding, and her lips droop down as if being pulled by heavy weights.

She betrayed you, Eve. She deserves to die.

No... No, she doesn't. I love Freyda. *She didn't mean to do this. She was blinded by her preposterous love for this man... Gabriel. He brainwashed her and turned her against me. She needs me. Freyda needs me.*

I slap myself across the face and a warm, tingling sensation spreads over my cheek.

Pull yourself together, Eve.

I let out a loud breath, not wanting to move from my lying position. Under me, my living room carpet feels soft and plush, and little bits of its shaggy material tickle the back of my neck.

I'm afraid that if I get up, I will have to carefully consider my new reality—one in which Freyda has become the enemy. And what then? I need to locate their whereabouts and force them out of hiding, so I can make examples out of them both. That way, no one will ever cross me again.

I don't want Freyda paying for the crimes of a

man.

She betrayed you, Eve. The man didn't make her do this.

"Shut up!" I shout at the ceiling.

Suddenly, a faint knock resonates from behind my door. I ignore it, hoping that whoever came to visit me decides to return at a later time. Unfortunately, that's not what transpires. The knocking continues until finally, I shout, "Go away!"

While I realize it may be Trinity coming to give me an update on Freyda's whereabouts, I doubt she located her so quickly. This must be somebody else entirely, and I'm simply not in the mood.

"Eve?" comes a woman's voice.

Mary-Anne.

Oh, God. What does that intolerable woman want now?

I roll my eyes until it hurts.

Just go away.

"Eve, it's me," she says. "I heard a few women talking about how you were looking upset. Is everything okay? You can talk to me, you know."

Women noticed my mood? I can't even recall walking back to my room. After I discovered Freyda's betrayal, I was beyond infuriated; I was lost in my mind. They must have spotted me going up in the elevators. Was anyone else with me in those elevators? Why can't I remember anything?

I must have blacked out in my fury.

At once, I sit upright, comb my hair with my fingers, and stand. "Open door."

My door swiftly opens and in comes Mary-Anne,

looking surprised to see the door open up. Her round orange-brown eyes dart from me to the door as if she's waiting for an invitation.

Reluctantly, she steps inside. "Hey there, Eve."

I force a smile, something that feels nearly impossible at the moment. "Mary-Anne, what a pleasure, as always."

My face hurts as I maintain my smile.

"Are... Are you all right, Eve?"

"Close door," I say aloud, and the door slams shut behind her.

Deep down, I know I can trust Mary-Anne. She's like a loyal mutt, and anything I tell her, she'll take to her grave. While I might not want her to know everything, I have no one else to talk to. Wiping my grimy forehead with the back of my hand, I say, "No, not really. Something terrible has happened."

A deep wrinkle sinks between her brows and she sits down on my white sofa, resting her hands on her blue pant legs. "You know you can tell me anything."

I breathe out loudly, fighting every urge to burst out crying.

"I've been betrayed by a dear friend," I say.

"Betrayed, how?"

I observe her for a moment, pondering whether to keep her in the dark about the details. As much as I hate Freyda for what she's done, I don't want any harm coming to her. And if Mary-Anne discovers that Freyda is behind a murderer's escape, it may change her perspective of me. She must remain blind to the truth.

"It doesn't matter," I say. "I don't want to bore you

with details—"

"You never bore me, Eve."

I brush off her comment, make my way around the glass coffee table, and sit next to her. She reaches for my shoulder, and surprisingly, I don't cringe or pull away. Her touch is warm and soothing, precisely what I need right now.

I'm beyond devasted, and I'm afraid that if I don't let her comfort me, my pain might revert to rage and I'll end up doing something far worse than cry.

"Have you told your friend how you feel?" she asks.

I shake my head. "Our relationship is severed, and I can't find her anywhere."

Mary-Anne pops one of her thin reddish eyebrows as if to say, *Really? You can't find her?*

She then points her chin at my coffee table and I can't help but smile. Sometimes, I forget that Mary-Anne is the one who gave me the Monarch Suite. She knows everything there is to know about this room, including the coffee table's built-in map of Elysium.

"It's complicated," I admit.

She drops her chin onto her fist and sighs. "Yeah, I get it. People can be complicated. Everyone's got their way of thinking, their own life experiences, and their own beliefs. Sometimes, I think it would be way easier if we were all the same."

She pauses, watching me carefully as if awaiting a reaction. Is this some sort of mind game?

"What?" I ask, even though what I want to say is, "Why are you staring at me?"

"Wouldn't you agree?" she asks.

Why is she behaving so oddly?

"If people were more like robots, or if they could be programmed, life would be much easier," she adds."

I let out a soft laugh. "It would prevent a lot of problems."

I think back to Freyda and to what she's done. If only she were a robot, I could have ensured that she never left my side. I would still have my partner... my best friend. Instead, she turned on me. After everything I've done... she went behind my back and fucked everything up.

I stare wide-eyed at my shag carpet, wanting nothing more than to lie face-first in it and die.

"Eve?"

I unclench my fists, speckles of blood sitting at the tips of my fingernails.

"Are you all right?" she repeats.

I want to yell at her and accuse her of being a half-brained ape for needing to ask me if I'm all right. Isn't it obvious? I'm anything but all right. Freyda did this to me, that fucking bitch.

"You look like you're getting angry," she says.

I turn to look at her, my eyes so large I feel them drying out.

Be careful, Eve. Mary-Anne isn't the enemy, and if you turn on her, you'll have no one.

I try to smile, but instead, my lip twitches. Unable to hide my anger, I turn away from her.

She touches my back, and I flinch.

"Eve."

When I don't respond or even turn back to look at

her, she adds, "May I show you something?"

I'm not exactly in a show-and-tell kind of mood. If anything, I'd much prefer she leave. I'm about to ask her for some time alone when she says, "It's something I never showed Vrin, but I think you might appreciate it."

This captures my interest. I turn back around, my anger dissipating. Mary-Anne kept a secret from Vrin? Why? Now, I'm curious.

"What is it?" I ask.

Her eyes shift from side to side as if inspecting my room for spies.

"We're alone," I say. "You're safe here."

Without saying a word, she jerks her head sideways, signaling me to follow. I make it a point to leave my Luminous Sphere behind as she leads me into my bedroom. Why is she taking me into my room?

She moves toward my closet, and I'm about to tell her to back off, but I remind myself that Mary-Anne knows this room better than I do. Despite me spending hours searching the place up and down, I'm certain there are things in here I still know nothing about.

Opening my closet doors, she steps inside the dimly lit space. She glances at me, but only briefly, before dropping to her knees and reaching toward the corner where the carpet meets the white trim. With her thumb and index finger, she pinches the carpet and raises it.

Intrigued, I step closer, watching her every move.

She peels it back enough to reveal a flat

rectangular plank of wood with a groove carved in the middle. It's deep enough for her to insert her finger and lift the entire thing away from the floor. Under it is a secret compartment—one that I imagine could easily fit several books. She opens it up delicately, brushing away cobwebs, and extracts a black metal box no larger than my fist.

I lower myself to her level. "What is that?"

With her thumb, she strokes the lid. "This"—she pauses, her eyes locking with mine—"might be the answer to all your problems."

CHAPTER 21 – GABRIEL

The girl fidgets in her chair, pulling at her thumbs. It's obvious she's nervous, and I don't blame the kid. I'd be nervous too if everyone was depending on me to steal a laptop from Elysium and bring it back down here.

The plan sounds simple, in theory, but it won't be easy. This girl has no experience in high-stress situations and if she breaks under pressure, we're all fucked.

She grabs her long brown braid over her shoulder and starts playing with its tip.

"Emily," Lucy says. She flattens a palm on the girl's leg, trying to get her to calm down. "I know you can do this, okay?"

Emily nods fast, but it doesn't look like she's convinced. "I need instructions. Like, detailed instructions."

Freyda slides her chair closer and grabs Emily's hand. "Relax, okay? I'll tell you exactly what you need to do."

Emily nods again.

God, does that kid ever look like Castor. I think back to my days out in the wild and how Castor—a guy I once thought was a complete idiot—turned out to be one of the most amazing guys I'd ever met. Still hurts me that he got killed. All he wanted was to find his daughter. Before they sent me to prison, I held on to the necklace he carried everywhere with him. A necklace with the letter E engraved in it.

When I first saw Emily, I automatically wondered if she was Castor's kid.

Is she? She looks a lot like him, right down to that single freckle on her left cheek.

"You know the computer engineering class?" Freyda asks.

Emily looks at her but doesn't say anything.

"What's the teacher's name again? Mrs. Pomski?"

Lucy answers for her. "Yeah."

"When you get back up inside of Elysium," Freyda says, "go find Mrs. Pomski after school and ask her if you can join her class."

Emily bites her lip. "But registration is over. How am I supposed to pull that off?"

"Don't worry about that," Freyda says. "Teachers like enthusiastic kids. All you have to do is tell her you had an epiphany, and you want to work on computers. You think it's the future of our world and you want to be a part of that future."

Emily smiles. "You sound like a commercial or something."

"What can I say?" Freyda says. "I should have been an actress."

I disagree with that, but I keep my mouth shut. Freyda's too bold to fake her way through life. I'm surprised she managed to keep her mouth shut by Eve's side this whole time.

"Let's say I get in," she says. "How am I supposed to sneak a laptop out of the classroom?"

"No one said this would be easy," Freyda says. "It could take days, maybe weeks. What you'll want to do is take on an extracurricular assignment. One that allows you to bring a laptop into your room for the evening."

Emily's jaw drops as if Freyda just asked her to determine the Earth's distance from the sun.

It's 92,955,807 miles.

Not sure why, but that number always stuck with me.

If only Freyda would bring that up one day. I'd come across as one hell of a smart guy.

"What if they change the code to get in?" Emily asks.

Smart girl.

She has every reason to believe Eve and her puppet would do that. If these kids are being monitored the way Lucy believes they are, then guaranteed Eve knows they went into the underground tunnels. They may not know where to find them under here, but they'll figure it out. If Lucas managed to memorize the access code to this room, it means it's documented somewhere.

We all share a moment of silence, trying to find an answer for the girl.

Lucas is the first to speak up. "We'll have to find another way to communicate. Remember where you put your Luminous Sphere?"

Still tugging at the tip of her braid, Emily nods.

"Well, if you can't get in, I want you to leave me a

note under that box. I'll come by every night to take a look. All you have to do is write down a time for the next day, and I'll be there to open the door for you."

Lucy stirs in her chair. Poor girl. It's obvious she's freaking out inside. There are so many what-ifs in this scenario that it's easy to imagine this whole thing failing. I don't say anything, though. In situations like these, blind hope is better than fear. If we screw it up, at least we tried. But if we don't try, we're screwed anyway.

"That's a solid plan," Freyda says. "If you get caught, remember your position: you're *not* on our side. Say whatever you have to in order to convince Eve that you're against us. It's the only way you'll save your skin."

Emily nods again like she's been doing for the last ten minutes. She knows the plan, and she knows what's at stake. What she doesn't know is whether she can pull this off.

What this girl needs is encouragement. Something to push her forward. I realize what I'm about to do is a longshot. I could be totally off and come across as an idiot, but I don't think I'm wrong. It's a feeling in my gut I can't explain.

"Your dad would be proud of you," I say.

Her eyes nearly double in size. She jumps to her feet, and her bottom lip quivers like a screw left on top of a washing machine during the spin cycle. Any second now, she's going to break down.

Fuck.

Did I make a mistake?

Am I putting the mission at risk by doing this?

No, I don't think so.

This girl is full of anxiety. Even when she tries to hide it, I can see it bubbling under the surface. I think her dad has something to do with that. The not knowing. That's what eats a person alive.

"You're Castor's girl, right?"

She takes a step toward me like she's about to say something, but nothing comes out. She parts her quivering lips, but then sucks in a sharp breath and seals them. I know what she wants to ask. She wants to know if he's still alive. She knows he isn't. I can see it in her eyes. But she needs me to say it. Needs confirmation of what she's been thinking for years.

"I'm sorry," I say. "Your dad gave his life saving mine."

I wait for the waterworks, but nothing happens. She nods slowly, breathing in as if counting every second.

"Emily?" Lucy asks. She wraps an arm around her small shoulders. "Are you okay?"

Emily's gaze remains fixated on my new boots. Her brain's going haywire. I need to say something else.

"Your dad was a good friend of mine." I smile at the thought of his mug. "My best friend, actually. He wasn't like the other rebel men out there. He was one of the few good guys."

Her lips start trembling again and her eyes darken to a bloodshot pink.

"He spent every day looking for you. He even held onto this little necklace—"

She reaches for her throat, clasping at something

invisible.

"I had it," I say. "It's in my room, if they haven't tossed it. I promise you that I'll do everything I can to get it back for you."

She looks up at me with big watery eyes. "Thank you."

But she isn't thanking me for promising to get her necklace back. She's thanking me for bringing her peace. For finally ending this lifelong misery of hers. I nod briefly to acknowledge her words, then glance over at Freyda. She's watching me like she's never done before. There's a softness in her eyes. A look that makes me feel like I'd be a great dad.

I've thought about it before, but with the world we live in, it isn't possible. No way am I bringing a kid into this place.

I smile down at Emily and pat her on the shoulder. "If your dad were here, he'd tell you that you can do this."

CHAPTER 22 – LUCY

Emily looks like a different person entirely.

It's almost as if someone lifted hundreds of pounds off her shoulders. Ever since I've met her, all she's ever talked about is her dad. She'd often tell me that maybe he was still out there, searching for her. Little did she know, he was. It breaks my heart to imagine that Emily will never see her dad again, but she doesn't seem as upset as I imagined she would be.

If anything, she looks relieved.

I pull my arm away, realizing she doesn't need my comfort.

Lucas clears his throat, no doubt trying to break the awkward silence. "Is there a Sharpie somewhere in here?"

Freyda aims her chin at the kitchen. "Second drawer by the sink, on the right."

Lucas seems impressed with her recollection abilities. He thanks her, gets up, and goes to find the marker. He comes back with the cap in his mouth, testing the marker's tip against the skin of his palm. He nods to himself as if saying, *It still works,* and moves close to Emily.

"May I?" he asks, tugging at the bottom of her

shirt.

"Sure, if you aren't a perv about it," she says.

He frowns at her with that cap still in his mouth, and I can't help but smile. That's the Emily I know and love. The girl who isn't afraid to crack jokes, even when the world may be falling apart around us. I haven't seen this side of her since before she got pneumonia and nearly died.

Lucas lifts the bottom of her shirt, but no higher than her belly button, and inverts the material. On the inside of her white top, he scribbles something. I have to tilt my head to see what he's doing.

2558

9779

"What's that?" I ask.

He pulls the cap out of his mouth, puts it on the marker, and points its tip at the first number. "This is the key code to get inside the underground tunneling system." He slaps the marker against the second number. "And this one gets you inside this room."

"Couldn't I just knock?" she asks.

Lucas lets go of her shirt and straightens his back. "You could. But you never know when you might need this information. Whatever you do, don't wash this shirt." He pauses, scratches his shin, and adds, "Well, never mind, it's permanent. But don't let anyone see those numbers."

Emily's eyelids go flat as if Lucas just told her that she needs oxygen to live. "I'm not a moron, moron."

He playfully searches the ceiling. "Well..."

Letting out a wicked laugh, she slaps his chest. He pulls away, nearly dropping the marker on the floor, and laughs with her.

"Come on." He grabs his flashlight off the table. "I'll get you out of here."

"How am I supposed to come back in?" she asks. "I don't have one of those." She wiggles her finger at Lucas's flashlight.

Freyda sticks a finger in the air. "Hold on. I've got you covered."

She enters the kitchenette and rummages through the drawers. When she finds what she's looking for, she beams and raises the small pin to eye level.

"What the heck is that?" Emily asks.

It's flat and no larger than a marble. Freyda pins it to her shirt and presses down on it. Without warning, a bright light comes blasting out of the little gadget, forcing me to look away.

"Are those—" Gabriel says.

Freyda unpins the little light and kisses it. "Yep. DotLites."

Gabriel smiles—something I've rarely seen him do. "Holy shit." His eyes dart our way. "I mean crap. I mean—"

Freyda looks at us, her brows all out of whack, and points a thumb at Gabriel. "Can you believe this guy? How old are you? Sixteen? Seventeen?" She smacks the air and turns to Gabriel. "For fuck's sake, Gabriel. We aren't dealing with toddlers, here."

He clears his throat, and I feel uncomfortable for the guy. It's apparent he's spent most of his life away from children and teenagers.

He forces a tight-lipped smile at us. "Right."

Freyda smacks his shoulder and approaches Emily. "Here." She pins the DotLite to her shirt. "When you leave, slip it into your pocket. You don't want anyone knowing you have one of these, okay? To turn it on, all you have to do is—"

Emily presses the pin, and the light turns on.

"That's it," Freyda says. "And to turn it off—"

Emily presses the button again and the light vanishes.

"Well, look at you," Freyda says. "You're a pro."

Emily smirks. "What about the battery life?"

Lucas chimes in. "Don't worry about that. Those things were designed for the military. They have built-in charging capabilities. The battery basically recharges itself. It combines negative capacitance—"

I touch Lucas's shoulder and he stops talking. As much as I admire his intelligence, we don't need the details. Especially details we don't understand or will never remember.

"All right," Emily says. "I'm ready."

Lucas points toward the kitchenette. "Um, hey, can I have one of those—"

Freyda tosses him a DotLite. It bounces in his palms several times before he finally snatches it.

"Thanks," he mumbles, pinning it to his shirt. "I'll be right back."

He leads Emily toward the front door, and right before they exit, I shout, "Wait!"

They both turn.

"I'm coming with," I say.

"Lucy, you don't have—" Lucas starts.

"When you come back, you'll be alone," I say. "I

think it's safer if we travel in pairs."

Lucas parts his lips to argue, but Freyda cuts in. "Lucy's right. We should stay in pairs from here on out. We can't assume we're safe down here. It's only a matter of time before they send forces to look for us."

I rush to Lucas's side, feeling a bit like a burden. While it might reassure me to be with him in those dark tunnels, I'm not much help to anyone. I have no combat skills or useful experience. But what I do have is a lot of time ahead of me with an ex-cop and an ex-marine. Before exiting through the door, I say, "Hey, Freyda. When I come back, can you teach me how to use a gun?"

She smiles at me the way mothers do when they're proud of their kids. "You bet. I'll teach you how to fight, too."

CHAPTER 23 – EVE

The chip is no larger than my pinkie nail.

With gloved hands, I grip it between my thumb and index finger, inspecting it with one eye. "This is our answer?" I say.

In my peripheral, Mary-Anne nods like an eager chihuahua. "Yes. The Zytek chip. Vrin abolished the other copies, but months later, I happened upon this little guy."

Squinting, I shift my focus to Mary-Anne. "Why didn't you tell her about it?"

She swallows hard and becomes fidgety, like a fly caught in a spider's web. I realize my question sounds like I'm attempting to trap her, which I am. I want to ensure we are on the same side.

"B-b-because, Eve. I see value in this. It's a tool. I never understood why she destroyed the technology."

I smirk. She's passing the test.

"But in the right hands," she continues, "I think this could change the world."

I stare at the chip's blue and green design, my heart full as the closet light sparkles off the tiny row of crystals. I've never seen anything like it before. It doesn't resemble the kind of electronic chip you'd find in a computer or technological equipment. There's something unique about this design. Every few seconds, a small streak of blue light glimmers across its surface, almost as if containing a life force within.

"Explain it again," I say.

Mary-Anne scours through the pile of papers that sat underneath the chip only moments ago. "Here it is." She pulls out a small blue binder and opens the dusty cover. "Do you want the detailed description, or—"

"I want to know what it does," I say.

Mary-Anne runs her finger across the white paper until she lands on something. "Case study number eighteen: host has become entirely complacent. Immediate response time when given an order. No apparent sign of hesitation or noncompliance."

I watch the blue shimmer across the small chip. If I can get this inside of every woman in Elysium, they will surrender to my demands. It's obvious that the men of this place have brainwashed them. This little gadget will allow me to reconfigure their minds. It will allow them to see the truth once again. They need this. They need me.

"Come," I order, and Mary-Anne follows me out of my room.

I lead her into the elevators and down into the basement. As usual, the lights are dim and flicker overhead, giving off an eerie ambience. I wish someone would fix those damn lights. But in a sense, it calms me. I enjoy the tranquility. I lead her into the monitoring room, where I hope to run into Quinton. As I turn the corner, we come face-to-face.

He jumps, the cardboard box in his arms bouncing. "Oh, Eve. Wow. You startled me."

I stare at him.

"I, um, I'm putting equipment into storage. H-h-how can I help you?"

"That can wait," I say. "I need you to do something for me."

He immediately places the box down, wipes his hands on his pants, and fixes his glasses. "Of course. Anything. Yep. Anything you need. Just say the word."

I walk past him and he follows me back into the monitoring room. Carefully, I open my gloved hand, revealing the Zytek chip. He lowers his face closer to my palm until his silver-rimmed glasses slide down the bridge of his nose. He pushes them back up and stares at the chip with his mouth agape—an unattractive posture he should consider improving.

"What is that?" he asks.

"Do not concern yourself with its purpose," I say. "Can you replicate it?"

He reaches for it and I curl my fingers into a fist.

"S-s-sorry. I'm sorry. I shouldn't have reached for that." He smacks his head. "God, you're such a moron, Quinton."

"It cannot come into contact with human skin, do you understand?"

He freezes, his mouth splitting into a huge grin. "It's bioengineered," he says. "Wow. I mean, wow." He runs a hand through his greasy blond locks and paces the room. "I've heard of technology like this, but I've never actually seen it up close."

He moves toward me again, so I open my palm.

Placing his hands on his waist, he leans forward, his jaw dropping again. "May I?"

I hesitate. But if I want this thing replicated, I need someone with the right skills to work on it. What has me sick to my stomach is that this chip is the last of its kind. If he fucks this up by damaging it, it's game over.

"This is the only copy," I warn him.

He nods fast and a bead of sweat drips down his forehead. "I understand. I'll guard it with my life."

"No one is to know about it, either."

Again, he nods. He turns around and plucks latex gloves out of a box. He then slips them on and carefully reaches for the chip. My stomach churns the moment he grabs it—I'm instantly plagued with visions of him dropping it and Elysium's future shattering to pieces.

"Be careful," I say.

Without looking away from it, he says, "Oh, don't worry. I will." He rushes it under a microscope and places it down gently. Then, with a back as round as a turtle's shell, he inspects the chip. "Holy crap. This is something else. I mean, look at this. There are live cells on this thing. They seem to be feeding the electrical current. I've never seen anything like it before."

"Can you replicate it, or not?" I ask.

He pulls away, a red circle around his eye. "I-I think so. Give me twenty-four hours. And I'll need full access to the lab."

I'm about to yell at him for proposing such a ridiculous time frame, but I remind myself how advanced this piece of technology is. Replication won't be an easy feat, and I need to grant him all the time he needs.

Clasping my hands together, I say, "All right. I will return in twenty-four hours, and you may use the lab as you see fit."

The wait will be excruciating. But I've gone this long without the use of brainwashing equipment. I suppose I can be patient for another day. Mary-Anne gives me two thumbs-up and grins from ear to ear—a look that nauseates me. As much as I appreciate her enthusiasm, sometimes I wish she would tone down her emotions.

When I order Mary-Anne to follow me and she obeys me like a trained military canine, I get a glimpse of precisely how Elysium will be moving forward. Soon, this is how all women will behave around me, and everything will finally be as it should.

CHAPTER 24 – GABRIEL

The kids leave with Lucas guiding the way. Right before he closes the door behind him, he presses his DotLite, and a blinding flash of white lights up the tunnels.

"Wish we'd had those on our way down," Freyda says.

I can't bring myself to respond. The truth is, I'm a bit worried about our game plan. I'm an ex-marine. Plans are what I follow. But this whole setup feels like a giant gamble. There are too many variables and way too many uncertainties. What will happen when we run out of food down here? Sooner or later, we'll have to resurface, and we're all going to pay for our crimes. I'm not afraid of doing time in prison. What scares me is the idea of Freyda's life being taken from her. She's young, vibrant, and has her entire life ahead of her.

So do I, but I have a habit of putting other people before me.

Those kids, too. They're entering adulthood. They don't deserve to be locked up behind bars. I wish someone would take Eve down once and for all. Maybe we'll get lucky and she'll ruin her rulership all on her own.

Then again, she reigned over Eden for years. She's a dangerous woman, and many people underestimate her.

"You okay?" Freyda asks.

"Hm?" I mumble.

Shit.

She caught me in my head.

And I can't lie to Freyda. I'm not a good liar to begin with. Mama always taught me that honesty is the best policy, even when it hurts. The only way I can get around to avoiding the truth is by finding an ounce of it, somewhere, and convincing myself that it's the whole truth.

"I'll be okay," I say.

She presses her cheek against a closed fist. "Is that so?"

She's on to me.

I love that about Freyda. She's so insightful. She doesn't show it, though. She's hard on the outside, but on the inside, she has the biggest heart I've ever known. She cares about people, especially me.

I scratch the back of my neck. "I don't like our plan. There. I said it."

This seems to amuse her. I don't get what's so funny about what I said. Smiling, she pats my hand on the table. "Welcome to the club, Gabriel."

"Why are we going along with it, then?" I ask. "Not only are we putting an innocent girl's life on the line, but we're setting ourselves up to be caught. If they catch her, it's only a matter of time before they'll get her to talk."

Freyda pouts her lips. It's the kind of look that tells

me she isn't all that concerned. "Don't get me wrong, Eve can be a monster. She can do some pretty harsh shit. But hurting a little girl? Not her cup of tea. She loves women. It's the reason she lost her mind. All she's ever wanted was to protect us. I'm not worried about Emily. Even if they catch her, they won't hurt her."

"They might lock her up."

"Maybe," Freyda admits. "But not for long. Eve will somehow find a way to blame you or Lucas for this. Trust me. She'll say that the men were responsible for our horrible actions. That you somehow managed to manipulate us into doing your bidding."

"That's fucked," I say.

She laughs. "Yeah, especially since it's usually the other way around." She wiggles her pinkie finger.

"I'm not wrapped around your little pinkie," I say.

"Not yet." She wiggles it some more.

She's so fucking beautiful that I can't even argue. I'd do anything for this woman.

"So, what?" I say. "We wait and hope for the best?"

She leans back in her chair, the wood making a faint creaking sound. That's when I realize most of my hearing has come back.

"Pretty much," she says.

It isn't long before Lucas and Lucy return, both looking blue. I don't blame them. They sent their friend on some impossible mission. And there's no telling when, or if, she'll even come back. I wish that girl all the luck in the world, but I won't hold my breath.

"All done," Lucas says, entering the room. "I think

she'll be okay."

Lucy doesn't look convinced.

"Hey," I say, and Lucy's bright green eyes dart my way. "She'll be okay. She's got Castor's DNA."

Lucy tries to smile, but it looks forced, like she's chewing on something rotten in her mouth. "I hope so."

After what Freyda told me about Eve, I'm a bit more relieved about the situation. I hope she can pull it off, but it's good to know that if she fails, she won't get killed or locked up for life. To me, that makes all the difference.

"You must be tired," I say.

Lucas and Lucy eyeball each other. They both look exhausted, like they spent the last twenty-four hours venturing through the Sahara desert.

"You should rest," I say. "There's a cot in that room." I point to where Freyda and I were only a few hours ago. "I'll change the sheets."

I realize it's pretty gross to ask someone to sleep in a bed you just had sex in, but what choice do we have? There's only one bed in this place, so we're going to have to get used to sharing it. And they don't need to know about the sex.

"I'll make some coffee," Freyda says, sliding her chair back. "We should rotate shifts. We'll keep watch while you sleep, and then vice versa."

Both Lucas and Lucy seem to agree with this, but they look too tired to answer.

"When you're all rested up," Freyda adds, "I'll teach you how to use a gun."

Lucy's lip pulls up at one corner. "I'd like that."

I leave the main space to clean up the bed. A few minutes later, Lucy and Lucas appear behind me, yawning. "I'll close the door," I say. "Rest up. You may end up needing your strength."

CHAPTER 25 – LUCY

I feel bad for ever doubting Gabriel.

He seems like a decent guy all around, and with the way he looks at Freyda, I can tell his heart is in the right place. I force a smile at him and thank him for the fresh sheets. The room itself is about the size of two Elysium rooms combined, which isn't big at all. Against the wall is a small cot that looks big enough for only one person. Atop it are clean gray sheets, though they don't smell clean—they smell like they've sat in a box for years.

I don't mind. At this point, I'll take anything. I'm so exhausted from all the crap we've had to deal with over the last few hours. It's a lot. That, and I've barely slept since I found that footage on my H-Cap. I'm emotionally drained. My godmother wants to find me, I want her dead, and now we're hiding in some underground tunneling that looks as ancient as the dawn of time.

"I'll sleep on the floor," Lucas says, searching the tight room.

What's he looking for? Something soft to lie on? Laundry? He pokes his head inside the closet and pulls out a fluffy winter jacket.

"Don't be stupid," I say. "If Gabriel and Freyda fit on here, we can make this work."

He stares at me, likely trying to figure out whether I'm joking. But I'm not joking. The truth is, all I want is to be against him. I want that feeling of security in his solid arms. I need it.

"Please," I add.

His features soften and he moves toward me. "Y-yeah, of course. I'm sure we'll fit."

He smiles like he's uncomfortable and gestures for me to climb on first. Facing away from him, I lie on my side, inching closer and closer to the wall until my nose almost touches it. The cot squeaks as Lucas climbs in behind me, the warmth of his body calming me in an instant. Awkwardly, he places a hand on my hip. It's like he's waiting for permission to hold me. Rather than say anything, I grab his hand and pull it up tight against my chest.

He lets out a hot breath against my neck and squeezes me tight.

* * * * *

Eve chases us, looking inhuman with her elongated limbs and hollow black holes for eyes. She opens her jaw, her chin drooping low and reaching her chest, then screams so loudly that a murder of overhead crows flies off the forest's dead branches.

"Hurry!" Lucas shouts.

He pants as he runs, his feet crushing dead leaves and dry twigs.

I try to keep up, but I can't.

It feels like I'm trying to run underwater—like I'm being chained down by some invisible force.

Why can't I run?

I glance back again, and this time, Eve laughs—a sinister sound that sends chills up my spine. Her suit, usually crisp and white, is covered in so much red that it looks like she emerged from a pool of blood.

"Faster!" Lucas cries.

I'm trying.

But it's as if the harder I try to run, the slower I become, and the closer Eve gets.

I look back again.

She smiles at me, revealing a mouthful of yellow incisors.

"Eve, stop!" I plead, but it's like she can't understand me... like she doesn't even speak English anymore.

She moves faster, reminding me of the Flash, an old superhero. With her long, disproportionate legs, she sprints over fallen tree trunks and large boulders as she charges at me.

There's no escaping her.

Lucas reaches for me, but suddenly, his hand crumbles apart and floats into the lifeless forest like a dandelion in the wind.

"Lucas!" I shout.

When I turn around again, Eve pounces through the air, her mouth expanding to the size of my body.

I try to move, but my legs remain stuck in the ground as if I've fallen in quicksand.

Why can't I move?

I raise my hands to shield myself, but it's too late.

She swallows me whole, and everything goes black.

CHAPTER 26 – EVE

I pace around my room, my bare feet dragging through my shag carpet. Every few seconds, I glance up at the wall clock. In thirty minutes, precisely twenty-four hours will have passed since I requested to have the Zytek chip replicated.

Has Quinton succeeded? Will I find good news when I descend into the basement? The clock's needles tick as slowly as a snail moving through molasses. These last few minutes are excruciating. Perhaps I should simply go down now. Will half an hour make all the difference?

Nodding firmly at nothing, I charge toward my bedroom door.

"Open door," I order.

It swooshes open, and to my surprise, Trinity stands stiffly in front of me.

"Eve," she says, matter-of-factly.

I pull my chin back. "Can I help you?"

"May I have a word?" she asks.

Now?

"Can it wait?" I ask.

She hesitates, which leads me to believe that whatever she wants to discuss must be urgent.

Sighing, I step aside and invite her in. She walks in with her head held high.

"Close door," I command.

The moment we're left in the privacy of my room, Trinity clears her throat. "The people of Elysium are getting antsy."

"Antsy?" I repeat. "What does that—"

"Irritated. Agitated. Impatient."

I clench my teeth. If there's one thing I hate more than disobedience, it's being cut off midsentence. She must sense my fury. She immediately bows her head. "My apologies."

Shaking my face at the ceiling, I say, "I didn't ask for synonyms. Why are they growing agitated?"

This subject seems difficult for her to talk about. Why? Is she afraid to insult me?

"Spit it out, Trinity."

"Your leadership, Eve," she says, and my back stiffens.

Compose yourself, Eve. This is business. Listen to what she has to say. "What about it?"

"Well—" She makes hand gestures in the air as if trying to glue tangible words together. "You've been preoccupied with this whole Lucy thing. You've put a lot of your energy into it, which means you haven't been focusing on the people of Elysium."

My first instinct is to lash out at her—to accuse her of disrespecting my position.

She isn't wrong, Eve. You've put no effort into Elysium since you've taken control.

I don't respond, and instead, wait for her to dive into specifics.

"Two fights have been reported in Elysium's East Wing this morning. There's talk of Gabriel being on the loose."

I scowl at her. "How did that information—"

"I don't know," she says, and immediately stops talking when she realizes she cut me off again.

"Go on."

"You know how things are here in Elysium, Eve. People talk. Someone may have spotted something, and then the rumor spread like wildfire from there. Either that, or the prison guard opened her mouth."

"Or Lucy," I say, biting the inside of my cheek to keep myself from losing my shit.

"It's possible," Trinity says. "But she may not even be involved in this. All I know is that the women are terrified, and that fear is turning into anger. I would highly suggest you prepare a speech to calm everyone's nerves."

I bow my head and pinch the bridge of my nose. "Schedule a meeting in the Hub for three o'clock this afternoon. I'll ease everyone's minds."

Trinity nods and begins walking backward, prepared to leave the room.

"These fights," I say, "were they between women? Or men?"

"Women," she says.

I'm a bit stunned to hear this, but at the same time, it should come as no surprise. Women tend to act out when they're afraid, oftentimes by attacking other women. If Quinton played his part accordingly, this panic and chaos will be a thing of the past.

"Thank you," I say. "You're dismissed."

She leaves my room, and I wait a few minutes before rushing down the hall and toward the elevators. As I descend, I spot Mavis and Perula sitting on a bench in the Hub. I haven't seen those two in days. They bicker, their backs rounded and their salt-and-pepper hair pulled over their shoulders. Mavis, as usual, is much more animated than her timid twin sister Perula. She throws her arms in the air, her mouth a gaping hole. I wonder what they're up to. The last time I spoke to them, they were assigned to a greenhouse right outside of Elysium. Have they managed to maintain the gardens? I think back to the Devil's Tea they used to concoct for me and how complacent the women of Eden became after sipping on the hot beverage. If only the twins knew what my new plans were. If everything works out as it should, the Devil's Tea will be child's play in comparison.

When I reach the basement, my heartbeat quickens. What if Quinton has failed? What if he has damaged the chip? An abundance of fearful thoughts race through my mind as I march toward the laboratory.

It's a corridor away from the monitoring room and resembles nothing like it. It's a condensed version of a scientific laboratory with microscopes, balances, beakers, test tubes, clamps, and a whole other slew of items I can't pronounce.

Overhead, white lights hang from cable wires, filling the room with a glow that reminds me of a hospital. I've only ever been in the basement's laboratory once before, and Trinity often tells me that it is being underused. There are many things our students could be researching, but the problem is that I do not want them to have access to the basement.

There is another lab situated on the main floor, in one of the school's classrooms, and another in a building entirely separate from Elysium. This building, also known as Elysium's Study Hub, is operated by some of the finest minds in our society—the Binaries. Scientists of varied backgrounds spend hours in this lab, studying quantum biology, synthetic biology, organic electronics, and other advanced fields I have no understanding of. They are the reason we as a species continue to advance. Without them, none of us would be standing here, inside of New Eden, which is why I feel so strongly about young minds receiving an education as early as possible.

Someday, the Binaries will be gone, and it will be up to the subsequent generation to fill their shoes.

While I considered asking the Binaries for help, I can't risk it. They're extremely progressive and would never agree to duplicating a chip capable of brainwashing a human being.

As I walk into the lab, a subtle scent of lemon and ginger enters my nose. It isn't strong, but it's enough to make me breathe in again.

"Oh, Eve," Quinton says, his face turning sideways.

He's hunched over something with a pair of silver tongs in his left hand. "Just finishing up... One last touch. Aha. Got it."

When he spins around, he blinks hard, his bloodshot eyes double their size behind a magnifying visor headset. He tilts his head back to look at me, blinks again, and removes the visor. "Sorry—I, um. Yeah. It's done."

"Have you slept?" I ask.

His eyes dart toward an empty coffee mug. "Um, I don't know. I think so. Maybe not."

As much as I appreciate how hard he's worked on this, lack of sleep is one of the surest ways to cause an accident.

"Have you succeeded?" I ask.

With his tongs, he reaches for the chip under his microscope. But as he raises it, I notice his hand trembling slightly. It isn't overly evident, but it's enough to cause my mouth to go dry. I reach into my pocket and extract my favorite pair of black leather gloves.

"Give me that," I order.

Slowly, he moves his tongs toward me and descends the chip into my gloved palm.

"This is the replica?" I ask.

He nods. "Yes. A perfect copy. It took a lot of work. I mean, I had to isolate the—"

I raise my free hand and he stops talking. I don't care about the details, nor about how much work it took to create an exact copy. The truth is, it doesn't matter. It could have taken the boy a week to complete, and I would have still demanded one be made.

Elysium currently houses approximately 6,500 bodies.

To insert a chip inside of every individual would take approximately eighteen years of continuous work. That number, however, could be cut down dramatically if more students took part in the replication process. And if they were chipped, they would do precisely as told.

"Will it work exactly like the original?" I ask, peering down at the tiny chip.

He opens his mouth, then bites his lip. "I mean. Yeah. It should. I wasn't sure what it was for, at first, but now it's obvious. This thing is engineered to make biological changes in the body. Or, more specifically, the brain. It's fascinating, really—"

"Will it work?" I say, my tone coming out colder than before.

" Y-yes. It'll work."

I stare at the tiny chip as Quinton goes on about cell reprogramming, firing neurons, bioreactors, and other words I don't care to ever remember.

The only sure way to ensure its functionality is to test the piece of technology on a live organism. Although I'm not entirely certain how it works, I do know that it is activated when coming into contact with human skin. Without warning, I grab Quinton's wrist and slap the chip against the inside of his forearm.

He immediately stops talking by sucking his lips inward, suddenly looking inhuman. His big bloodshot eyes roll up at me, almost pleadingly.

"I'm sorry, Quinton, but we must be certain of its functionality."

Slowly, I remove my gloved hand, only to find a small red square imprinted on his forearm. The chip is gone, and for a moment, I wonder if perhaps I dropped it. I pull away, searching the floor. My heels tick as I take a few steps back, while Quinton stands still, almost like a robot.

"Quinton?" I ask.

"Yes, Eve?"

I tilt my head to the right.

"If I were to ask you to replicate the original chip again, what would be your answer?"

"I would happily oblige," he says, matter-of-factly.

I lean forward, inspecting his eyes. He observes me as if waiting for permission to breathe. "I want you to create another dozen copies of these chips," I say. "And I want it done by tomorrow."

"No problem, Eve. I will get started right away."

He turns away and begins gathering all sorts of tools and gadgets.

I'm too stunned to say anything else. So instead, I grin from ear to ear as I imagine a better version of Elysium—the New Eden I've always wanted.

CHAPTER 27 – GABRIEL

Freyda draws circles on my arm, smiling warmly at me in a way she's never done before. "You're good with them, you know. And what you did yesterday for Emily, that was pretty amazing."

I smile back. I never pegged Freyda as the type of woman who'd want children, but with the way she keeps looking at me, it's becoming obvious. As much as I enjoy the looks she's giving me, it pains me. How can I tell her that bringing a kid into this world isn't what I want? That it isn't fair?

"The kid only needed a bit of motivation," I say.

"You know, that *kid* is sixteen," she says. "I get that you haven't been around many teens over the last few years, but you should stop calling them that. They don't like it."

"Always looking out for other people's feelings."

She shrugs with one shoulder. "Someone's got to."

As I stare into her beautiful mismatched eyes, I can't help but imagine a life different from this one. What if we weren't living in a postapocalyptic world? What if society were to rebuild itself in only a matter of years? Would my view on children change? Would I want a family with Freyda?

Yeah. More than anything.

The idea of having a mini Freyda fills my heart with a joy I can't even begin to explain.

I fucking love this woman.

"So how will we get around the whole sex issue?" she asks.

I'm a bit taken aback by her boldness, but I like it. "You mean because of the kids—the *teens*?"

She smirks at my attempt to correct myself. "Yeah, because of them. We can't exactly keep using that bed. It's disrespectful, and honestly, it's gross. I wouldn't want to sleep in there knowing the two of them got their funky on."

"Know of any other places down here?"

Lost in thought, she shakes her head. "I mean, I remember seeing something below us."

"As in deeper than we already are?" I ask.

She doesn't even have to nod for me to know that's a *yes*.

"You didn't happen to bring the plans with you, did you?" I ask.

She tilts her head and flattens her lids. It's a look that translates to *Do I look like a moron to you?*

"Do you have any idea how many there were?" she says. "Piles and piles of papers. I scoured through everything as fast as I could so I wouldn't get caught."

"Where were they?" I ask.

She hesitates. I'm betting they were somewhere she shouldn't have gone.

"Vrin's old office."

My jaw drops. "As in Eve's new office?"

She breathes in, her chest expanding. "Yep. That

one."

I'm not sure whether to give her shit for being so reckless or kiss her for being so damn hot.

"How did you even get in there?"

"Doorstop," she says like it's nothing.

"You waited outside the office for Eve to come out?"

She shrugs. "Yeah, around the corner. It was risky, but I managed to pull it off."

I still can't believe she went through all this trouble to get me out.

"What did you do with the blueprints on this place?" I ask.

"Toilet," she says, and I could kiss her. "Tore the sheet up into small shreds and flushed them."

"You're incredible, you know that?"

She winks at me as if to say, *Yeah, I know*, then goes back to staring at nothing. "About a mile away from there, there's a latch door. It's the entry point into the sub-architecture. There were a lot of other papers about it, but I didn't have time to go through them. There are also other resting hubs like this one down here, but we'd have to walk around blindly until we find them. I looked for the one nearest to the prison."

"So why don't we go for a walk?" I ask.

She bites her lip and aims her stare at my groin. "Just a walk, huh?"

I smirk. "Well, that depends on what we find."

"We can't be long," she says. "If they wake up"— she throws her chin out toward the small bedroom— "they'll wonder where we went."

"Like you said, they aren't *kids*," I say. "And it's their second night here now. They'll be fine."

She doesn't seem too impressed by my smart-ass comment. "Fine, let's go."

Standing, she holsters a Glock and hands me another one. She marches into the kitchen, grabs a pair of DotLites, and pins one to her shirt. I grab the other one and place it right in the middle of my chest.

"Whatever you do," she says, "don't go firing your gun down here unless you absolutely have to."

That's a given. A hole inside this underground architecture could ruin everything. The pressure system would go out of whack, and gases like methane would start to seep in. I already know this, but I don't say anything. Freyda likes to feel like she's running the show, and I have no issues with that.

Sometimes, I think Freyda forgets what I used to do for a living. Maybe my gentle side gets in the way of her remembering that I was trained to kill. Trained to run all sorts of operations much more dangerous than this one. She either forgot, or she doesn't want to know that side of me.

She leads us out of the room and back into the large metal tunnels. This time, everything is much clearer. The light from our DotLites expands up the sleek walls and even illuminates the ceiling. The floor, chipped and rust-colored, looks white under the brightness of our lights.

This is so much better than using a flashlight.

With my unloaded gun, I aim straight ahead, prepared to intimidate any potential attacker. I highly doubt anyone is living down here. If they were, they would have consumed all the food in our hideout. If I were to guess, I'd say that aside from a few repair engineers, no one's been down here for years.

We walk for a while until finally, Freyda stops midtrack and points her gun at something. I don't see it at first, but when she turns her chest, the wall lights up. It's another door, similar to ours.

I want to ask her whether she saw that on the plan, but it's better if I don't speak. My voice will echo down the tunnels, and if by any chance someone else is living in here, they'll hear us. She gives me an uncertain look and shrugs. Slowly, she reaches for the security pad and punches in the same code as the one she did for our room. The pad beeps once, a blue light flickering on the top, and beeps again, this time followed by a red light.

Freyda shakes her head. She doesn't know the PIN, which means there's no going in there. Jerking her head sideways, she continues down the tunnel and takes a left. I'm about to ask her how much farther it is when she stops abruptly and points the barrel of her gun at a cavernous opening in the tunnel. It's about the size of a closet, and on the floor is a large hatch similar to those found in submarines.

She turns to smile at me but winces and looks away when my light blinds her. So I turn it off. It's not like we need two of them right now.

"This isn't what I was looking for, but let's check it out," she says softly. She taps her boot on the hatch and I reach for the wheel.

Using all my strength, I tug sideways. Once, twice, three times. Finally, something loosens, and a loud creaking sound echoes down the tunnel. The door easily weighs over a hundred pounds. With my feet planted firmly on the ground, I pull it up and it rests against the wall.

Freyda smiles up at me, and this time, I'm the one to frown and raise a hand in front of my eyes.

"Sorry," she says.

"I'll go," I say, stepping toward the opening.

She smacks my chest. "Yeah, I don't think so, buddy. This is my treasure."

I laugh. "All right, go ahead. I'll be right behind you."

Looking like a kid with a shiny new toy, she hops into the hole and latches onto the metal ladder. One boot at a time, she descends into the darkness. From above, all I see is her black silhouette and her white light bouncing off the ladder in front of her. When she reaches the bottom, she looks up. The light surrounding her is too bright for me to make out her features, but I get the feeling she's pretty happy about what's down there.

"You have got to see this," she shouts.

Her light dims as she walks toward something I can't see. I get that she's excited with whatever's down there, but I wish she'd wait for me.

I place my boot onto the ladder's first step, prepared to begin my descent when suddenly, everything down below goes black. Did she turn off her light? And if so, why would she do that?

"Freyda?" I call out.

Nothing.

"Freyda?" I try again.

She doesn't respond.

Something's wrong.

I tighten my grip around my gun and drop myself down to the bottom of the ladder.

CHAPTER 28 – LUCY

I wake up with a racing heart and clammy skin.

When I realize I'm not being chased by a monstrous version of Eve, my heartbeat slows down. I wrap an arm around Lucas, thankful to be in his arms for a second day in a row.

He breathes slowly, his chest rising every few seconds. As I wipe my mouth, I watch him. He sleeps peacefully with his mouth open, and all I want to do is reach for that dark stubble of his. It suits him—the stubble. It gives him an edgy look that I find attractive.

I wrap my arm tightly around his abdomen and lay my head back on his chest. For a moment, I forget all about Elysium and Eve. All that matters is Lucas's body against mine. I feel safe, protected, and whole.

He mumbles something, licks his lips, and moans. Slowly, he cracks his eyes open. The moment he meets mine, he smiles down at me and I smile back.

"Good morning," I say, blinking hard.

"Is it?" Lucas asks.

"What?" I say. "Morning? I have no idea. I can't keep track of time down here."

It could be nighttime, for all I know. Being here with Lucas, somewhere under Elysium, feels like a getaway. Nothing matters down here. I should be worried about Emily and thinking about whether she's succeeding with our plan, but I'm not. There's nothing I can do about it.

"How'd you sleep?" he moans.

I press my cheek against his chest. "Great."

With his thumb, he caresses my shoulder. "Same."

We lie quietly for a few more minutes, listening to each other breathe until a grumbling sound vibrates under my palm.

I laugh. "You hungry?"

"Starving," he says.

Grunting, I push myself into an upright position. The bed is so small that I have to use his chest for stability. But I don't mind. I could spend every night like this.

Yesterday, we woke up to the smell of cooked pasta, but today, there's no smell slipping underneath the bedroom door. I wonder what Freyda and Gabriel are up to. Maybe today, I'll cook.

"Guess we'd better check what there is to eat around here," I say.

Yawning, he slips his legs off the bed and stands, stretching until his back cracks. "Come on. I'll make you something."

I don't argue and follow him out into the main room, but to my surprise, Freyda and Gabriel aren't here.

"That's weird," I say. "Where would they have gone?"

Lucas scours the space, poking his head inside the bathroom and even inside the large closet near the front door. It's filled with thick, military-style jackets, boots, and a box of guns.

"This doesn't make any sense," he says. "Why would they leave?"

I bite my lip, lost in thought. Did I misjudge Freyda and Gabriel? Was this their plan the whole time? To abandon us? Maybe we're nothing more than a liability to them. *Kids*, as Gabriel likes to call us.

"Maybe they left us."

Lucas scoffs. I can't tell if he's upset, or if he thinks I'm being crazy. "No way. They wouldn't do that. Why would they do that?" His footsteps become heavy as he searches the same places over and over again.

"They aren't here," I say.

Frowning, he pulls out a chair and sits down. "There has to be an explanation. Maybe they went out looking for additional supplies."

"We have everything we need in here," I point out.

I try to convince myself that Freyda wouldn't do something like that. She wouldn't abandon us while we're sleeping. Freyda and I may not be best friends, but I like to think I know her well enough: she wouldn't stab me in the back.

If she left with Gabriel without the intention of returning, that would be a form of betrayal, and Freyda's too good of a person to do something like that. If anything, she'd be blunt about it and tell us they don't want to take part in whatever plot we're carrying out against Eve. But she does want to be a part of the plan. She has to—she has just as much to lose as I do. If we don't take Eve down, we're all going to suffer.

Gabriel is a wanted fugitive, and if Freyda gets caught, she'll be punished for aiding and abetting—a punishment Eve will probably want to deliver personally.

"Let's wait it out a bit," I say. "If they aren't back in a few hours, then we can start to worry."

Lucas agrees and moves into the kitchen, behind the counter. He reaches inside a cupboard and extracts a clear pouch full of beige powder.

"What's that?" I ask.

He crinkles his nose. "No idea." He then jabs his finger on the pouch and says, "Oh, here it is. Pancake mix. Just add water."

"Pancake without egg?" I say. "How's that even possible? Oh God... Eggs."

He sighs. "Yeah, I'm gonna miss them, too. That, and fruits, and vegetables."

I'm suddenly reminded of Mavis and Perula, and I can't help but wonder what they're up to. Have they discovered a space similar to their Herb Shack? Are they back in the business of growing things? Then, I think of Nola and wonder if she's worried about me. Has she realized I've gone missing? Does she regret pulling away from me? I hope so. I'm still hurt that she believed Eve over me, but I don't blame her for it. Eve is a master manipulator. She could convince someone to sell their soul for a bottle of water.

Defeated, I slouch in the wooden chair.

In the kitchen, Lucas pulls out a frying pan, the sound of clanging metal echoing around us. But he stops moving when he notices me. He stands still, a large frying pan in one hand and a pouch of pancake mix in the other. "Hey, you okay?"

I sigh. "Think so. Guess it finally hit me that we're stuck down here."

He places the pan down gently and joins me at the kitchen table. When he reaches for my chin, I look up at him. "Don't think of it that way. We aren't stuck. We chose to come down here. Stuck would be if Eve had imprisoned us, and I can guarantee that's exactly what would've happened if we'd stayed up there." His sharp canine tooth makes an appearance, and I immediately feel calmer. "Think of it as... us preparing for a revolution."

I roll my eyes. "Right. Because I want to hear that word after everything that's happened."

"It doesn't have to be a bad thing, Lucy. The world we once lived in became toxic. You saw it firsthand. You, as a woman, lost your rights. Doesn't that bother you?"

"I was only a kid," I say.

"But you aren't anymore. Imagine living in that old life. Imagine not being allowed to vote or to speak up against any man. Being told what you can or can't do."

Why does he care so much? He isn't a woman.

"You need to care, Lucy. This is huge."

I realize how bad things were, but it's hard to feel it when it didn't directly affect me. Mom took good care of me and protected me from all the awful crap that was going on around us.

"What does it matter to you if I care?" I ask.

"Everyone should care," he says. "My parents didn't risk their lives joining the underground revolution for nothing. Revolutions mean something.

People should have the right to live in a democracy—not in a twisted version of it that gives us a pretense of power. Millions of people died so that people like you and I could have a better life." His brows come close together, and I sense the anger radiating from his body. "This isn't about you or me, Lucy. It's about everyone up there." He points at the ceiling. "They're all being manipulated by a woman who cares only about herself. She's going to ruin everything people like my parents died trying to uphold."

His chest heaves with every breath, and I stand up, wrapping my arms around his body. "I... I'm sorry," I say. "I didn't think of it that way. You're right. You're absolutely right. A few months spent in isolation down here is nothing if it means protecting thousands of lives in Elysium."

He holds me tight, his hot breath beating against the top of my head. "Exactly."

CHAPTER 29 – EVE

My heart pulsates in my throat as I make my way down the corridor and toward the elevators.

"They're ready," Trinity says, her voice blaring out of my Luminous Sphere.

I wave dismissively and my sphere lowers itself near my waist. Although I haven't yet prepared a speech, I know precisely what I am going to discuss—Gabriel. Over the last few years, I've learned that the only way into the hearts of my women is through compassion and honesty. Unlike male soldiers, women cannot be forced into blind compliance. They require tender care and guidance. Otherwise, they will begin to speculate and discuss among themselves. They question and bicker.

If I have any intention of continuing my reign here in Elysium, I must come forward with the truth.

As I descend in the glass elevators, numerous people from within the Hub turn to look at me. This moment will be defining. I haven't spoken to the people of Elysium since I took power after Vrin's death. As Trinity mentioned, I've been so lost in my head that I haven't taken the time to care for my people.

Today, that changes.

The elevator doors glide open and I step out, head held high.

While many women watch me with adoration, others scowl at me as I walk past them. A few men stand next to their wives, mothers, or sisters, matching their expression—whatever it may be. It's apparent that they support the opinions of those they love.

At the far back of the room stands ex-military men with wide chests and rounded shoulders. Out of everyone in the room, they are the ones I am most concerned about. They glower at me with such hatred that I envision them charging straight for me the moment I turn my back.

But I know nothing would come of it.

I have too many women prepared to fight to the death for me.

Trinity joins my side, along with another dozen women clad in military gear. They carry assault rifles against their chests and avoid eye contact with the population.

While I don't typically demand such a high level of protection, I would say it's a required precaution given recent events. I walk up to the podium next to a massive window on the external side of the Hub. Through it, a dull light penetrates the gray, overcast sky, barely warming me. The season has proved to be dull and lifeless, and without many trees around Elysium, it's difficult to admire autumn's beauty. There's a forest in the distance, which I sometimes gaze at from my suite's window, but it's far, making it difficult to appreciate its charm.

Everything is simply dying.

I walk up the two steps leading onto the large platform and stand behind the podium. Soft bickering spreads throughout the Hub, but it comes to an immediate stop when I raise a hand.

Mustering all of my strength, I smile sweetly at everyone. "Welcome," I say.

No one responds. Half the crowd believes me unfit to rule, while the other half is too stunned by my presence to even open their mouths.

"I owe you all an apology," I say.

The crowd shifts slightly—angry women soften their features, unclench their fists, and watch me carefully. They weren't expecting such a bold debut to my speech.

"It was beyond selfish of me to allow my mental state to interfere with my ability to rule."

By mental state, I'm referring to the trauma I endured when I *found* Vrin's body. If I can extract pity from them, or at least understanding, perhaps I can steer them in the direction of my choice.

"Finding Vrin the way I did has affected me. The blood, her pale face..." I lower my head, feigning despair. "But as ruler of Elysium, you deserve better." I elevate my head again—a symbolic gesture signifying that I am ready to let go of any personal attachments. "I understand you may have concerns, and I would like to take this time to address them."

No one speaks, but the hostility in the room has dissipated. While there are still a few men staring scornfully my way, most of the crowd has let down their guard.

When no one speaks up, I clear my throat. "You may have heard rumors circulating. Rumors of Vrin's murderer escaping." I pause as mouths drop and a sense of panic begins to spread. "Unfortunately, these rumors are true."

An uproar shakes the Hub, sending vibrations up the podium and into my fingers. If I allow them to bicker too long, anger will replace fear, and some may even be so bold as to do something regrettable. I raise a hand again, and the crowd grows silent once more.

"I assure you that we are doing everything in our power to catch the fugitive," I say.

A woman with two young daughters at her sides steps forward. "That isn't good enough, Eve. How did this happen? How can we ever feel safe again knowing the prison is compromised?"

My first instinct is to narrow my gaze onto this woman. How dare she speak to me in such a manner?

This is business, Eve. Nothing is personal here.

"I understand your frustration," I say. Her jaw splits like she's about to say something else but I cut her off. "Our prison compound lacks certain security measures. While Vrin might have believed in rehabilitation and second chances, I do not—at least not for such heinous crimes."

I must be careful with how I approach the topic of Vrin. She was loved by many in Elysium, and it's important I speak of her with admiration and not with hatred.

"While I appreciate the hard work Vrin did for Elysium, there are certain things, such as prison security, that I believe require more attention."

Nods fill the room as my voice carries across the Hub.

"Where is he now?" someone asks.

Only hours ago, Trinity informed me that she believes Gabriel and Freyda fled into Elysium's underground infrastructure. I am currently considering my options to sweep the area, but I want to be careful with how I approach this. I do not want anyone knowing Freyda is behind this. Gabriel needs to be the villain.

"We believe the fugitive has managed to get underneath Elysium," I say.

"Underneath?" someone asks.

"Yes," I say, matter-of-factly. "Elysium is built atop a supporting infrastructure that houses our water filtration systems, along with other components that contribute to our heating and cooling."

While I understand the concept of it—as explained to me by Trinity—I am no engineer and I do not pretend to understand what is sitting beneath us.

"Should we be concerned?" one woman asks. She pulls on her son's shirt, pressing his back against her hips, and wraps a protective arm across his little chest. "We have children, Eve. Is this man still a threat to us?"

"No," I say. "I assure you that this man is simply on the run and would not be foolish enough to set foot inside of Elysium. As an additional precaution, however, I will be assigning patrol guards to each floor."

The women—mostly the mothers—nod in unison. It's obvious that what matters most to them is the safety of their children.

Tightening my grip around the podium, I add, "I will die before harm comes to your children, do you understand?"

This seems to work. Those who glared at me only minutes ago now watch me like sheep in front of their shepherd. They *want* me to guide them. They *want* my protection.

"Are there any other concerns you would like me to address?"

The crowd remains silent.

I clear my throat. "Commencing next week, I would like all children of Elysium to be registered for school."

A few mothers whisper, but no one protests. Not only do I want an educated society, but I'm growing rather tired of having children run about during regular hours.

"In addition, I believe it would be in everyone's best interests for us to review our roles and responsibilities."

The whispering gets louder. I can't tell if they're upset, or simply curious. The problem we've faced since arriving at Elysium is that some of my women—those from Eden—did not continue to pursue work. In a sense, it has been a chaotic free-for-all. Unless someone is severely disabled and cannot perform their job duties, everyone should be contributing to our society.

What I believe most women will find exciting is

the idea of a career change. Judging by their reactions, it would appear that Vrin was not one to encourage such changes. I, on the other hand, want my women to feel motivated. Performing the same duties over and over again becomes monotonous.

"I am thinking a rotational shift," I say. "What are your thoughts?"

I typically don't care to ask an audience for their feedback, but if I include them in the decision, they can't blame me for any dissatisfaction that might arise in the future. Furthermore, offering your people a chance to provide input builds trust. It builds a connection like no other.

One man at the far back clears his throat—a deep grumble—and emerges from the crowd. "Um, if I may—"

The sound of chafing echoes throughout the Hub as everyone turns to look at him.

"They say it takes six months to learn a job. What if we pick two different professions and swap every six months?"

Several nods fill the room and I rub my chin. As much as I despise the fact that a man spoke first, I cannot reject his idea—in fact, it's rather good.

I turn my attention to the crowd.

One woman, in particular, grins so wide the corners of her lips nearly meet her earlobes. She elbows the woman next to her and says, "I've always wanted to work in agriculture."

Her friend doesn't look as impressed. Clearly, many people are not comfortable with change, but they will simply have to get over it. This rotation will keep everyone's minds sharp and prevent a great deal of depression.

I spot Nayma in the crowd and call her up onto the platform.

She readjusts her blue-rimmed glasses and comes rushing up the stairs with that tablet she carries around with her everywhere she goes. "Yes, Eve?"

"Can the Luminous Spheres interact with people? Meaning, would it be possible to send out a survey to everyone's spheres and have them answer it?"

Again, she pushes her glasses up the bridge of her nose, her dark eyes on me. "Absolutely. It could even be individualized so that we can keep track of every answer."

I touch her shoulder tenderly. "Wonderful."

Then, I approach the podium again. "This evening, you shall receive a survey offering you the different career paths available. Note that positions requiring high levels of education will not be on the list."

"Do you have examples?" one woman asks.

The only position I can think of that would be excluded is that of a doctor, so I turn to Nayma for guidance.

She smiles sweetly and quicksteps her way to the podium, her beige shoes barely making a sound. She taps the microphone, her back unattractively rounded. "Medical professionals—including veterinarians—engineers, postsecondary teachers—"

"Teacher," one woman whispers, her hands clasped in front of her humongous smile.

"Physicists, astronomers, computer scientists—"

As Nayma goes on to list a few more professions,

I can't help but notice the defeat in some of my women's eyes. It's obvious that all they've ever wanted is to do something meaningful, yet they were never allowed the opportunity to study the field.

"Scientists—"

I reach for Nayma's shoulder and she stops talking.

As some eyes roll toward the ground, I smile to myself. In a moment, I will become everyone's favorite leader.

"Thank you, Nayma," I say, and she leaves the platform. "As you can see, the new rotational shift regime will apply mostly to standard trade jobs. That being said, I would like to take this opportunity to announce a new program I would like to pilot."

Several people light up like dogs being shown a piece of meat.

"I understand that some of you were never allowed to study in your field of interest."

They hang on to my every word. And they should. What I'm about to reveal could change everything.

"In addition to the rotational-shift initiative, I would also like to offer a career-reset option."

Several gasps echo throughout the Hub.

"Those of you interested in pursuing a high-level job will be permitted to take night classes delivered by some of Elysium's brightest minds."

This time, the crowd explodes into an excited banter.

"Can you imagine, Lorna? Me, a doctor?"

"Well, you always talk about it!"

For the first time since I've arrived at Elysium,

everyone appears genuinely happy. I've given them something Vrin never could—hope.

Smiling to myself, I elevate my chin. Now, my people will follow me to the ends of the earth. And for those who should choose to defy me, well, Quinton will soon have the solution to that problem.

CHAPTER 30 – GABRIEL

"Drop the gun," the man orders.

I stare at his eyes, wondering who's behind the metal plate mask. It accentuates his cheekbones, his chin, and his jawline, making him look somewhat deformed. I've never seen a mask like it before. Around us are blinding pot lights, and I raise an arm to fight off the glare.

The last thing I want is for Freyda to get hurt, so I do what the man says. I slowly lower my gun onto the metal floor.

"Kick it away," he orders.

It's hard not to do what he says when he has a huge knife pressed in Freyda's throat. She watches me, calculations running through her mind. I can see it from here. She's trying to figure out whether it's safe to take the guy out. I know Freyda. She'd be able to do it. With two moves, the guy would be on the ground with a broken wrist and his own knife at his throat.

But we know nothing about him. Is he alone? Are there others? What's his background? It would be stupid to attack someone without having all of that information.

I kick the gun away, a scraping sound filling the area.

"State your name," he orders.

I'm getting pretty pissed off watching him dig his blade into Freyda's throat, but I have to stay calm.

I raise my hands in submission. "Gabriel Rodriguez. I'm from Elysium."

I don't bring up my military ID number. For all I know, this guy could be a huge military-hater.

He watches me carefully, his dark eyes narrowing behind the holes in his mask. Based on his reaction, he knows what Elysium is. Does he also know it was once referred to as Area 82? I left that part out on purpose. If I use the term, he'll know I'm ex-military.

"And her?" he asks.

"Freyda Mills," I say. "She's with me."

I realize the last part was pretty obvious, but I didn't know what else to say.

"State your purpose," the man says.

"Look," I say, trying the genuine approach. "We aren't here for any trouble. We were exploring the tunnels because we're stuck down here."

"What do you mean, *stuck*?"

I look at Freyda briefly, who gives me a look that says, *Go ahead, you can be honest.*

It's a huge gamble. What if this guy is with Eve? Then again, no man in their right mind would work for Eve.

"I was framed for a crime I didn't commit," I say. "And Freyda here got me out of prison. Now, we're on the run. If we resurface, Eve—"

"Eve," the man says. "Eve Malum?"

So he knows her.

Slowly, his grip around Freyda's neck loosens. He pulls away and raises his mask, revealing an unsightly burn scar down the right side of his face. Over his lips is a brown mustache that matches his bushy eyebrows. He's a big guy with wide shoulders and a large chest and even a bit of a belly. "Eve Malum is wanted for the murder of President Price," he says soberly.

I glance at Freyda. What the hell is going on here? Who is this guy?

"General James," the man says. "Edmond James." He extends a hand and I shake it.

He has a solid grip and a stiff posture. Military? He has to be. He glances down at my boots. "You guys military?"

I hesitate.

"Twenty-sixth division," he says, forming a fist over his chest. "Ground operations."

I guess that's my cue.

"Black Marine," I say.

He seems surprised. "Holy shit. So you took part in—"

"Everything," I say shamefully.

He watches me carefully, no doubt trying to figure out if I'm one of the brainwashed Black Marines.

"It was a nightmare," I admit.

"I'm sorry to hear that," he says, breaking his stare.

He seems genuine about it.

"And you?" He points at Freyda.

"Ex-cop," she says.

A smile stretches his face and he plants his large hands on his belt. "I can't believe this. Never in a million years did I think anyone from Area 82 would come down here. Or, I guess as you call it now—Elysium."

There's a moment of silence between us. I'm still trying to wrap my head around this. Why is a military guy hiding out under Elysium? He must sense my confusion.

"We aren't here on mission, if that's what you think," he says.

That's exactly what I was thinking, which only confuses me more.

"Some of us are military, others civilians," James says. "We've been living down here since the war."

"Are you from Area 82?" I ask.

He shakes his head. "No way. We had intel from the inside and we came in through the underground system."

What's he saying? That the tunnels lead outside of Elysium?

He laughs. It's a deep, rumbly sound that fills the dark room.

"The twenty-sixth division was working a covert operation before all this shit went down. We were tasked with infiltrating Area 82 to gather intel on their techniques."

"Military against military?" I ask.

He nods, looking sad about it. "It's too bad we didn't shut them down before the war started. Maybe all of this could have been avoided."

"So you were looking to bring down the Black

Marines?"

Again, he nods. "The operation was huge. It went against the president's orders, but we couldn't stand around while a bunch of men were being brainwashed into hating women. I mean, how the fuck does anyone let something like that happen? Those were some real sick sons of bitches, and I hope they're all dead."

He pauses, probably realizing he put his foot in his mouth. "Sorry," he adds.

"Don't be," I say. "You're right." I take in a long breath. "So you were the good guys."

Freyda looks as shocked as I am. I wish I'd known about them when I joined the Black Marines. It would have given me hope. Maybe I wouldn't have become so hateful and tainted. To me, most men were monsters. No one was standing up against the injustice. But the truth was, countless men and women were fighting the good cause underground. I wish I could have been a part of that.

"This place was already here, but we added to it," he says, raising his palms to showcase the surrounding space.

Only then do I see where we're standing. Behind James is a long rectangular room with matte metal walls on either side. In front of the walls are huge turrets with their muzzles aimed straight ahead. I open my mouth to ask him about them, but he raises a palm and says, "Yep, they would've killed you."

I swallow hard.

"Lucky for you, I happened to be doing a routine inspection on these bad boys when I heard a hatch open up. Let's just say if we lived in the old world, I'd be telling you both to buy a lottery ticket right about now."

I glance over at Freyda, who seems as freaked out as me.

"They're sensored?" I ask.

He nods. "It's to prevent anyone from accessing our base."

My jaw drops. Base? How much digging did they do under Elysium? How much did they *add*?

"I think you'll be pleasantly surprised," James says, jerking his head toward the heavy-duty vault door at the back of the room.

Those turrets aren't making my first step all that easy.

"They're deactivated," he says. "Do you think I'd come in here with those things on?"

He's right. And if I start doubting everything he says or does, he'll think we're up to no good.

I have to find the perfect balance.

"Trust me," he adds. "If I hadn't deactivated them"—he turns to Freyda—"you'd be nothing but a pile of bloody guts right about now."

Freyda gives me a look that translates to *The man has a point*.

I nod and follow him to the door, my gaze never leaving the giant machine guns. In a sense, it's reassuring to know that those things are here. After all, if Eve or any of her followers decide to come hunting for us, they won't succeed.

The last thing I want is for someone to die following Eve's orders, but I also don't want Freyda and me to get caught. It's a shitty situation all around.

Freyda stops walking halfway across the room, right in front of the turrets. It makes me uneasy, but I stay quiet.

"What about Lucy and Lucas?" she asks. "If they come looking for us—"

James squints at the ceiling. "There are more of you up there?"

"Only two," Freyda says. "They're teenagers who also happen to be on the run from Eve."

James seems to cringe every time we say Eve's name.

"If you want," he says, "I can send someone up to fetch them safely."

I hesitate. What if this is a trap? We know nothing about this guy. Freyda seems to sense my hesitation. Forcing a smile, she touches the man's shoulder. "Thank you for the offer, but I think that'll spook them more than anything. Gabriel and I can go after them later."

James eyes us both. It's obvious he's doubting us. I don't blame the guy. We could have an army waiting up there. An army organized by Eve to infiltrate this underground base.

"I would be more comfortable sending my men," James says plainly.

I want to argue with him, but I understand where he's coming from. If we put up a fight, we'll become the enemy, and it won't take long before we find out what it feels like to be blazed by a dozen turrets.

I look at Freyda and sigh. "We want to trust you, James, we honestly do. I think it's fair to say you're feeling the same way about us."

He nods slowly, his mustache twitching.

"But I promise you that upstairs, all you'll find are two scared kids." I glance sideways at Freyda. "Well, teenagers. But I get it. I'm certain protocol says that anyone entering your base is forced to remain on-site, which means you can't have us leaving yet."

Again, he nods. At least I'm on the right track.

"And we're okay with that," I continue. "Heck, we'd much rather be hiding down here than where we were. But can I make one request?"

He grips his belt again, his belly sticking out. "Of course."

"Can you show us around before we give you the coordinates to our friends? We want to make sure that if you send men to retrieve them, they'll be coming down to a safe environment."

He pauses, clearly thinking this over. "That's fair."

I'm about to thank him when he smiles, his mustache expanding, and says, "I hope you're ready for one hell of a tour."

CHAPTER 31– LUCY

"Aren't you the least bit worried?" I ask.

Lucas is hard to read. I realize it's only been an hour or so, but I'm still freaking out. It makes little sense that Freyda and Gabriel would take off like that.

"Not yet," Lucas says. "You shouldn't be, either. Those two have pretty crazy backgrounds and advanced tactical skills. I sure as hell wouldn't want to go up against either one of them, let alone the two combined."

I smile. He has a good point. With my fork, I grab a piece of my pancake and twirl it through my maple syrup. It crumbles easily and doesn't taste like the pancakes we had in Eden, or like the ones Elysium offers, but it's not bad. I'm happy to have it at all.

"How's your pancake?" Lucas asks as if reading my mind.

With syrup dripping from the sides of my mouth, I give him a thumbs-up. Smirking, he finishes cleaning up the kitchen pan and spatula and joins me at the table. He places his plate on the table, pulls out a chair, and sits down. Before taking a bite of his food, he reaches for my hand.

"We're gonna be fine," he says.

I hope he's right.

I want to believe that Gabriel and Freyda will be back any minute, but a nagging feeling in my gut tells me something is wrong.

What if they don't come back?

CHAPTER 32 – EVE

"Oh, Eve, that was amazing," Mary-Anne says.

She rushes to my side, trying to keep up with my long strides. At first, I ignore her, but when I remember who I'm dealing with, I stop walking. Mary-Anne isn't the type to leave anyone alone, especially me. Besides, I owe her everything. After all, she introduced me to the Zytek chip.

"Thank you, Mary-Anne."

She takes in my words as if she were ingesting a drug and her face splits in half with a goofy grin. "So, how's the thing going? You know—"

I narrow my eyes on her—a look meant to warn her to be extremely careful with how she proceeds with this conversation.

She pulls at an invisible zipper over her mouth. "S-s-sorry, Eve."

If anyone will be useful at my side, it's Mary-Anne.

"Come," I say, leading her toward the elevators.

She trots behind me, whistling a tune.

As I walk, I spot Miss Henry mopping away in the Hub's corner. She looks tired as she does every day, maneuvering her wet mop in long strides. She glances up at me and smiles—something she's never done before.

I imagine Miss Henry is already anticipating a change of work. What field she will be interested in pursuing? Being a cleaner is not something I could handle daily.

I offer her a sweet smile and lead Mary-Anne into the elevators and down to the basement.

When we're out of everyone's view, she turns to me, fists shaking at her sides like she's about to explode. "Did it work? Oh, tell me it worked!"

Smirking malevolently, I say, "It worked."

She shrieks and I take a step back. "S-s-sorry, Eve. I can't believe this. I mean... can you imagine how this will change everything? Finally, we will be able to rebuild society the way it should have always been."

I don't appreciate her use of the term *we*, but I keep my thoughts to myself. Mary-Anne is simply excited, and considering she is the one who introduced me to the chip, it's no wonder she feels as though we're partners in this venture.

I make my way through the basement corridor, envisioning the progress Quinton must have made by now. Did he manage to recreate the dozen copies I requested of him? I realize it's only been a few hours, but now that he's under my spell, I imagine he's working much faster.

Something else hits me. Have there been any ill side effects to the chip? Is Quinton still... alive?

I hurry into the laboratory, my heart pounding hard with anticipation. The moment I enter, my mouth goes dry.

"Stop it," Quinton says, pulling away from Trinity.

Trinity reaches over his shoulder, trying to yank a pair of tweezers out of his grasp. "You're exhausted! Go lie down. I'll manage down here."

Quinton pulls away from her again, a menacing scowl deforming his face. "I don't obey *your* orders."

I step into the laboratory and Trinity's head turns to the side.

"Eve," she says.

I'm about to ask her what she's doing down here when I remember that she often patrols the basement.

"Can you please tell Quinton to take a break?" she says. "Look at him."

Quinton's sunken, bloodshot eyes dart my way, but only briefly. He resumes his mission, hovering over the microscope with silver tweezers in one hand and a strange cylindrical tool in the other.

She isn't wrong—Quinton looks awful. Perhaps ordering him to continue replicating the chips was a foolish idea. If he collapses, he won't be able to continue his work for me.

"What the hell could be so important?" Trinity takes another step toward him, but I step closer to Quinton.

"Quinton, could you please head back to your room?" I say. "I think it's time you get some rest."

Like a brainless robot, he pulls away from the microscope and smiles at me. "Of course, Eve."

Trinity isn't having it. She reaches for his arm and stops him midtrack. "What the hell is this about, Quinton? Have I done something to offend you? I asked you a dozen times to take a break. I might not be Eve, but I still have authority over you."

He doesn't respond. Instead, he stares at me as if awaiting a command.

Trinity crinkles her nose at him, looking like she's on the verge of roaring like a lion.

The easiest solution would be to explain everything to Trinity, but how can I trust her? She once served Vrin, and Vrin went through a great deal of trouble to ensure that all of the Zytek chips were destroyed. For all I know, Trinity shares that same belief as her former leader.

"Trinity, stand down," I order.

Her features still hard, she turns to me. "Eve, what is this about?"

"Let the boy go," I say.

She does as told, though it's apparent she isn't pleased with how the situation is unfolding.

Forcing a smile, I say, "It's my fault. I asked Quinton to look into some forensic evidence and made him promise he'd keep his research private. I never meant to keep anything from you."

"Forensic evidence?" Trinity arches a brow and moves toward Quinton's microscope.

Mary-Anne looks as uneasy as I'm feeling.

"Yes," I blurt, moving closer. "It's regarding Lucy's disappearance. This might sound silly, but I had some of her baby hair, and I asked him to perform a complete analysis to help us locate her whereabouts."

Trinity isn't buying it. With a dimpled chin, she leans over the microscope.

Mary-Anne looks at me, horror-struck, but I shake my head as a way of telling her, *Don't get involved.*

Quietly, I move toward Trinity and the microscope.

"What the hell..." Trinity mutters. She hunches even more, her neck disappearing into her shoulders. "This looks like—"

Finally, she turns her head sideways, her features twisted so drastically you'd think she consumed a spoonful of mustard. "Is this what I think it is?"

Her words come out as more of an accusation than a question, proving to me that Trinity is not, nor will she ever be, on board with the Zytek project.

I play coy.

"I can't very well see what it is you're looking at, Trinity. I don't know anything about this science stuff. What are you talking about?"

She turns away from me again, prepared to grab the chip with Quinton's prongs, when I spot a small jar of chips with a sticky note that reads: completed.

He did it.

Without thinking, I reach a gloved hand inside and extract one of Quinton's copies. Trinity doesn't hear me approach—her new discovery is too much of a distraction. Carefully, she grabs the chip with Quinton's tweezers and pulls it out from underneath the microscope. At that same moment, I slap the duplicate chip against the back of her neck. She flinches, dropping both the tweezers and the chip onto the counter, and reaches for the back of her neck.

I step back.

Looking confused, she rubs at her skin as if a

spider bit her. But nothing is there. Her skin has completely absorbed the chip, leaving nothing more than a faint red mark.

Fascinating.

"Trinity," I say, and she stands upright like a soldier on duty. "I want you to find Lucy and bring her to me."

Without blinking, she says, "Absolutely, Eve."

And with that, she marches out of the laboratory, never once looking back. Mary-Anne gapes at me as if I were walking on water.

"Wow," she says. "I mean... I imagined it went something like that, but... wow."

I arch a brow. "And we're only getting started."

CHAPTER 33 – GABRIEL

James takes us through the large slate doors without looking back at us. It's like he knows we're too interested in this place to try to run or attack him from behind. And why wouldn't we be? An underground society? That's pretty damn cool to me.

Besides, it sounds like we're all on the same page. When we mentioned Eve, James appeared disturbed by it. I believe him when he says they've been after her for a while. Eve Malum has made one hell of a name for herself, even in a world without technology.

Word gets around.

The woman who killed the president. The woman who saved countless souls and rebuilt an entire self-sustaining society. The fact that survivors from the city were searching for Eden says a lot about word of mouth.

I have no clue what James plans to do with her when he catches her. Not that I care. That woman is volatile. She deserves what she has coming. And if that's life behind bars, justice will be served.

Mama always taught me that everyone has a story. Even the bad guys. When I think of Eve, I sometimes remember that. I wonder what kind of woman—or girl—she was before all of this happened. Did she smile a lot? Did she laugh? Did she have friends or family? I don't know anything about her. But it doesn't matter. Her mental instability will lead to a second war, and we can't have that.

"This is one of our exit points," James says, huffing his chest at the closed door behind us. He points at the large letter G above the door. "Exit G, to be specific. We have seven in total, three of them leading directly into Elysium's underground system."

"And the other four?" Freyda asks.

James exudes pride. "Outside."

Outside, I think. Freedom. Fresh air. As hard as it was surviving the wild, I miss the freedom. I miss waking up in the morning along with Mother Nature and watching the birds play in the trees and listening to their joyful singing. But I wouldn't go back. It's one of those things where the memory is more enjoyable than the actual situation. Sure, I miss it, but my life was at risk every day. Living in a society changes that. You wake up feeling safe. I shift my focus to Freyda. And I get to wake up and see that face.

James marches down a corridor, his broad shoulders drawn back. Unlike Elysium's underground tunnels, the walls and floors down here are shiny, almost as if they're polished regularly. They must have cleaners who take care of stuff like that.

He leads us to a regular-sized door with a panel to its left. "This here leads into the main city. Only authorized personnel such as myself can access the exit points.

"City?" I say.

He gives me a smug look, reaches for the handle, and opens the door.

White light floods the gloomy tunnel and reflects off the tips of our boots. I squint, but only for a second until my eyes adjust. We step out onto another sturdy platform and move toward a wall made entirely of glass.

The moment I step up to it, my jaw goes slack.

How is this even possible?

Freyda breathes out. "Holy shit."

"Not bad, huh?" General James says.

Not *bad* is the understatement of the year. Through the glass and down below—at least several hundred feet—is a massive open space full of people, machines, weapons, and plants. It seems as though everything is divided into sections, like a city built of Legos. At the far back is a giant section that takes up half the city, easily the size of three football fields. It looks like a greenhouse of some sort. Innumerable white lights hang above green plants as people in green jumpsuits move through the aisles, inspecting the vegetation. At the other end of the greenhouse is a large metal bin full of fruits and vegetables.

"Pretty simple," James says. "Right there, you've got food and water filtration." He points at the greenhouse, then moves his finger across the glass, bringing our focus to the section under it, which seems divided by a large metal wall. "And right there, you've got artillery and defense systems. Over here are materials, clothing, you name it."

"What's that?" Freyda asks, pointing beyond the greenhouse.

"Living quarters," he says.

It's like looking at a building without a roof. A live, 3D architectural plan. Hundreds, if not thousands of rooms, spread out beyond the greenhouse. They don't appear to have access to the city, but there are other larger rooms that look like they were designed for social gatherings. People seem to flock to those rooms the most.

"No one has a ceiling?" Freyda says.

James's mustache twitches. "They do, sort of. It's camouflage technology. It ensures that we have eyes everywhere at all times. For the people down there, though, they can't see us. To them, it looks like there's a ceiling in place."

Pretty smart. Seems a lot better than having cameras set up everywhere.

"Do they know—" Freyda starts.

This seems to amuse James. He pulls his finger away from the glass. "We're all about transparency here. We don't believe in keeping secrets or being sneaky around our civilians. Everyone knows they can be seen from above."

I glance sideways at Freyda, wondering if she's thinking what I'm thinking. When the general catches me staring, it becomes obvious that my thoughts aren't private.

He elbows me in the shoulder. "Don't you worry, sport. At nine p.m. sharp, the blinders come on. Anyone interested in performing extracurricular activities..." He clears his throat. "Well, that's up to them. We've only ever had to turn off the blinders twice in the middle of the night, and both times was to locate a lost child."

"So, there haven't been any internal threats? No one attacking each other?" I ask.

He shakes his head. "We control our people without being restrictive. That's the whole point in being honest and open with everyone. No one feels like they're being taken advantage of, or taken for a ride. The moment we suspect a threat, they're removed from our facilities. Everyone knows the rules."

"What about them?" Freyda asks, pointing down toward the city. "Security?"

James nods.

I lean forward to take a peek at what Freyda's referring to. Down below are men and women clad in black uniforms. In their grip are heavy advanced rifles that look like they could shoot lasers.

"I'm happy to report that we've never had to resort to their services," James says.

As much as I hate the idea of living in a place with guns constantly around me, I understand the logic. We don't live in a society with laws anymore. Having to rely on brute force, or at least the threat of it, is the only sure way to keep people in line."

"Come," he says. "I'd like you to meet someone."

He leads us down the corridor, along the glass wall and through another set of doors. It's a path I know I'll never remember, but it doesn't matter. It's not like General James, or whoever is in charge around here, will grant Freyda and me access to this floor. It's clear that civilians live down below in the city.

When we arrive at a set of double doors, I know that whoever's behind there is important. How? Well, on either side of the doors are two huge guys with heavily powered assault rifles. They stare at me like they're waiting to be given the order to shoot. I can't tell if it's because Freyda and I are wearing outsider clothes, or they're only doing their jobs and trying to look as intimidating as possible.

And I thought I was a big guy. These two are easily over six foot five and two hundred and fifty pounds of raw muscle.

James doesn't pay much attention to them. He leans toward what appears to be an intercom, and presses a small red button under the speaker. "General James here. Two inhabitants of Elysium located and confined."

No voice comes back.

Instead, the doors open with a loud click to reveal another set of guards armed from head to toe.

"General James," comes a pleasant yet authoritative voice. "Come in."

James leads us into the room. It's carpeted, which feels nice in contrast to the hard metal surface we've been standing on for hours. Across from us is a large wooden desk, and behind it, a woman with dark brown skin, short coiled hair, and a harsh square jaw that makes her look like someone you wouldn't want to piss off. She appears to be in her midforties, with only a few patches of gray hair on either side of her head. The top appears unaffected. Her arms are defined and muscular, easily seen through the fabric of her uniform.

"Names," she says indifferently.

"Freyda Mills," Freyda says.

"Gabriel Rodriguez," I say.

James steps aside as the woman stands and moves toward us. Like her soldiers, she's clad in something I would have worn during my Black Marine days. For all I know, that's exactly where the uniforms come from.

She holds her arms behind her back. "What do you report, General James?"

The general puffs out his chest. "Not a threat, Commander Thompson," he says. "They're fugitives from Eve Malum herself."

The commander's dark eyes widen a bit. "Eve Malum?"

The general nods.

She turns away and paces across her office. "Please tell me—"

"I'm afraid Vrin has been eliminated," says James.

Thompson stops pacing and pinches the bridge of her nose. "That's why we haven't been able to make contact."

General James nods.

The commander's eyes suddenly turn on us. "How many more of you are there?"

I hesitate, but Freyda doesn't.

"Two," she says. "We'd like for you to—"

Commander Thompson flicks a finger in the air and two of her guards exit the room.

"Don't worry about your friends," she says. "We'll have them brought down here safely."

There's something genuine about her. I don't know the woman, but I can tell we're on the same team. Crossing her arms, she adds, "We'll prepare the mission."

"What mission?" I say.

The commander looks up at General James.

"Ex-Black Marine and ex-cop," he says as if reading her mind.

She rubs her chin. "Black Marine?"

Black Marines aren't popular around here. Based on what James told us earlier, this group was designed to fight against Black Marine corruption. Most of my comrades were brainwashed into becoming cold-blooded killers. How does this woman know I'm safe?

"Yes, ma'am," I say. "Though I assure you that I took no part in fighting women during the war. In fact, I've shot my own men more times than I can count. I'm surprised to still be alive today. I fled the moment everything collapsed and have been on the run ever since."

She sizes me up. "Thank you for the clarification."

It's not like I need to take a lie detector test for the commander to believe my story. No brainwashed Black Marine would ever talk badly about their own. They'd fight to the death and go after anyone who disagrees with the beliefs that were implanted in their brains.

If I were one of them, it would have been obvious the second I stepped foot down here.

"Black Marines are few and far between these days," she says candidly.

I can tell by the tone of her voice that she's really saying, *We've eliminated as many as possible.*

I have no problem with that. As much as I'd prefer to see these men rehabilitated, I'm not sure it's possible. Their brain chemistry has been completely altered, and with all the horrible things they did during the war, like slaughtering innocent women and children, they'd never be the same again. Killing them is almost a mercy. And it goes without saying that many of those men were already psychopaths to begin with.

"How many armed men would you say there are in Elysium?" the commander asks.

Freyda and I look at each other.

"None," I say.

The commander pulls her face back, small folds forming under her chin.

"Eve stripped all men of their weapons," I say. "She's armed women, instead."

The commander plants two hands on her hips. "Interesting."

She pauses, observing the tips of her boots. "Protocol remains the same. Zeros only."

I turn to James, who clearly understands what she's talking about.

"Zeros?" I ask.

"Tranquilizers," James says. "We don't want to kill these people."

"Even if you have tranquilizers," I say, "you can't waltz in there. You may avoid using lethal force, but that doesn't mean you'll receive the same courtesy in return. I guarantee you that the women carrying guns will do whatever is needed to protect Eve."

The commander smiles at me. It's not a sweet

smile that makes me want to become friends with her. It's a terrifying look that tells me she knows what she's doing and that she's a force to be reckoned with.

Let's just say that I'm happy to be on her side.

CHAPTER 34 – LUCY

I wake up to the annoying sound of something scraping or chewing.

What is that? I jolt upright in our tiny bed, elbowing Lucas in the process. He groans, pulls at the small sheet we're sharing, and rolls over. I try to follow the sound with my eyes, but all it does is move along the base of the wall before disappearing.

It must have been a mouse.

I rub my dry eyes, wondering how long we've been asleep. Across from the bed is a small clock with the top half of its red digits missing. Guess they burned out over the years.

I climb out of bed backward, doing my best not to squish Lucas in the process. I make my way into the kitchen and living room, met with nothing but silence.

For a second, I stop breathing. Sometimes, this helps calm my thoughts.

Freyda and Gabriel—they're still missing.

Something's wrong.

Lucas might say I'm being paranoid, but I don't think I am. Mom used to tell me that I have a gift for intuition—that I should listen to my gut when I feel something isn't quite right.

And right now, I feel like nothing is right. They didn't simply decide to leave us behind. Something happened. I can't say for sure that they're in danger, but I don't think they're coming back.

Still holding my breath, I swing around, prepared to charge straight into the bedroom when Lucas's tall figure appears.

He rubs at his bloodshot eyes. "Hey."

I don't respond. I can't. I'm afraid that if I do, I won't be able to shut up about how Freyda and Gabriel need our help.

"They aren't here," he says, scanning the living room. He sighs. "All right, let's get some gear and go out there."

I perk up. "Are you serious?"

I figured he would keep brushing me off... telling me that it was only a matter of time before our friends came back. But the fact that he's suggesting we go out into the tunnels tells me that he's as worried as I am. Either that or he wants to ease my anxiety. I can't tell which one it is.

"Yeah, I'm serious," he says. "This isn't normal. I'm starting to think something might have happened."

I swallow hard.

"Not necessarily a bad something," he quickly corrects. "But *something*. They don't strike me as two-faced people, you know? They both seem pretty up front and honest."

"I can't speak for Gabriel, but yeah, Freyda's a good person," I say. "She wouldn't help us come up with a plan and then take off."

Lucas scratches the stubble on his face, then

points to the cabinet near the entrance. "Guns are in there, right?"

I nod slowly. As much as I want to carry a gun, I know nothing about them. He must sense my hesitation. Smirking, he moves toward the box and pulls out two black handguns.

I blink hard.

He does something to them, but he moves too fast for me to see what he's doing. There's clicking going on, and the next thing I know, two black cases full of golden bullets come falling out of the gun's grip. He sets the case aside and inserts a new one—an empty one.

"What're you doing?" I ask.

"Giving you an empty mag," he says. He twirls the gun in one hand, offering me its grip.

I reach for it. "Mag?"

This seems to amuse him. "Magazine," he says. "It's where you store the additional bullets. You know, before they move up into the chamber once you load your gun."

"Chamber?" I say. The gun feels cold and heavy in my palm.

He scratches at his brow and gives me a handsome smile. "You don't need to know anything other than this—never point the gun at anyone unless you're about to shoot them or threatening to shoot them."

"I thought you said this thing was empty!" I say, now wanting to put the weapon down.

"It is," he says. "But that's not the point. It's a habit you need to ingrain in yourself. There's always a small risk that a gun wasn't properly unloaded. You never *ever* want to be pointing it at anyone, okay?"

"So this part here?" I say, pointing at the tip.

"That's the barrel," he says.

"Barrel," I repeat.

He moves toward me, positions the gun in my palm, and gets me to stand with my legs parted. With a warm hand, he presses my lower back and sets me in position. "Arms straight ahead. Shoulders forward. That's it."

For a moment, I forget that I'm holding a gun. His touch causes goose bumps to explode all over my body.

"You've got it," he says, his grin tickling my cheek.

"So what's the point of carrying this if it's empty? What if I need to shoot someone?"

His smile disappears. "Would you?"

"Would I what?"

"Shoot someone."

His words feel like a heavy weight on my chest. Would I shoot someone? What kind of question is that?

"If you had a gun pointed at another human being," he says, "could you pull the trigger?"

I swallow hard. I'm not so sure I could.

He rests a hand over the barrel of my gun and lowers it. "You aren't a killer, Lucy. That's not a bad thing."

"Well, it is a bad thing if I need to protect those I love." The second that last word comes out, I push my cheek with my tongue and turn away from him. "Well, those I care about. You know what I mean."

He doesn't make it awkward. "Yeah, I do know what you mean, and that's why I'm here. If someone needs to take a shot"—he jams a loaded magazine into his gun, pulls something back, and a loud clicking sound comes out of it—"then I'll be the one to take it."

"You've done this before," I say.

He doesn't answer. Lucas never told me he knew anything about guns. He said he dealt mainly with computers and electrical systems, and that he'd caused the death of countless soldiers due to his manipulation of those systems.

I had no idea he knew how to shoot.

"Twice," he finally admits. "My dad taught me how to shoot. After he was killed, I stayed in the house for a few weeks. I found my dad's gun safe and got in. The next day, two guys broke into our house and I shot them both point-blank."

"I... I'm sorry."

He shakes his head. "Don't be. This is the world we live in."

"Wish it wasn't." I grimace.

He forces a smile. "Isn't that why we're doing all this? To take Eve down and make sure we have a better shot at the future?"

He's right. That's exactly why we're fighting so hard to remove Eve from power. We have a chance at recreating a new world—one in which people don't feel the need to carry guns for basic survival. The world caused this.

He heads into the kitchen and comes back with two DotLites. "You sure you're ready for this?"

It isn't like we have any other choice. He pins the

DotLite onto my shirt. "Don't worry," he says. "We'll find them, okay?"

I hope he's right.

I grip the gun in my hand, careful to keep the barrel away from Lucas. "All right, let's go."

He leads us through the door, letting it close loudly behind us. It's a grim sound that makes me wonder if we're making the right decision. We were safe inside that room. And I'm no soldier. I stay close to Lucas and follow him down the tunnel, our DotLites brightening the path ahead of us.

I wish we'd had these things on our way down.

Lucas raises his gun, keeping it held firmly ahead of him. I do the same, even though I know my threat is empty. But Lucas is right—the sight of a gun is usually enough to make someone in their tracks.

If someone were to attack us, they'd have no way of knowing my gun is empty.

Empowered by this, I tighten my grip and move forward like it's loaded.

We're about to make a left turn when I hear something behind us. A footstep. I spin around, my bright white light following my movements, and glare into a narrow tunnel.

Lucas does the same. "Everything okay?"

"I heard something," I whisper.

He takes a step forward and squints down the tunnel. "Could have been a rat or a mouse."

He's probably right, especially now that I know there are mice down here.

I turn the other way and we continue our path deeper into Elysium's underground tunnels. We make another turn, and this time, I hear the sound again.

This time, it's swift and light.

I twirl on the spot, hoping to catch the perpetrator in their tracks, but it's too late. Something pinches my neck—it feels like a bug bite— and my vision blurs. I reach for my neck, imagining I might find a protruding dart, but I can't reach. My muscles are seizing up.

Lucas suddenly does the same thing I did— reaches for his neck and winces.

I blink hard and open my mouth to call out his name, but nothing comes out.

There isn't time to do anything else. I fall to one knee and everything goes black.

CHAPTER 35 – EVE

I pace across my room, wondering if my heels have indented the floor by now. Every time I get anxious, I wander across the same location over and over again.

Why haven't I heard from Trinity? The last time we spoke, which was several hours ago, she assured me that she'd located Lucy's general whereabouts—under Elysium. She mentioned something about locating Lucy's Luminous Sphere in a box, which means Lucy descended into Elysium's underground tunnels to avoid being traced. Trinity also assured me that she would scour the place until she found her. It's been several hours since then. Has something happened to Lucy? Have Gabriel and Freyda harmed her? Kidnapped her?

I search the ceiling, allowing the ticking sound of my silver-rimmed wall clock to ease me.

Calm yourself, Eve. If anyone can bring you, Lucy, it's Trinity with a chip in her brain.

Is the chip truly in her brain? I wonder. Where did it go? The skin appears to absorb the piece of technology, but there's no telling where it implants itself.

It doesn't matter.

What matters is that Trinity is as eager to locate Lucy as I am, which means she will succeed no matter the cost.

Though I'm not certain how much longer I can torturously stand here, awaiting an update from Trinity. I must do something. I must preoccupy my mind.

Pausing my pacing, I charge straight for my door, reach the elevators, and descend to the seventh floor. Rarely do I ever visit the other floors, but the seventh floor happens to be where Quinton resides.

Room 715, I recall.

Women offer sweet greeting gestures as I walk past them feeling like a goddess. Ever since my speech in the Hub, women now watch me with adoration. It's as if they believe me responsible for offering them something they haven't felt in a while—joy.

You are responsible, Eve. You're the reason these women are happy and safe. You're their everything.

I walk faster, my steps seeming lighter.

You are their reason for being.

"Good morning," I say as I pass several women.

They're shy in their response, almost as if unworthy of my presence.

When I reach Quinton's door, I knock once, twice, then three times. Finally, the door swooshes open, and out comes a groggy Quinton with puffy pink eyes and pillow marks on his right cheek. His pajamas, sky blue cotton material with a snowflake pattern, look crinkled and in need of a good wash.

"Good morning," I say coldly.

"Eve." He appears flabbergasted to see me.

"I need more," I say. "I want you to return to the basement and resume your work."

With robotic movements, he brushes past me and trots down the corridor.

I'm about to remind him that he's still in his pajamas, but there's no use. He's already on his way to the basement.

CHAPTER 36 – GABRIEL

Freyda looks as worried as I'm feeling.

It's been an hour since Commander Thompson ordered two men to retrieve Lucas and Lucy. Why is it taking so long? Freyda cranes her neck and looks through the dark glass ceiling. Like me, she's probably wondering if we're being watched right now.

"You think they're okay?" she asks.

I want to reassure her and tell her that everything's fine, but the truth is, I have no idea. There's no telling if Lucas went back to the main entrance to check for Emily's signal. And if he did, Trinity could have been waiting for him.

I try to act cool, but my lip twitches.

"Great," Freyda says. "Thanks for keeping me calm."

Sighing, I get up from my chair and wrap my arms around her. "All I know is that those kids are tough. Whatever is going on, I'm sure they're fine."

I want to believe that. I know Lucas is tougher than he lets on. He looks like the kind of guy who has experience in combat, even though he never once talked about it. Lucy has enough anger in her to bring down all of Elysium. She wants vengeance for her mom. This could be a good thing or a bad thing depending on the situation. She doesn't have any combat skills, but she has a purpose and that's what matters.

"What if Lucy and Lucas refused to come back with James's men?" Freyda asks. "They have no way of knowing they're the good guys."

I squeeze her shoulders. "I wouldn't worry about that. We made it clear how to approach them. I can't imagine them wanting to stay inside that tiny room when there's an entire city down here."

Freyda touches my hand on her shoulder. It's warm, comforting, and makes me want to kiss her neck. "Yeah, I know. I'm sure they're fine. I'm a little worried, that's all. It shouldn't take over an hour for an extraction operation."

Turning away, I tap my fingers on my biceps. I keep telling myself that any second now, General James will open the door with Lucy and Lucas at his side. I'm about to share my vision with Freyda when the door swooshes open and my heart skips a beat.

General James steps inside with two armed men at his sides. He looks defeated, like a doctor on the verge of giving a loved one terrible news.

The kids aren't here.

"What happened?" I asked.

Freyda jolts up, joining me at my side.

The general shakes his head. "I'm sorry. We searched everywhere. There was no sign of a teen boy or girl."

"That doesn't make any sense!" Freyda growls. "They were up there."

I try to wrap my arms around her again, but she pulls away. There's no point in trying to console her. Freyda has every right to be upset. If they weren't up there, then where are they?

"We searched the room you provided coordinates to," James says. "We have reason to believe they were there recently. In the sink were plates with sticky maple syrup, which means they must have eaten before heading out into the tunnels."

"So maybe they're walking around—"

"We looked everywhere," James says. "Only two options remain. One, they exited through where they originally came from—"

"They wouldn't do that unless—" Freyda tries.

"Or two," the general continues, "they were captured and extracted from the tunnels."

I ignore the second option. "They wouldn't have left like that. It doesn't make any sense. Even if they'd received word from Emily, no way would they be stupid enough to go back inside of Elysium."

"Then it's option two," Freyda says begrudgingly. "Someone got to them first. Whether they caught them at the entrance or in the tunnels, I can't say. But someone has them. I'm telling you."

"Then we need to get up there," I say. "If we don't stop Eve now, there's no telling what she'll do to Lucy. Or worse, to Lucas." I turn to Freyda. "You know what that woman is capable of."

Freyda's so worked up she looks like she's on the verge of crying.

"You need to get your soldiers up there, General," I say. "Please."

General James scratches at his mustache. "I'm sorry, but I can't send armed soldiers into an area full of civilians. It'll be a bloodbath. We have protocols in place in case of a hostage situation, but this isn't a typical hostage situation. Eve doesn't want anything in exchange for their lives. Can you imagine how many innocent lives will be lost if we go up there, guns blazing?"

Freyda grabs her hips so aggressively it makes a smacking sound. "Then what do we do? We can't sit here and do nothing. I'm telling you, General, Eve Malum will murder Lucas and then convince everyone that he's a monster who corrupted her godchild."

James sticks his belly out, lost in thought. I can't even imagine how many scenarios are racing through his mind right now. And whatever he decides, he'll have to run it by the commander. Even then, there's no guarantee she'll approve. Like James says, they weren't prepared for a situation like this. No one imagined Elysium being overtaken by a lunatic, or that its civilians would actually follow that lunatic.

This is one hell of a messed-up situation.

"I'll prepare an extraction team," James says.

"For Lucy?" Freyda asks. "And Lucas?"

"No," the general says. "For Eve."

I can't tell if this is supposed to be a joke. Given how quickly things are escalating, I highly doubt the general is trying to get a laugh out of us. He must sense our confusion.

"Eve is the threat," he adds. "If we can remove her from the equation, we can attempt infiltration without being met by hostility. If Eve is present, her people will do anything to protect her."

"And how do you propose we remove Eve from the equation?" I ask.

The general sticks his thumbs inside his belt. "I never said it would be easy. But I believe our best course of action is sending in a Trojan horse."

A Trojan horse? How could he possibly do something like that? Eve isn't an idiot. She'll never let random people inside of Elysium. Especially after what happened in Eden. Letting me in is what caused all of this in the first place. If she could go back in time, she would have remained inside of Eden's walls and wouldn't have migrated here, even if it meant a great deal of her women would die of the virus that was spreading at the time.

"I have a team of specialized women," James continues. "They'll pose as stranded survivors outside of Elysium's gates."

Freyda scoffs. "I know you want to believe Eve will let in innocent women, but there's no guarantee—"

"Not women," James cuts her off. "Children. We'll include children with these women."

I get where James is going with this, but it still doesn't guarantee anything. Now that Freyda and I—wanted fugitives—are on the loose, Eve will be extremely stringent. She may refuse access altogether, even if kids' lives are involved. She'll rationalize that risking the lives of her people, including thousands of women and children, isn't worth saving a few.

"I don't care what Eve thinks," says General James.

"We'll make sure that the people of Elysium see the survivors."

Freyda stops pacing and pulls at her plush bottom lip—something she does when she's thinking hard. "If we can get the civilians concerned for these strangers, Eve won't have a choice but to let them in. Eve hates to look like the bad guy."

General James winks at her. "Bingo."

CHAPTER 37 – LUCY

I wake up to a loud ringing in my ears and a throbbing pain in my neck.

Where am I? My body is sore, almost as if I spent the last few hours sleeping on a concrete floor. Yet, the surface under me feels soft and plushy. A bed? I crack my eyes open.

I'm lying atop a bed with an oversized shackle around my left ankle. It's heavy, cold, and hurts my skin. When I tug at it, a heavy chain drags across the sheets.

Where the hell am I?

The room is clean—almost too clean—with its smooth royal purple bedding, its dustless bedposts, and its spotless windows. The ceiling, white and full of hand-designed swirls, makes me dizzy. I've never seen anything like it before.

I breathe in, two conflicting smells entering my nostrils: the smell of lemon and alcohol combined with the mouthwatering scent of fried eggs, bacon, and baked potato.

Is someone cooking? I glance down at my shackle. The chain appears to lead somewhere underneath the bed. Either that, or around the post. It seems as though I have enough slack to stand up and walk around a bit, but not enough to exit the room.

I crawl out of bed as quietly as I can, the heavy chain links striking each other. Under my feet is a soft beige carpet that feels like a cloud beneath my heels. If it weren't for the shackle digging into my ankle bone, I'd appreciate the carpet's texture. I move forward, baring my teeth as the chain drags heavily behind me.

I'm going to give myself away.

Suddenly, the door creaks open.

Though I'm tempted to lunge back into the bed and pretend to be asleep, I don't have time.

Eve comes waltzing in carrying a white ceramic plate topped with fried eggs, sizzling bacon, and potato wedges with crispy browned skin. Next to it is a small mountain of ketchup.

I forget to breathe.

Eve.

She smiles at me as if we've gone back in time and she's brought me a cookie at Mom's.

This woman is insane. How can she smile at me after what she's done? And worse, after learning that I *know* what she's done? How can she stand there and act like she's done nothing wrong? As if all is forgiven?

"I dread to think what you were being fed in that awful place," she says. "I prepared you a fresh breakfast. You know me"—she twirls a finger next to her ear and lets out a giggle that makes me uncomfortable—"I've never been much of a cook. But I think you'll be pleasantly sur—"

"What the fuck do you think you're doing?" I say.

Although she stops talking, her smile doesn't fade. It's creepy and makes me want to squish her lips together until she can't smile anymore.

"I... I've made you breakfast, my sweet Lucy."

I scoff so loudly it hurts my lungs. "My sweet Lucy? Have you lost your mind? Oh, wait, yeah you have. A long time ago. You're delusional. You're fucking delusional, you know that?"

Her lip twitches, but her smile remains intact. "You appear slightly aggravated. I suppose that's understandable, given that I chained you to my bed. I assure you, my dear, that it's only a precaution until I'm certain that your brain is back to being as it should be."

"My brain?" I say. "What the hell—"

She waves dismissively and lets out a high-pitched laugh. "The boy, my sweet Lucy. It may be difficult for you to grasp this, but he's brainwashed you. I don't know what he's done to you, but he's taken you away from me."

She's fucking insane. Nothing I say will get through to her. I want to lunge at her and strangle her with my chain, but she's out of reach.

"He's made you believe that I somehow harmed your mother. My sweet Lucy, you know that I would never—"

"You're lying!" I say. "You're lying, you fucking bitch!" I yank at my chain and it rattles loudly, forcing her to step back. "You killed my mom. I saw you. I watched you do it."

Her features twist as if I'm breaking her heart. She looks devastated. Does she believe her own lies? She's trying to make me think I'm crazy. I'm not the crazy one. She is. I know what I saw.

"I have proof on my H-Cap, and you know it. That's why you took it from me!"

She crinkles her nose. "My sweet Lucy, what on Earth are you talking about?" She aims the plate of food toward the bedside table. Atop it is my H-Cap. "Yes, I took your H-Cap, but only about an hour ago. I extracted it from your room and brought it to you. I know you have wonderful memories—"

"You're lying!" I shout.

My voice cuts out. Why is she doing this?

She fans her face like she's on the verge of crying. "He ruined you... my dear Lucy. I can't believe you would think me capable of doing such a horrendous thing." Her eyes water, but I won't give in. This is what Eve does. She's a master manipulator. "Ophelia was my best friend." She frowns this time and her thumb whitens around the plate of food. "That boy has implanted false memories in your brain. I would never lay a finger on your mother. Do you hear me?"

The confusing part is that deep down, I want to believe her. I want to believe that this whole time, I've been subjected to brainwashing techniques and my thoughts are not my own. If only if it were so simple. If only I could wake up and realize that Eve was still my godmother... that she still loved me. That I still loved her.

But she's a monster. As I stare at her bright, bloodshot eyes, all I see is evil.

She fans her face again, kneels, and places the food on the floor. Carefully, she inches it a bit closer to me before standing back up.

"I won't subject myself to this abuse," she says. "I've done nothing to deserve this. I love you, my sweet Lucy, and when you're ready—"

I lunge forward again, my chain clanging so loudly that she flinches.

She lets out a strained breath, wipes her eye, and turns around. But before exiting, she points at a door next to the bed. "The en suite bathroom is located there, should you need it. You should have enough length to reach it. And I promise you, my dear Lucy, that I won't give up on you. I love you, and you will come to your senses, no matter how long it takes."

I want to tell her to go fuck herself, but I can't. I'm too shocked by what's happening to say anything else. I once thought that witnessing Eve talk to herself was frightening, but that memory pales in comparison to this.

Eve believes her own lies. Somehow, she's convinced herself that with enough time, we'll reunite as a family—that all will be fine, and we'll return to how things used to be when Mom was around.

That'll never happen.

She can keep playing her games all she wants, but she'll never get my love.

CHAPTER 38 – EVE

As I close my bedroom door behind me, my heart feels like it's going to burst.

My Lucy... My sweet Lucy. What has that boy done to her? He's stolen her from me. I clench my fists, my fingernails painfully digging into my palms. He will suffer. I will make sure of it. Because of him, Lucy now believes that I've killed her mother. How could she think such a horrible thing?

You did kill Ophelia, says a little voice in my head.

"I did no such thing!" I cry out.

I clear my throat at the sound of my voice reverberating off the walls of my room. Straightening my posture, I fix my white overcoat and reattach one of its loose buttons.

I'm not a murderer. I'm a good person.

You're losing sense of reality.

I grit my teeth. Someone is behind this. Perhaps the boy. Someone is attempting to implant memories in my mind. I know it. I feel it in my gut. No way would I ever harm my best friend. I understand, now—that memory is false.

You're a cold-blooded killer.

"Shut up!" I hiss, pulling at my hair.

I move swiftly through my suite and slap myself across the face, hoping this awful voice will disappear. What is wrong with me? Why can't I make it stop? Did Lucas do this to me? He appears to have quite the fascination with Lucy. It would make perfect sense. Perhaps he's messed with my mind to distance her from me. It's the perfect plan, after all.

He knows how I feel about men and must think that I'm the only thing standing in his way.

But I won't allow it. I won't allow some boy to destroy my family and to make me out to be a cruel villain.

None of that matters now, anyway. Trinity assured me that the boy would be taken care of. All that matters now is ensuring that Lucy comes to her senses. It may take a few days, but eventually, she will realize that I'm all she's got. I'm the only person who truly cares about her, the only person she can trust.

My throat swells at the thought of my godchild. I wipe my burning eyes, swallow hard, and aim my gaze at the ceiling.

Everything will be okay.

"Everything will be okay," I repeat aloud. "Everything."

I force a smile, and a sense of tranquility washes over me.

"Everything will be okay," I repeat.

Lucy has been returned to me, and soon, she will love me again as she once did.

I grin at the thought.

My sweet Lucy.

She'll be hungry again in a few hours. I wonder

what the kitchen is serving today. Exhilarated, I begin to fantasize about the next few days with Lucy. I could grab a movie from the library and make popcorn. She always did love popcorn.

Feeling like a new version of myself, I make my way to my suite's door and call out, "Open door."

It slips open and I step out to find Trinity standing strong with her back pressed against the wall.

"Thank you," I say, grazing her cheek. "You've brought Lucy to me, and I couldn't be happier."

She doesn't respond. Ever since I put that chip in her, it's as if happiness is no longer in her repertoire of emotions. Not that Trinity ever expressed much joy to begin with.

"What about the boy?" I ask.

"He's being contained inside an isolation unit," she says. "Locked away for treason."

"Good," I say. "And what about Gabriel and Freyda? Have you found them?"

"No, my queen. I was unable to locate the two. Would you like me to continue searching for them?"

I frown at the thought of those two holding hands. "No. Let them rot down there. Let's focus our energy on the women of Elysium instead."

"What do you need of me?" she asks.

"For now, continue watching my door unless something more pressing comes up. No one enters, and Lucy stays inside. Am I clear?"

"Yes, my queen."

CHAPTER 39 – GABRIEL

"How long have you been down here?" James asks.

"A few days," I say.

"Good. Then it shouldn't be too hard on you," he says. "I've had men surface to our aboveground bases after spending months underground. We usually give them sunglasses. You should be fine. The sky is overcast today."

"Like walking out of the movies in the afternoon," Freyda says.

I hold on to that thought. What I wouldn't do to take her to the movies on a date. Maybe one day, we'll get to experience that again.

We walk up a long corridor with a ceiling at least twenty feet high. It reminds me a bit of a ramp you'd find leading into an underground parking lot. They use this ramp for vehicles, too.

James makes a gesture at the two guards standing on opposite ends of the massive garage-like door. Not only does it begin to open vertically, but behind it, another horizontal platform splits open, revealing a gray, overcast sky.

"You guys are well hidden down here, aren't you?"

James looks back at me. "Absolutely. We can't risk

anyone breaking in."

The brightness isn't as bad as I thought it would be. I'm sure being around artificial light helps with that. It's not like we've been cooped up inside some cave with no light whatsoever. I squint at the brightness, but only for a few seconds. Freyda doesn't seem bothered at all.

We walk up the ramp and into the crisp autumn air. It smells clean and pure, like it's filtrating my lungs. Near the opening is a vast forest with dying orange leaves and bare branches. Aside from that, there isn't much else. No outposts, nothing. Only nature. I guess they don't want any sort of indication of a military base. It's a smart approach.

James readjusts his bulletproof vest and presses a button. "Bring 'em up," he says.

The sound of an engine turning echoes from inside the tunnel we came out of. Out from the darkness comes a set of headlights, followed by a sand-colored rover the size of a Jeep. Driving the thing is Commander Thompson, who looks like she was born for this. With an arm hanging out of the driver's window, she maneuvers the beast of a machine with a single hand.

She pulls up next to us, lowers her tinted aviator sunglasses, and says, "Get in."

James climbs in next to her and Freyda and I move to the back. Without warning, she presses on the gas, causing my head to fall back, and drives through tall grass. The rover's wheels flatten the blades as we move, making a weird hissing sound. Behind us, the horizontal door closes, a layer of artificial grass covering the external panels. If I hadn't come out of there just now, I'd have no idea that a door even exists.

"Where are we going?" I ask.

Commander Thompson turns her head as she drives, her voice carrying with the wind. "Three miles from here is an outpost. Our infiltration team is waiting for us there and is being prepped as we speak. We have a few monitoring systems inside this outpost. We won't have eyes or ears inside of Elysium, but we'll be able to watch them until they're brought inside."

"With drones?" I ask.

James turns around this time. "No, that would be too obvious. We implanted cameras on some trees around Elysium a few years ago. The bark camouflages them. So far, we've had no problems."

I remain silent and grab Freyda's hand. She gives me a bit of a squeeze to say, *We've got this.*

Poor Freyda. She's worried about Lucy. So am I. There's no telling what Eve has planned for her, and with how she feels about men, I don't even want to think about what she'll do to Lucas. Chances are she'll blame the guy for everything. If this extraction team doesn't succeed, we're fucked.

It's our only chance.

I don't voice my concerns aloud. What's the point? Commander Thompson and James seem to know what they're doing. They've been around for a while, and they have all the right equipment. I'm sure that whoever they're sending in there will get the job done.

We drive in silence, the rover's wheels easing over bumps and rocks along the way. The suspension on this thing is out of this world. Finally, Commander Thompson slows the vehicle, though I don't understand why. I can't see any outpost for miles.

It must be underground.

The commander parks the rover, turns off the engine, and hops out like she has springs for legs. She walks through the tall grass and toward a large boulder in the middle of nowhere. Is there a switch on that thing?

But then, out of nowhere, something flickers, distorting what I thought was a boulder only seconds ago. Seemingly out of thin air, a building the size of a small house appears, its black glass windows shimmering with a blue current.

"What the hell?" I say.

James lets out a playful laugh. "Pretty neat, huh? Do you have any idea how long it took us to develop this sort of camouflaging technology?"

I blink several times to make sense of it. Freyda seems as surprised as I am, though slightly more excited. She beams like someone who finds a $100 bill on the ground. "Holy shit. I've heard about this in my police days, but they were only rumors."

Commander Thompson walks ahead without looking back at us. Two guards at the front doors step aside and allow her inside. When we approach, James says, "They're with us," and the soldiers lower their guns.

The first thing I notice when we step inside are all the computers, the wide screens, and flickering lights. This must be one of their control hubs. I wonder what else they control or monitor from this station.

"We've got eyes and ears all over the place," James says. "And we continue to expand every day."

He points at a large screen above the heads of two young women and a young man who appear to be hacking away at their keyboards.

On the screen is Elysium, standing tall underneath a gloomy overcast sky. Every few seconds, the cameras alternate, and I see Elysium from a different angle.

"So no eyes at all on the inside?" I ask.

James shakes his head. "Unfortunately not. Vrin didn't feel comfortable sharing inside footage with anyone from the outside. She was a smart woman. We always respected her decision."

"So how do we know this mission will work?" I ask.

James isn't a moron. The guy knows what he's doing, as does Commander Thompson. But for my own peace of mind, I need to know. Eve may be power hungry and sometimes blinded by hatred, but she isn't an idiot. This whole operation could go belly-up if we underestimate her intelligence.

James winks at Thompson like they're sharing some inside joke. Either that, or they've planned this long and hard for years. Before James can explain anything, the commander removes her aviator glasses.

"The women selected for this mission are the best of the best," she says. "If they can't pull this off, no one can."

That thought is comforting, though it still doesn't explain to me exactly how this will unfold.

James leans forward and narrows his gaze through the outpost's tinted window. "They're here."

On the other side of the window is another beige rover pulling up through the untrimmed grass. It parks and two women and four children step out of the vehicle. The children all appear to be between five and eight years old.

"Let me introduce you," James says, exiting the post.

We follow him out into the open air as the newcomers approach us, dressed like they've been traveling through these fields for months. The first agent to approach us—a middle-aged Asian woman with long black hair and a prominent jaw structure—extends a hand.

"Mori," she says.

I shake her hand. "Gabriel."

She has a firm grip that makes me think she knows how to operate all sorts of weapons.

The second woman goes on to do the same thing. "Sanchez." Her shake is also firm, and her dark eyes never leave mine. "Puerto Rico?" she asks me in Spanish. Behind her back hangs long brown, almost black hair, which appears to be housing blades of grass.

"Yeah," I say, a bit taken aback. "But born and raised in the states."

She smacks my shoulder hard before letting go of my hand. "Same. Nice to meet you, Gabriel."

Freyda steps in, almost shoving me aside.

"Freyda," she says.

Sanchez smirks when she gets a good look at Freyda. "Better hold on to this one, chico," she says, her attention lingering on Freyda.

She gives Freyda a full up-and-down look and bites her bottom lip.

Well, I wasn't expecting that.

I wrap an arm around Freyda's shoulder. "I'm holding on to her, don't worry."

Freyda doesn't pull away. She seems to like it when I take control.

Sanchez smirks and turns her attention to James, her posture immediately shifting. She stands stiff, as does Mori next to her, while the children gather backpacks from the rover.

"I take it you've been debriefed?" General James says.

Both Mori and Sanchez nod, though Sanchez is the one to speak. "At headquarters, sir."

"Good," James says. "The trek from here is approximately ten miles. You'll have to go on foot."

"Yes, sir," Sanchez says.

Although they both act like soldiers, you'd think they'd traveled through time from the Middle Ages. I know this is intentional. They need to look like survivors. Dirt covers their faces, arms, and necks, and they're both clad in brown and green mesh that looks like dishrags sewn together. Sanchez's boots are falling apart at the seams, and Mori is missing a pant leg altogether.

I remember that look all too well. I lived it for years.

The kids, too, wear torn and stained clothing. They drag their ripped backpacks behind them, which I assume contain only basic items like a bit of food and some water. They can't be showing up at Elysium with advanced technology in their bags, or they'll blow their cover.

"When the lights go out, we'll send our team in," James says.

"Yes, sir," Sanchez says, hands held behind her back.

James reaches for both their shoulders. "Do well."

The women turn around, warning the kids to stay close. As they walk toward Elysium, which isn't even visible from here, they shrink in size.

"Lights, sir?" I ask.

James taps his temple. "All we need is to get them inside."

I wait. He's going somewhere with this.

"See that little girl?" he points to the smallest one who looks no older than five. "She's carrying a jammer."

"An EMP?" Freyda asks.

"Something like that. It's concealed inside a teddy bear. Once they're inside, all they have to do is activate it. The lights go out, we go in. I already have three teams in position, waiting for my command."

"So you'll have the advantage," I say. "You'll be ready with NODs before they even get to theirs."

Freyda scrunches her nose at me.

"Night optical devices," I say. "Or, better known as night vision goggles."

James grins. "Exactly."

CHAPTER 40 – LUCY

I rub at the inflamed skin around my ankle, feeling like a cheese grater attacked it. This shackle is rough and cold, and I'd do anything to take it off.

I follow the chain to the bottom left bedpost. It's wrapped around the bed's leg and locked in place by a padlock. If this bed didn't look like it weighed over a thousand pounds, I wouldn't be so discouraged.

Sighing, I drop myself down to the ground, my back grazing the side of the mattress. I throw my head back into the plush texture and growl.

There has to be a way out of this.

I stick a finger between the shackle and my ankle bone, trying to ease some of the tension, but it only makes the pain worse.

As I stare at the ceiling, I can't help but wonder... Where's Emily? Is she all right? Did Eve discover that she was part of our plan to expose her? Does she even know we've been caught? Oh God... Emily. I hope she's all right. I wish I could go find her and tell her everything. I'd tell her to stop looking—to stop trying to help us. It's no use now. Eve has me tied up like a wild animal, and I have no clue what she's done with Lucas.

Knowing Eve, she probably locked him up somewhere. Lucas is a male, after all. She thinks he's the reason I hate her, which makes this situation incredibly dangerous. If Eve was able to murder Vrin in cold blood, there's no telling what she'll do to the boy she now believes is the reason I'm trying to take her down.

How can she believe that, anyway? Is it all an act, or does she believe herself? If it's the latter, we're all in serious danger. The woman's lost her mind, and it's not like she had much of it left to begin with.

I envision Lucas locked up in a cell, and my stomach churns. What's he thinking about right now? Is he thinking about me? Is he as worried as I am? Probably. He thinks Eve wants me dead. So did I, until she showed up in here with breakfast.

My gaze lingers on the cold plate of eggs, bacon, and potatoes. As hungry as I am, I don't want to eat anything made by Eve's monstrous hands. I'd rather starve to death.

It's irrational thinking, I know. If it gets to the point of having to make a life-or-death decision, I'll choose the food. But there's plenty of time before then. If I could only get out of this damn thing.

In movies, some people go so far as to dislocate their body parts to remove their shackles. I wouldn't even know how to do that, and to be honest, I'm too afraid to. To dislocate a thumb is one thing, but a foot? Yuck.

Blowing air out through my tight lips, I rock my head back and forth, slamming it into the mattress every few seconds. "Come on, Lucy, think."

There has to be a way out of here.

I reach for the bed's leg post, sliding my palm against its luxurious finish. It's made of solid mahogany, and the only reason I know that is because Mom once found a mahogany dresser at a garage sale for twenty dollars. She couldn't stop talking about it for months after that.

"Can you believe it? Twenty dollars for this thing. I can't... I can't believe it. Do you have any idea how expensive mahogany can be?" she'd said over and over again.

I remember getting annoyed by how repetitive she'd become, but right now, I'd do anything to go back and listen to her rant endlessly about that dresser.

The wood feels smooth and cool against my thumb as I follow the grooves and patterns. As I reach about halfway down, however, something sharp pokes me. I pull away to find a droplet of blood on the tip of my index finger.

Did something bite me?

Curious, I lean sideways to peek under the bed. I reach the same spot, careful this time. What is that? A splinter? Mom always said mahogany didn't splinter easily. With my fingernails, I pluck at the splinter until it makes a faint splitting sound and separates from the foot of the bed. It's about two inches long and hard to the touch. With the splinter now horizontal, I twirl it until it snaps off.

I swing my body out from underneath the bed and examine the splinter. It's hard and as sharp as a needle. Although I have no idea what I'm about to do,

I have to try. Holding the splinter firmly between my thumb and index finger, I stick its sharp end into the shackle's keyhole. It's awkward and takes a bit of practice, but I get it in.

Like in the movies, I start pressing and twirling the wood, trying to unlock the mechanism on the inside.

"Come on," I mumble under my breath.

It feels like I'm hitting something, but I could be imagining the whole thing. Truthfully, I have no clue what I'm doing.

I poke harder, hoping something will unlock, but nothing happens. Frustrated, I jam the splinter even farther and something snaps.

"Damn it," I mutter.

The splinter comes out in two pieces.

There goes my chance of ever getting out of these.

What am I supposed to do? Sit here and wait for Eve? Pretend to be happy when she shows up? It would probably work, but I can't bring myself to do it. As much as I want out of this mess, I can't pretend to care about someone who murdered my mom.

CHAPTER 41— EVE

Mary-Anne observes me with a twinkle in her eye.

"You seem awfully chipper," she says.

I can't help it. How could I not be? My sweet Lucy is waiting for me in my room. Finally, we'll be a family again. As much as I want to share this with Mary-Anne, I don't. She wouldn't understand. If anyone finds out I'm holding a young girl captive, they'll think me a monster.

If only they understood that the true monster is Lucas. I may be holding Lucy captive for now, but in time, she will see that it is for her own good. She will come to realize that Lucas brainwashed her into believing me capable of dreadful things.

She will see through his lies.

I light up. "It's a great day."

Mary-Anne shifts her focus toward the twelfth floor's lunchroom, where dozens of women and a handful of men sit around tables, jabbing their forks into vegetarian shepherd's pie. As odd as the recipe might sound, it's rather delicious with its spiced lentil base.

The atmosphere quiets as Mary-Anne and I enter the room. One woman wearing a pearl necklace stops midbite, bits of lentils falling back onto her plate. She drops her fork, blots her mouth with a decorative napkin, and says, "We have a spot right here, Eve."

The women around her stir in their seats like excited children waiting for recess.

"Thank you," I say politely, making my way into the kitchen.

Behind the glass counter stands Muzella, our floor's chef. She's known in all of Elysium for her vegetarian dishes, and many people from different floors often come here for her food.

"Eve," she says, nodding next to her lentil-covered spatula. "Care for a bite?"

"Yes, please," I say, and she scoops a messy ball of lentils, corn, and potatoes onto a white ceramic plate. She then places it atop the glass dome between us and I reach for it.

"On the house," she says, shooing away my Luminous Sphere.

Mary-Anne goes to nudge me in the ribs but stops midair, likely recalling how much I despise being touched. "Royalty treatment," she says through the side of her mouth.

Muzella serves her without smiling and moves on to the cash register, which isn't exactly a register—it's a tablet. She punches something into the gadget and on the other side of it, a price in bold font appears:

$4.00 – K12

"Payment, K12," Mary-Anne says, and the screen flashes green before showing "Transaction Complete."

If only they'd had this technology in the old world.

At the time, the idea of wrist chips completing payments impressed me, but these spheres are even more advanced. Without even extracting our spheres, we're able to simply say the word *payment* followed by the receiver's code, and through voice recognition, the sphere sends a signal for payment.

I never agreed with a currency system in Eden, but now that I've experienced it in Elysium, I wouldn't change it. Everyone receives a base salary that allows them to obtain essentials, with additional wages for performing work at different levels.

Mary-Anne grabs her plate and plucks a fork from the cutlery booth. She follows me toward the woman with the pearl necklace, and we sit down.

The air is quiet and heavy until the woman with the pearl necklace screeches her fork and sets it aside. "We've all been discussing our career aspirations, Eve."

She talks to me as if awaiting a gold star.

"That's wonderful," I say. "What are you planning on doing?"

My question seems to excite her even more. She slouches over her plate. "Well, I've always wanted to be a teacher. I mean, I know we already have teachers, but I'm hoping some of them will also be looking for a change."

The woman sitting next to her—a strange-looking lady with overly short bangs and close-knit eyes—bares a set of crooked teeth at me. I can't tell if she's smiling or trying to intimidate me, but by the way she's stirring in her seat, I'd say she's thrilled by my presence. "And I'm looking into studying engineering." She laughs, an unpleasant chortle. "I mean, it's always interested me. I couldn't afford it at the time, 'cause, ya know, school costs money and stuff. And I ain't never had lots of money."

Clearly, with a vocabulary like yours, you will never succeed at becoming an engineer.

Despite my judgmental thoughts, I squint at her. "I'm sure you will do a fantastic job."

She lets out another choppy laugh that makes me want to get up and walk away.

Fortunately, a distraction comes along before I feel the need to make an excuse to leave. From the elevators comes Trinity. She moves swiftly, her fists balled on either side of her rapidly scissoring legs.

As soon as she spots me, her features harden and her speed doubles. Something is wrong.

I drop my fork atop my shepherd's pie and stand. "What is it, Trinity?"

She clears her throat as if contemplating whether to announce it in front of everyone.

Touching Mary-Anne's shoulder, I excuse myself and hurry over to Trinity. "What is it?" I whisper.

"We have a situation," she says.

I give her a stupid look meant to signify *Well, spit it out already.*

Rather than responding, she turns her head slightly to the side, and I follow her gaze. Although difficult to see through Elysium's thick glass, I spot a crowd gathering on the other side of the twelfth floor—a multitude of colors blending.

I frown. "What's going on over there?"

"Newcomers," she says.

I don't waste time interrogating her. Instead, I march my way past the elevators and down the corridor. Behind me, chairs screech and rapid footsteps follow. When I reach the other side of the floor, men and women part, creating a clear path to the now grimy and fogged window.

Without saying hello to anyone, I hurry to the window and peer outside.

Down below, several yards away, a small group of newcomers approach our walls—two women and four children, to be precise. One of the women walks with a limp, while the other supports her by wrapping an arm around her torso. Their clothes, torn rags, make it clear to me that they've been traveling in the wilderness for quite some time.

I know I should feel sorry for them, but I don't. Only recently have I acquired the title of leader in Elysium. The last thing I need is for newcomers to enter our kingdom and tarnish everything I've worked so hard to build.

What if their beliefs are different from ours? What if they have news of the outside world? Of other survivors? Of other bases? It will disrupt everything. I think back to the documentation I found in Vrin's office. What if this is only the beginning? Perhaps they've come looking for a habitable place with the promise of returning to their people.

Elysium may still have capacity, but if we start bringing in survivors, we will run out of space and resources.

You and your people were migrating survivors, too.

I glower through the window, wishing my

thoughts would silence themselves.

I'm nothing like these people. I'm not a leech. We came from Eden bringing experience, resources, and knowledge. What do they bring to us? More mouths to feed.

You can't let them inside, Eve.

"Survivors!" someone calls out, and everyone turns to me.

I grit my teeth.

I may be the leader—the one with the power to decide between two choices—but right now, I don't have much of a choice. If I don't allow them inside Elysium, my people will view me as a monster.

Behind me, Trinity catches up, waiting for a new command.

I leave the crowd and approach Trinity. "Bring them in. But I want them isolated. At least until I can speak with them privately and we can ensure they aren't a threat in any way."

"Yes, my queen," she says, before turning around and rushing toward the elevators.

Sensing that all eyes are still on me, I twirl on my heels, clasp my fingers together, and grin as wide as I can until my back molars ache. "I'm sure you're all as excited to meet the newcomers as I am. They have to go through an isolation period to ensure they aren't carrying any contagious virus. Once that's done, I will set up a meeting for introductions."

Animated discussions ensue, and I turn around, my smile instantly vanishing.

CHAPTER 42 – GABRIEL

Freyda stares at the live feed like she's watching the Super Bowl. "I wish we had eyes on the inside."

She looks sideways at me, probably thinking what I'm thinking: why not hack our way inside? Before either one of us can voice this, General James cuts in. "Me too, but we couldn't risk it. And before you say anything"—he sticks out a flat palm—"breaking into their system would only put them on high alert."

How did he know what we were thinking? Must be a side effect of working in this field. Always on mission mode, thinking of ways to have as many eyes on our target as possible.

I'm about to comment on how if the hack is done right, no one will know. But Freyda chimes in before I can.

"He's right." I'm a bit surprised to hear how quickly she's agreed with this stranger, but Freyda isn't one to agree with anyone only to be nice. "This is Elysium we're talking about," she continues. "They have Binaries living there, which means they have top-notch systems in place."

"I see your point," I say. "It still sucks."

James laughs and pats me on the back. "That, it

does, but I can assure you that those women we sent in are some of my finest agents. They'll get the job done."

I stare absentmindedly at the screens, fantasizing about Eve being dragged out of Elysium with cuffs around her wrists. Is that how it'll play out? Probably not. There's no way her people would ever let that happen. Some of those women are so brainwashed by Eve that they'd stand in front of machine guns to save her life.

If that isn't brainwashed, I don't know what is.

"This could take a little while," James says.

I know he's right, but it's hard to look away. I'm scared to miss something. What if they send out some sort of signal and we miss it? But then I remember that this isn't my mission. James has other agents working the case, like the row of young men and women wearing headsets and currently monitoring the feed.

I'd say we're in good hands.

But I'm nervous.

If we don't get this right, everything could be over.

"I'd like to show you something," James says.

He leads us away from the monitoring station and toward a blue metal door at the back of the control hub. How is there even a door there? This place is pretty compact. I can't imagine another room on the other side of that thing.

He opens the door but doesn't walk in right away. There's nowhere to walk... What is this? A closet? I peer over his shoulder, and that's when I spot it: a hatch door on the floor, similar to the one we came through underground.

"There's a switch here to open the hatch, but as you well know"—he turns to me—"you can also open it manually."

"Yeah, a hundred pounds of manual," I say, still feeling the ache in my shoulders.

James laughs. He reaches for a switch at the back wall. At his feet, the hatch door's wheel spins once, and something unlocks. He waits patiently as the door opens. It must be some sort of hydraulic system.

"Why didn't the other door have a switch like this?" I ask, rolling my shoulders. "Would have made our lives way easier."

"You think?" he says, still laughing.

"Does this lead back to the base?" I ask.

James shakes his head. "Nope, not this one. Every outpost has an underground facility in case, well, you know. We like to have eyes on the surface, but it's always good to have a backup plan."

He turns around, finds the ladder, and descends into the hole.

We follow him down.

The second our feet land on the metal floor, elongated fluorescent lights flicker overhead. There are about six long bulbs attached to the ceiling, but only two of them turn on.

"Looks like you need replacements," I point out.

James grabs his belt and looks up at the lights. "Oh, no. That's intentional. We rotate the powered lights to conserve solar energy. Besides, no one needs that much lighting down here. It gives people headaches."

I think back to the old days when I used to shop at grocery stores with Mama. The lights always annoyed me.

He reaches for another switch, and a bunch of equipment powers on. At first, it's a soft humming sound, but then high-pitched beeping enters the mix, and blue and orange lights flicker across the back wall.

Only then do I notice that the upper half of the wall is a screen similar to a built-in TV. It turns on, displaying footage of something familiar. Something...

I turn to James, but all he does is light up and jerk his chin toward the screen. Confused, I take a step toward the footage. Although I'm staring right at the screen, I can't believe what I'm seeing.

"Is that—" I try, and Freyda takes a step forward.

"Washington, DC," she breathes.

On the screen is live footage of Washington DC. Most of its buildings are dark and gloomy, and broken glass covers the streets. But what has me flabbergasted isn't the destruction... it's how clean the city looks in comparison to how it looked after the war. Most of the streets are empty of cars, which wasn't the case a few years ago. Every few seconds, the footage shifts to a different spot in the city.

Military vehicles are parked on the sides of the streets, and men and women clad from head to toe in white astronaut-like suits are moving around, cleaning debris, and working on electrical fixtures. People in construction attire load beams of metal and wood atop their huge trucks before they move on to the broken windows throughout the city.

My throat swells at the sight of it. This whole time, I imagined everyone killing each other until there was no one left, but now that I'm seeing this, it's obvious that we all want the same thing... to fix the damage this war caused.

"We've restored power to a portion of the city, and we have men and women working on surrounding areas."

"Since when?" Freyda says.

She looks as shocked as I feel.

"Project Rebirth," comes Commander Thompson's voice. She lets go of the ladder and moves toward us. "We started the mission approximately ten months ago after making contact with other military bases throughout America. We restored power in crucial areas and succeeded in our communication efforts with other countries. Half of the people you see on that screen are from Canada, Australia, and the United Kingdom. They were hit hard by the war, but not as hard as we were, and have since agreed to lend a helping hand."

"And what about the gender ratio?" I ask.

I don't want to come across as ungrateful, or negative, but the gender ratio issue is what caused this whole thing in the first place. Well, it sparked it. Greedy, power-hungry humans are what caused the war.

"It would appear the issue is still present," says the commander. "But the top scientists of the world are currently investigating the issue and working on an approach to balance the ratio. We're living in the twenty-first century." She raises her hands in the air to showcase the room we're standing in. "If we can camouflage an entire building, there's no need to control the population through inhumane tactics. Decisions made by President Price and his followers were horrendous, and we have no intention of continuing his methods."

I'm beyond relieved to hear this. There are so many thoughts rushing through my mind that I can't pick a single one. I rub my forehead, trying to let it all sink in, when Freyda throws her arms around my neck. I catch her, squeezing her tight against me as my throat swells.

"We might just make it," she breathes into my neck.

CHAPTER 43 – LUCY

I wake up to the sound of stomping in the other room. Peeling my face away from the carpet, I sit upright. How long have I been out? My neck is sore from sleeping on the floor, as is my back and oddly, my right knee.

What kind of weird position did I sleep in?

A cupboard suddenly slams shut and I flinch.

Has someone broken in? My heartbeat quickens.

Although I want to get up and see what's going on, the smarter move is to wait here, hidden on the opposite side of the bed. What if someone is after Eve? What if they've found a way inside her suite?

"Fucking bullshit," comes Eve's voice.

I guess it isn't an intruder.

Slowly, I stand up and tiptoe my way over to the bedroom door. I can't reach it, and it's closed, but I can hear better at this distance.

"What the hell did you think would happen? That you'd live happily ever after?"

"No, that's not what—"

"You fucking idiot."

The stomping continues.

I want to imagine her yelling at someone, but I

know all too well that Eve's gone off the rails again. She's talking to herself, which means something must have happened. Is this about me? Probably not. I don't think she'd be dumb enough to make herself look like a psycho in front of me, especially if she's trying to reunite our twisted family.

I get the feeling that whatever happened, it's caused her to forget that I'm even here. Eve is all about her image. If she knew I were listening, she'd straighten up, fix her white overcoat, and force a grin so big she'd get crow's feet.

"What if..." she continues. "What if, maybe, no... That won't work. Or, will it?"

I picture her pacing across her living room, tapping a finger on her chin.

"Stop trying to—just fucking stop it."

What the hell is she going on about? I consider coughing or making some noise to get her to stop acting so deranged. Admittedly, it scares me more than when she pretends to be overjoyed. At least when she's being overly nice, it's because she wants to uphold a positive image, so she's careful with her words. But when she starts talking to herself, there's no telling how far she's gone or what she's capable of.

Something hard suddenly hits a wall and glass shatters.

"Fuck!"

There's a long pause, until finally, she says, "It's not like you haven't brought survivors in before, Eve. You've saved countless lives."

"That was different!" she cries in a different voice. It's hoarse and strained. "I'm only now starting to build a reputation here. I can't... I can't..."

What's she doing now? Pinching the skin above her nose? She does that a lot.

The silence returns.

Survivors, she mentioned.

Does this mean people are trying to enter Elysium? It would explain her neurotic behavior. Eve hates to lose control. She must have had a whole plan outlined in her head—a plan intended to last several months as she builds a name for herself here in Elysium. I guess newcomers weren't part of her plan. It might sound trivial, but to Eve, it probably feels like the end of the world. She has a way of blowing stuff up in her head and making things out to be way worse than they are.

A few survivors. What's the big deal? Are they male? Maybe that's the problem. And if it is, she can just deny them access. I bite my lower lip, trying to figure this all out. Eve's image. No, she can't deny them access. If anyone else knows about the survivors, they'd never forgive her for keeping Elysium's doors closed.

That's it.

That's why she's so pissed off.

She's being forced into making a decision she doesn't want to make.

The bedroom door suddenly blasts open and my heart nearly climbs up into my throat. Eve comes barging in, her hair erect and greasy.

"L-L-Lucy," she stammers.

Her glazed eyes suddenly brighten to their usual sky blue.

She's coming to.

"I um—" She goes for the bridge of her nose again, this time clenching so hard that wrinkles bulge over her fingers. "I'm sorry. I didn't realize." She straightens up, a fake smile cracking her face. "How are you doing?"

I stare callously at her. *How am I doing*? How does she think I'm doing? She has me chained to her bed like a prisoner.

She must sense my anger. She waves dismissively. "I apologize. That was a stupid question. You're chained at the ankle and"—she scans the plate of cold food on the floor—"I see you haven't eaten."

I clench my jaw, holding back a slew of harsh words I'd love to throw at her.

"I will bring you some lunch shortly. How does a sandwich sound? You always did love your cucumber sandwiches—"

"Stop it!" I say. I can't do this. I can't hold it in, even if I'm afraid she'll lose her mind again. "Why can't you admit it, Eve? Admit you killed Mom. You're acting like you didn't do it, but I saw you, okay? I saw the video."

She pulls her face back like I spat on her—like I'm the one insulting her. Does she not like being accused? This isn't an alleged accusation. It's a fact. I saw the video. It was real footage.

"Lucy," she says, her tone a bit harsher than earlier this morning. "I understand you've been through a lot, but I'm also dealing with a lot at the moment. I would appreciate it if you stopped making me out to be some horrible monster."

"But you are!" I say.

Her jaw clenches and muscles pop on either side.

Maybe I'm crossing a line.

She takes a step toward me, her fist balled next to her waist.

"Go ahead," I say. "Kill me, same as you did with Mom."

My heart's pounding so hard that it feels like my entire body is pulsating. Yeah, I'm terrified. But I'm also enraged. As much as I don't want to push her to the breaking point, I can't seem to stop. My anger outweighs my fear.

She scrunches her nose and balls her other fist, her face swelling to a candy apple red. But before she can lash out, she releases the long breath she was holding in and unclenches her fists.

"No," she says, now composing herself. "I won't harm you, Lucy. That's not who I am. I will return with lunch in an hour or so. And until then, I suggest you think long and hard about our next reunion. I love you, my sweet Lucy, but I will not subject myself to your abuse."

I'm about to say something along the lines of *What the fuck? You're a psychotic bitch*, when she adds, "Don't make me force you into submission, Lucy, because I certainly can."

She turns around and slams the door shut, causing a painting of two golden cats to fall to the floor.

Force me into submission? What the hell is that supposed to mean? The way she said that makes me think she isn't bluffing.

I swallow hard.

Eve is up to something... something horrific.

CHAPTER 44 – EVE

I thank Quinton and march my way back to the basement elevators with three chips in my gloved hand. One for Lucy, and two for the adult newcomers.

I truly hope that I will not have to use a chip on Lucy, but my patience is wearing thin and she's forcing my hand. I will not tolerate being yelled at in my own home. As the elevator ascends to the main floor, I play with the chips, admiring their intricate patterns.

They're so small, so fragile, yet more powerful than anything I've ever come across.

If only I'd thought about the chips earlier, I could have avoided making a fool of myself in front of Lucy. I was so caught up with being cornered into making a decision that I didn't take the time to think clearly. Instead, I allowed my emotions to take over.

This was an error on my part.

The elevator doors open swiftly and I gently clench my fingers around the Zytek chips. Soon enough, these newcomers won't be a problem. Stepping out into the Hub, I elevate my chin and walk straight ahead, avoiding eye contact with everyone.

I cannot allow any distractions right now. The

sooner I implant these chips into our new guests, the sooner my mind will be at ease.

"Eve!" comes Nola's voice.

Nola. I cringe. What does she want? She's already served her purpose by providing me information on Lucy. I no longer need her.

I try to ignore her, but her footsteps quicken. "Eve!"

Sighing, I stop walking.

"Eve," she says, "I'm so sorry to bother you. I, um, I was wondering if you've seen Lucy lately. I've been trying for days to bump into her, but I can never seem to catch her."

Does she feel guilty now? For turning on someone so dear to her? Lucy looked up to Nola almost as a mother. They were once close. That is, until I convinced Nola that Lucy was suffering from delusions and that she was a danger to herself.

Slowly, I turn to Nola, forcing my frown to soften. "I'm sorry, Nola, but I'm afraid I haven't seen her. I know she's been spending time with a young boy..." I tighten my lips to feign worry. "He seems like the kind of boy who might be a bad influence, if you know what I mean."

Nola reaches for her mouth. "Oh, no... This is all my fault. I should have never pushed her away."

Her eyes linger on me a bit longer than I'd like. If I don't say something now, she may consider blaming me for their distance.

"It isn't your fault, my dear Nola." With my free hand, I squeeze her shoulder. "You've only been trying to help her. I know that in time, she'll see that and appreciate the love you've always given her."

She scratches the back of her head, looking unconvinced. "I hope you're right, Eve. I hope she doesn't hate me."

"Oh, heavens no, Nola. Without question, Lucy loves you."

This seems to appease her. She clears her throat. "Well, if you do see her, can you please tell her I'm looking for her?"

"It will be the first thing I tell her," I lie.

"Th-thanks, Eve."

She bows her head, looking distraught, and I take that as my cue to leave. Irritated at the interruption, I walk faster.

"Trinity," I say, and my Luminous Sphere appears next to my lips. It flashes a vivid blue, listening to my every word. "Can you please confirm the room. Was it 103, or 105?"

No response.

"Trinity," I repeat.

She gave me the room number only minutes ago and told me the newcomers were ready to be vetted. She must be busy talking with them. I head down the corridor that leads to the prison facility but take a left turn before entering the prison. There are several dozen isolation rooms in this area of Elysium, most of which were used for patients suffering from pneumonia when we first arrived.

Although the rooms were built to house prisoners, Vrin never believed in that. Instead, she modified the spaces to act as hospital rooms, each with their own bed, sink, and washroom. While I may not agree with her leniency toward disobedience, Vrin set in place a good medical emergency system.

I walk past numerous empty rooms, all the way to the back where the corridor ends with a medium-sized window facing an empty field. It's covered in condensation, and at the corner, a bit of frost.

I head to room 103 first, but the door is open. This can't possibly be it. I peek inside—nothing. I turn toward the other side of the corridor, where another room sits with bold digits next to the door: 105.

This must be it.

I reach for the handle and open the door.

To my surprise, everything is dark. What the hell is going on?

I reach for the light switch. When the room lights up, I press a hand over my heart and gasp. On the floor is Trinity, out cold. I hurry inside, scanning every corner as if I'm somehow going to find someone hiding. Even the washroom is empty.

"Trinity!" I hiss.

I kneel next to her, grab her by the collar, and shake her. Her head bounces off the solid floor underneath, but she doesn't wake up.

Out of frustration, I try again, this time yelling in her face. "Trinity!"

Then, I catch a glimpse of something. Blood. Her lower lip is split in half, and droplets of red have trickled down her cheek.

Immediately, I spring upright and give the order. "Launch Lockdown Protocol."

My Luminous Sphere flashes red this time, and with a pleasant female voice, responds, "Please provide the access code."

Nayma gave me the access code the day I became leader, and I've since repeated it in my mind several times a day. I never imagined I'd need it so soon.

"69923F32," I say.

My sphere flashes wildly again before saying, "Lockdown Protocol Initiated."

A loud humming fills the air around me, followed by something that sounds like gears or motors turning. I rush out of the room in time to see a thick sheet of black slide down over the window, blacking out the entire corridor.

"Nayma!" I bark into my sphere. "I want all security personnel on the lookout for the newcomers. They've taken Trinity out, and they're somewhere inside of Elysium."

Her voice comes back through the small speaker. "On it, Eve."

I storm my way into the main Hub, howling at everyone to return to their rooms. In precisely five minutes, all doors will lock, which means those who haven't entered their rooms will be locked out in the corridors.

Panicked women and children scurry in all directions.

"Eve, what's going on?" one woman asks.

"We've been infiltrated," I say, wanting to grab the woman by the throat.

If it weren't for all of you wanting to bring these newcomers in, we wouldn't be facing this problem.

But she looks terrified, and I remind myself that this isn't her fault.

The Hub grows darker as black sheets of metal begin to mask the windows all around us.

Suddenly, that same robotic female voice spreads throughout hundreds of Luminous Spheres. "Lockdown Protocol in effect. Please return to your room immediately. Lockdown Protocol in effect. Please return to your room immediately."

Countless spheres flash red as they float through the air, following their owners. I spot Nayma near the elevators, guiding people inside while ensuring everyone remains calm.

"No more than twenty at a time," she says, monitoring each elevator.

Two female soldiers get involved. They walk briskly with their guns held firmly against their chests. "Sir, not this one. You'll have to wait."

"But my wife and daughter!" he cries.

The soldier presses a firm hand on his chest, pushing him back. "You can take the next one."

His wife looks terrified, almost as if saying goodbye for the last time.

It certainly won't come to that. All we have to do is find these infiltrators and shut them down. I'm not certain what their plan is, which is what is eating away at me. I know all too well the damage a few people can do. What if they've come to fry our systems? To strip us of our advanced technology?

A dozen guards storm through the Hub with automatic rifles.

Sergeant Layse, a forty-year-old woman praised many times by Vrin, smacks her boot on the floor. "Listen up, soldiers," she yells. "Groups of two. Sweep every floor. Two female suspects wearing unauthorized clothing. Three children may or may not be with them. Bring them in alive."

I'm tempted to say, *Shoot to kill*, but I don't. The truth is, I want to know who these bitches are. Did someone send them? What is their end game? What are they planning? The fact that they got past Trinity tells me they're dangerous.

The sound of guns being cocked echoes throughout the Hub, and the soldiers begin to split up.

"We can help," comes a man's voice.

I turn sideways to find a young man with a square jaw staring me cold in the face. He's muscular, which tells me he exercises daily. By the way he carries himself—two hands tucked behind his tight back—I can tell he used to be a soldier here in Elysium. Behind him are another dozen young men with their eyes fixated straight ahead into nothingness.

How can I trust them? They're men.

You need all the help you can get, Eve.

Not from men, I don't.

And then, I remember the Zytek chips tucked away in my palm.

Without hesitating, I grab one and reach for the man's neck. The second it makes contact, I smile at him. "Thank you for your bravery."

I go on to do the same thing to two more of the men. They reach for their necks as if having been bitten by a mosquito. I may not have a dozen chips on hand, but three is all I need to ensure they don't turn on me. Should the nonchipped soldiers decide to try anything, my new dogs will tear them to shreds.

I return to the first man, who appears to be the leader. "Bring those intruders in alive." I lean in close, lowering my voice. "And if any of your men try to turn on me or any woman inside Elysium, kill them."

The man nods, the veins in his neck bulging. "Absolutely, Eve."

"Layse," I call out.

She jogs toward me.

"Arm these men," I order.

She hesitates, and I find myself wishing I had more chips. My soldiers shouldn't hesitate—ever. Hesitation translates to doubt, and no one should doubt me.

It looks like she's about to ask me if I'm sure, so I say, "Now!"

She turns around and whistles, calling to another soldier.

I walk away as the sound of guns being cocked echoes throughout the Hub. Without my people roaming the halls, and with the sheets of metal blacking out the windows, it looks dark and desolate here, almost as if we're on the verge of emigrating from Elysium.

CHAPTER 45 – GABRIEL

General James storms through the control hub, rubbing the back of his neck.

He didn't anticipate Elysium locking down. I think the plan was to wait until nightfall.

"It's okay," he says when he catches Freyda and me watching him. "We've prepared for this sort of situation."

"I take it this wasn't the signal you were hoping for," Freyda says.

James smiles at her. "Not exactly, but this is life. Things don't always go as we plan. But we've got this covered."

I turn to the monitors when something dark appears in my peripheral. Black drones suddenly hover into the cameras' multiple views. They move swiftly and effortlessly with their propeller blades. To my surprise, they aren't the size of any drone I've ever seen before. They look to be the size of a motorcycle, only flat and more oval-shaped.

"What is that?" I ask.

James puffs his chest out proudly. "Carrier drones. Might not look like much from here, but inside each one of those is a soldier."

Freyda takes a step closer to the monitor.

"They're heading to the rooftop and drilling their way inside," James says. "I'm counting on my inside women to cut off the emergency lights. I'm not sure what led to the lockdown... Hopefully they're still active and haven't been subdued."

"That's a big if," I say. "What makes you think they'll succeed?"

James gives me a look that tells me I'm asking a stupid question. It's clear he has a lot of faith in this super team of his. To me, it's still a huge gamble. The whole plan was to get a team inside so we could cut their power. Somehow, their identity was compromised before this could happen, and Eve must have initiated a lockdown. It works for us, in a sense, because natural light is now out of the equation. But guaranteed they have emergency lights on, and if we don't cut those, James's soldiers will encounter bullets.

We need darkness if we want to have the advantage.

"They'll infiltrate through there," James says, pointing at the roof. "And once they're in, we'll have eyes and ears on the inside."

I stare at the screen, my stomach a tight knot.

This had better work.

CHAPTER 46 – LUCY

I stare at the blacked-out window, trying to figure out what's going on.

Did something happen? I've never seen anything like this before. I blink hard, trying to regain focus of the room. Everything looks either black or white.

Whatever is going on, it isn't good.

I hurry back to my spot on the floor, hoping to find another splinter. I can't give up. Lucas is out there, and he needs my help. But after spending several minutes reaching underneath the bed, I'm left empty-handed.

"This is bullshit," I mutter, slamming my heel down into the carpet.

The vibration makes my chain rattle, and I stop breathing to think. Maybe...

With my shoulder, I push underneath the bedframe, hoping to lift the leg high enough to pull the cuff out of. Unfortunately, the bed is way too heavy. I roll my shoulder back, knowing that by tomorrow, it will be bruised.

I try several more times until my shoulder feels so raw I can't apply any more pressure to it.

"You can't give up..." I tell myself.

I blink hard, trying to come up with another solution when something hits me. The mattress. Standing, I push the weight of my body against the side of the mattress until it starts to slide. This thing probably weighs over a hundred pounds, which isn't helping my escape. It slides halfway across the box spring, so I climb onto the bed and kick the rest of the mattress off. Thankfully, the box spring isn't all that heavy. Lifting it, I throw it on top of the mattress.

With knees bent and my back straight, I grab the base of the frame and pull up.

Nothing.

It won't budge.

I'm about to start swearing and stomping my feet again, but the last thing I want is to draw attention. If Eve returns early and catches me in here like this, there's no telling what she'll do.

Suddenly, I remember something.

Mom once told me that women carry their strength in their legs. She told me this when things were starting to get bad. Even though I was only a kid, she taught me a few self-defense moves and often reminded me to use my legs to fight if I could. Her exact words were "Kicking is always better than punching."

With that in mind, I return to the foot of the bed and roll onto my back. If I can't lift the damn thing using my arms, maybe I can push it up with my legs. I plant my feet against the wooden frame, my legs bent so far back that my knees graze my cheeks.

Holding my breath, I push as hard as I can. For a second, the pressure is so intense that I'm afraid my legs might break. A hot throbbing pain radiates into my thighs, but I don't give up. I need to keep trying.

I take a short break, breathe, then try again.

Something budges this time.

"Come on," I mutter, holding my breath as I push.

If I can lift the bed about half an inch, I'll be able to pull my chain out. I push again, this time pulling at the chain.

You can do this. You can do this. You can do this.

CHAPTER 47 – EVE

I hurry to the emergency stairwell. By now, the elevators will have locked in place, and I need to make it back to my room. In there, I will be safe and able to protect Lucy. There's no telling what these strangers want. For all I know, they're after me. I can't be too careful. I run up the twelve flights of stairs, feeling like my legs might melt by the end of it. My lungs ache and my muscles burn, making me feel older than I am.

"Open door," I say, reaching the top floor.

The access panel next to it flashes red, denying me entry.

Of course, the lockdown.

"Override lockdown," I order, and before my sphere can ask me for another PIN, I say, "08DT9."

The panel blinks yellow a few times before unlocking the door. I blast it open and run to my room, having to once again use the override code.

My door swooshes open and I'm about to step in when a dark figure lunges out at me. I don't have time to understand what's happening. The person crashes into me, sending us both flying into the wall across from my door. My head smashes hard into the corridor's drywall and I collapse on the floor, ears ringing.

Something cold suddenly tightens around my neck.

I blink hard until Lucy's face comes into focus. She sits atop me with both legs on either side of my torso. In her grasp is the long chain I used to tie her up with. She presses it hard into my neck until my eyes feel like they're going to pop out of their sockets.

"Admit it!" she says, saliva dripping from the corners of her lips.

Her nostrils widen as she pushes down harder.

"W-w-what—" I try, but she's crushing my vocal cords.

"Admit you killed Mom! And Vrin! Admit it!"

Why is she doing this? I clench a fist and swing for the side of her face. She manages to pull away a bit, though not enough. My knuckles hit her square in the jaw. Surprisingly, it does nothing but make her scowl even harder.

I try another swing, but my arm is growing weak. The impact is soft against her shoulder.

"L-L-Lucy... S-stop. Stop..."

Teeth bared, she doesn't even look like herself anymore.

"Admit it!" she screams in my face.

I claw at the chain, but it accomplishes nothing. "O-o-okay. I... D-did it."

Her features soften and she loosens her grip around my throat. Every few seconds, her brows come together before separating again. It's as if she's battling a roller coaster of emotions, trying to decide whether to cry or kill me.

This is my chance.

I ball another fist when suddenly, footsteps come stomping beside us.

Trinity?

We turn to look, only to find three men and a woman dressed in black military tactical gear. These aren't my soldiers. Who the hell are they?

"Sir, we have the target," one of them says, pressing something in his ear.

Who is he talking to?

He steps forward, his dark hair lightening to brown as he approaches one of the lit emergency lights.

Lucy pulls away from me and raises two hands on either side of her face. But these intruders don't seem to care about her, or about the fact that she was on the verge of killing me.

The man is staring at me.

He steps closer, his heavy military boots hitting the floor as he aims his rifle at my chest.

"Eve Malum, you are under arrest for the murder of Vrin Madden. Anything you say can and will be used—"

"Vrin?" I sneer, my voice raw. I sit upright and rub at my throat. "Who the fuck are you? You have no proof of anything."

"Actually, we have your confession," says the man. He turns to a woman with a blond ponytail standing next to him. He doesn't even have to say anything.

She nods and presses a small button on her vest. Suddenly, a holographic video footage blasts out into the dark space between us—footage of Lucy on top of me, strangling my confession out of me.

I glare sideways at Lucy, but she looks as surprised as I feel.

She didn't plan for this.

"Who are you?" I growl.

The soldiers ignore my question.

"Turn around and put your hands behind your back," says the leader.

I scoff. "You think you can waltz in here and kidnap me? Leader of Elysium?"

The woman with the video footage turns her head sideways. "Not yet, sir. Lights are still on."

What is she talking about? Are they planning on shutting down all power? What do they want? They're going to destroy everything I've worked for.

I can't let that happen. I won't. My women will never allow it. Once I release them from their rooms...

"Terminate emergency lockdown," I order, and my sphere comes zooming out of my pocket, flicking next to my face. "Access code 69923—"

Without warning, my Luminous Sphere bursts into a hundred bits. I'm forced to cover my eyes and ears and turn away. I stretch my jaw as my ears ring loudly, making me think I've gone deaf. When I open my eyes again, the man in uniform lowers his rifle.

That son of a bitch destroyed my sphere.

"You could have killed me!" I yell, pain radiating down my throat.

"Turn around," he orders. He isn't aggressive about it, but something tells me that if I don't comply, things will get heated.

"You can't do this!" I say.

"Turn around," he repeats.

This time, he grabs me by the arm and spins me around onto my stomach.

"You're hurting me!" I lie.

"And you've hurt a lot of people," he says. He fastens cuffs around my wrists and locks them into place. With his strong hands, he grabs me by the arms and pulls me up into a standing position.

The woman in tactical gear crouches in front of Lucy. "It's okay, love. We're the good guys."

It's obvious that Lucy wants to believe her, but she has no idea who they are.

The woman presses something in her ear and says, "Yes, Redhead. We found her here with Eve." She pauses, then narrows her eyes on Lucy. "Are you Lucy?"

Lucy's eyes double in size, as do mine. How do they know her name? How did they know mine? The woman pulls her communication device out and offers it to Lucy. "Someone wants to say hi."

Confused, I watch Lucy. What's going on? She hesitates, then grabs the little earpiece and holds it up next to her face.

A soft voice echoes in the earpiece and Lucy's eyes widen. "Freyda? What? How?"

Freyda.

Clenching my jaw, I take a fast step toward Lucy, but the man behind me holds on tight. "Not a chance," he warns.

"Freyda, you fucking traitor!" I scream.

Lucy frowns up at me and turns her head to the side. "What's going on? Yeah. Okay."

She goes silent. I'm dying to know what Freyda is telling her.

"Yeah, I can do that," Lucy says. She nods several more times before handing the earpiece back to the female soldier.

The soldier takes it and inserts it into her ear. "We can do that. We're waiting on—"

Suddenly, the emergency lights go out and I find myself staring at nothing but blackness.

"What the hell is going on?" I say, feeling as though my words are reaching no one.

The sound of shuffling resonates around me, but no one responds. Instead, I'm yanked by the arms and forced to walk backward down the corridor without a clue as to where I'm being taken.

CHAPTER 48 – GABRIEL

We sit in silence, our masks painted with green and black markings.

It reminds me of the old days when I first started my training as a Black Marine.

"Don't get too close, son," James says.

At first, I think he's talking to me, but when I turn to look at him, I realize he's aiming his order at the young soldier in front of me. The soldier kneels in the tall grass, extracts a pair of camo-green binoculars, and gazes at Elysium through small circular lenses.

"Still in lockdown, sir."

James nods and twirls his finger, commanding his group of infantry to split up. "Remember, no casualties."

"Is that what this is for?" Freyda asks, showcasing her new pistol. It's jet black and looks exactly like a regular semiautomatic gun. What gives it away is a small green logo at the base of the grip. It looks like a dart or an arrow. All I know is that it signifies sleep, so it's probably a dart. Unlike traditional tranquilizer guns, this one has immediate effects. Or at least, that's what James explained to us. That's huge. Some tranquilizer darts can take up to forty-five minutes to incapacitate a victim. And even then, there's no guarantee it'll even cause a person's lights to go out. It could simply sedate them. It's a huge gamble and not the type of firepower I'd bring to any battle.

But to have new technology that knocks someone out instantly? That's impressive. I wish wars were fought with this rather than lethal ammo.

General James points at Freyda's gun. "It's technically still pending approval, but you know how red tape is. And then the war happened." He rolls his eyes like he's talking about nothing more than bad weather.

"Stats?" Freyda asks.

James's lip tugs at one corner. "Ninety-eight percent accuracy. We're working to increase that to a hundred."

"Any fatalities?" Freyda asks.

Damn, that woman is good at gathering information. I'm lucky to have her by my side.

"One," James says. He sighs, his breath causing grass blades to waver in front of him. "But that was bad luck. Turns out the guy had a heart defect."

Freyda purses her lips as she inspects her new toy. "Those things are bound to happen. Can't beat yourself up. What counts is all the lives that are being saved. Where does the two percent come from? I imagine it isn't only from the single casualty."

"Good question," James says. "In short, really big guys."

I hold back a laugh. "Sort of like trying to take down a dinosaur, huh?"

"Yep," he says. "It sedated them, but they didn't go

down. We hesitated to fire a second shot. The dosage in these things is already high enough as it is. I mean, imagine—"

He stops talking and presses his ear. He doesn't respond to whatever is being fed through his earpiece, and instead, scowls at the horizon. Finally, he smacks his knee. "They're in."

"Who's in?" I ask.

"Mori and Sanchez." He beams like a proud father. "I knew they'd pull through. Turns out the first person who brought them in found the EMP device. That's why all of this happened. But they've managed to hack into Elysium's primary system: APHRODITE. The emergency lights should be out any second now. They're opening the East Wing's primary entry point for us. Take out as many armed soldiers as you can."

"What about my plan?" Freyda asks.

She's referring to the plan she made with Lucy only minutes ago. It's genius. But she's right to ask about it. How will they broadcast the video footage of Eve's confession with the power out?

General James doesn't seem bothered by her question. "You're ambitious. Always one step ahead of me." He pauses, cocks his gun, and adds, "Lucas, you said his name was?"

Freyda nods.

"We'll get him out, don't you worry about that." He hands us both night vision goggles and sets them on his forehead. "But we don't need him for your plan. We need to focus our resources on—"

"What?" Freyda cuts him off. "He's the best we have in computer—"

James raises a stiff hand, revealing his general side. "I understand your concern, Freyda, but as I said, we don't need him. The time it takes to retrieve him from his prison cell could mean life or death. Mori and Sanchez are already in the system. They're giving us a ten-minute window to incapacitate our enemy. Once that window is up, the lights are coming back on."

"And the video," Freyda says, though it sounds more like a question.

"Sanchez already has it ready for when the power comes on."

"Well, good," she says. "Because the second you revert the lockdown, you can bet your ass that Eve's followers will try to—"

"Lights out," James says, pointing the barrel of his gun at an Elysium so dark I don't even recognize the building. He presses his ear again. "Move, move, move!"

CHAPTER 49 – LUCY

Loud gunfire explodes nearby and windows shatter.

The female soldier leading me wraps a protective arm around my shoulders and stands between me and the glass. "We're in," she says.

Ahead of me, Eve struggles. "Let me go! You can't do this!"

Rapid footsteps come running toward us, and a high-pitched *pew pew* sound bounces off the corridor walls. What is that? It isn't gunfire. Why aren't these soldiers using bullets? Not that it matters. After the firing sound, I hear grunting and the thud of bodies hitting the floor.

Whatever they're using, it's working.

"This way," comes a husky voice.

More footsteps.

I hate this.

I can't see anything. All I can do is trust that these soldiers are the good guys and that they're taking me someplace safe. The darkness persists for a few more minutes until someone kicks a door in, and natural light floods the corridor. From inside the room comes the sound of powerful helicopter blades.

"Let me go!" Eve says, kicking wildly.

Another *pew pew* sound and Eve stops talking.

"Well, that worked," says the female soldier.

We enter a large storage room full of broken cardboard, old paperback books, and piles of clothing. Through the ceiling is a large hole the size of a car. It seems to have been carved through Elysium's metal and stone structure. What did they do? Blast their way inside?

I watch as the men lay Eve on a platform supported by cables. One of the men hops onto the platform with Eve, and slowly, they ascend through the hole in the roof. The sound of the helicopter blades becomes quieter.

"Where are you taking her?" I ask.

I know I shouldn't give a damn about Eve. She's a bitch who deserves whatever she has coming to her. But for some twisted reason, there's still a part of me that hopes they don't kill her. Deep down, I know she's sick and didn't intentionally kill my mom. I saw her crying in the video. I still hate her for it, but my emotions are all over the place.

"She's being taken to a secure holding cell," says the man who sent her up. He steps back when the sound of more helicopter blades returns and a powerful gust of wind blasts into the room, sending books sweeping across the floor. "Commander Thompson will decide what happens next."

I have no idea who this Commander Thompson is, but I can only hope she's fair. I know all too well how easy it is for power to get to someone's head. I wish we lived in a world where everyone's fate didn't fall into the hands of a single person or a corrupt government.

I hate corruption.

Come on," says the female soldier, gently pushing on my upper back.

For the first time, I get a good look at her. Despite her hardened features, there's a softness to her I can't quite put my finger on. She wears her hair pulled back so tight it makes her jaw look more rounded and her overbite more prominent than they are. She doesn't try to smile at me, but she doesn't need to. I know she's doing everything in her power to keep me safe. I can feel it.

She helps me up onto the metal platform and tells me to hold on to the handle in the middle. I grab on for dear life, terrified of how high up I'm about to go. She hops on with me, causing the platform to sway, and grips the large handle.

She then nods to the man next to us and he tugs hard on one of the cables—a signal to whoever is up there inside the helicopter.

Carefully, we ascend, and my stomach sinks.

The moment we exit Elysium's roof, I can't help but shift my head from side to side, taking it all in. Elysium, once a stunning piece of architecture full of massive windows reflecting the sun's hot rays, is now nothing more than a large brick edifice covered in slate black metal.

It's terrifying, but I don't focus on it for too long. Instead, my gaze lingers on the dozens of helicopters circling Elysium, and the men and women dressed in black charging through the fields. They all seem to be targeting the same entry point—Elysium's East Wing.

Did they blast their way inside there, too?

Cool wind sweeps through my long hair as the helicopter flies farther away from Elysium. I want to ask where we're going, but with the helicopter's propeller racing, I know my voice won't carry far.

We don't fly for long—maybe two minutes—before we begin our descent.

I watch as Eve's helicopter goes down first, lowering her platform onto the long grass. For a second, I feel bad for her. She lies unconscious, sprawled across the metal platform in her white dress suit, her short hair fluttering under the helicopter's powerful breeze. A dozen other soldiers circle her and unclasp the cables from the platform, allowing the helicopter to take off again.

One soldier reaches under the platform and presses something. Wheels suddenly expand underneath, creating a gurney.

Where are they taking her?

We're lowered down onto the grass, and another four soldiers come to help us off the platform. Unlike with Eve, they don't detach the cables. We walk off, and once we're clear of the metal slab, the helicopter takes off with the platform still attached.

In a panic, I stretch my neck to see where Eve is being rolled off to. I don't know a thing about these people. They could be planning to torture her for information. As much as I hate her, I don't want that for her.

"Relax," says the blond soldier. "No harm will come to her."

I'm both relieved and disappointed.

What the hell is wrong with me?

"Where are we?" I ask.

"Someplace safe," the soldier says.

Finally, she smiles, and my heart slows down.

"Come," she says, guiding me toward a huge boulder.

I walk around it, not understanding where I'm being taken, when we reach the other side. Mouth agape, I stare at something I never imagined seeing. At the base of the boulder is an opening with a metal ramp leading way down underground.

"You guys live underground?" I ask.

She squeezes my shoulder and waves at someone.

At once, a beige-colored rover driven by a scrawny, dark-skinned man comes rolling toward us. "Sohawn here will take you down into the waiting area."

"Waiting area?" I ask. "What am I waiting for?"

The soldier shrugs. "Friends? Family?"

I blink hard and she brushes her thumb along my cheek. "Trust me, it's better this way. Area 82 is no place for anyone to live. It's a military base. We'll ensure everyone gets to live in a real home."

"A real home?" I repeat.

She simply crinkles her eyes and urges me to get inside the rover. I climb in, feeling a bit uncomfortable next to a man I don't know.

But the second he smiles at me—a face-splitting grin full of white, Chiclet-like teeth—I feel at ease.

"Wah gwaan!" he says, overly chipper.

What does that even mean?

"Welcome, welcome," he adds.

I glance back at the female soldier one last time before Sohawn presses the gas pedal and leads me into the dimly light tunnel underground. "You're goin' to be so much 'appier 'ere, ma sweet girl," he says, his Jamaican accent thick.

He drives straight ahead, his dark bony arms steering the wheel as we roll down the ramp.

I have no idea what I'm getting into, but I have a hunch my life is about to change forever.

CHAPTER 50 – EVE

I wake up to the smell of humidity and mild detergent.

Where am I? A throbbing pain shoots from my wrists and up into my forearms. I'm bruised. Why am I bruised? The handcuffs, I remember. I stretch my neck and roll my shoulders, feeling something pinch.

How long have I been out?

I sit upright, only to find that I'm being held prisoner in some sort of containment cell.

Unlike Elysium, the walls aren't white, nor are they clean. They remind me of the inside of a haunted prison cell—the kind with stone blocks and cracks in the walls. The sheets, however, smell fresh. It's as if they cleaned out the cell specifically for my arrival.

I leap onto my feet and rush to the iron bars at the front of my cell.

"Hello?" I call out.

My voice carries down a dark hallway.

"Quit yer whinin', sweetheart," comes a woman's hoarse voice.

If I were to guess, I'd say she spent most of her life inhaling daily packs of cigarettes.

"Where am I?" I ask.

"Where d'you think?" she says like I'm a complete

moron.

I clench my jaw. She has no idea who I am. Although she can't see me, I straighten my posture and flatten the folds in my dress suit. It isn't quite as white as I'd like, but I'd much rather be wearing this than an orange jumpsuit.

"Been months since they brought someone else in 'ere," she says. "What'd you do?"

"Do?" I repeat. "I haven't done anything. I was only trying to protect my people—"

"Her people," she repeats. "Ya hear that, Chris? Her people." She scoffs. "Like she's some sorta saint."

Farther down, a man chuckles to himself.

There's no use talking to these people—they're mad.

"They keep tellin' us trial's comin'," the woman continues, "but hell, I'm startin' to think it's all bullshit."

"Trial?" I whisper to myself.

For Vrin's murder, you fool.

I pace the cell, my heel catching in a crack on the floor. I consider slipping my shoes off, but the floor is far too filthy. There has to be a way out of this. My people will come for me. They will save me.

Near the ceiling is a small window with iron bars, allowing only a faint amount of sunlight to slip through. Even if I had the strength to pry off those bars, I'd never fit through the hole.

"It's a new day, it's a new world, it's a new life," the woman sings, and I wish she'd shut that hole in her face. She sounds like a heap of crushed stone sliding out of a gravel truck.

Deeper down the prison, Chris joins her, making stupid beats with his mouth. He goes on to slap the iron bars and stomp his feet.

"A new world, comin' for us, baby," the woman keeps singing.

I roll my eyes.

What the hell are they talking about? We are in the New World.

The crazy duo shuts up the moment footsteps approach us. I hurry to the gate and press my cheeks against the cold metal. "Hello? Who are you? Where am I? I demand answers! Do you have any idea who I am?"

A dark-skinned woman suddenly appears in front of me, her short coiled hair sticking straight up. "Eve Malum," she says heartlessly.

Across her black uniform and over her breast pocket is a name tag that reads *Thompson*.

What is she? A prison guard?

"Commander Thompson," she says as if reading my mind.

Commander?

I take a step back.

"I imagine you're confused by your detainment."

I point a finger in her face. "You have no right—"

"You aren't what I imagined," she says, amusement tugging at her lips.

Do I entertain her? I furrow my brows.

"Your name has been passed from mouth to mouth since the war. I never imagined such a dangerous woman to look, so..."

Pathetic? Weak? Spit it out, you stupid bitch. I'll

make you regret your words.

"Where's Lucy?" I spew. "I swear to God, if you hurt her—"

She sighs. "I came here to meet the great Eve Malum but also to tell you that your trial date will take place approximately two months from now, in Washington, DC. I can assure you that archaic prison methodologies are a thing of the past, and you will be treated fairly and with decency while under our care."

Is this supposed to make me feel better? And what is she talking about? Washington, DC is gone. This woman is a lunatic. And I don't give a shit about any of that right now. I want to know where my goddaughter is.

"Where's my Lucy?" I say, hopping in one spot.

She elevates her chin, dimples appearing in her cheeks. "Your reign is over, Eve. I suggest you get comfortable."

This can't be happening. She's wrong. My women are loyal to me. And those with the Zytek chips... they'll follow me to the ends of the Earth.

The commander turns away from me, without a care in the world.

I should yell at her and accuse her of being a complete fool.

But I don't. Instead, I leer at the back of her head. "You're wrong, Commander. You will see."

CHAPTER 51 – GABRIEL

As much as I hate what Eve's done, watching the devastation spread throughout Elysium is tough. Men and women hold on to each other, some crying, others whispering. Overhead, the video footage plays over and over again as Eve confesses to murdering Vrin.

People are heartbroken.

A few others look at me almost apologetically. Like they're ashamed for having believed I was capable of murdering someone in cold blood. They took Eve's word for it. But I'm not angry with them. They didn't know better, and Eve has a way of making anyone believe anything.

I hope she's somewhere isolated right now, where she can't manipulate anyone else.

"Can you believe this is happening?" I ask Freyda.

She seems content, like she *can* believe it. "I've waited a long time for this... But I never imagined it would work out this well."

"Well?" I say, looking around me. This doesn't seem like it worked out *well*. Are we looking at the same thing? A mass of women and children sit huddled under blankets in Elysium's Hub, and most of them look terrified. General James's soldiers walk around with their tranquilizer rifles held firmly against their chests. Near the windows, Eve's soldiers are lying side by side, sedated and tied at the wrists.

"We need to start evacuating everyone," James says.

"Evacuating?" I ask. "What's the emergency? For most people here, this is home."

"Is it?" James says, and it sounds rhetorical. "There's no leader here anymore, and by the looks of it, some of these women will have to go through extensive therapy before they're back to normal."

I assume he's referring to the harm caused by Eve's brainwashing.

"Their anger is misplaced," James continues, eyeballing a crowd of glaring women. "Eve's taught a lot of women here to hate us men. And I get it. I understand where the hatred comes from. But if we want to move forward as a new society, we need to work together. Not against each other."

"I agree," I say, "but it isn't that easy. You can't tell everyone to pack up and leave. And you can't force them, either."

"Then we won't," James says like the answer is obvious. If he had suspenders, he'd probably pop them right about now. "We'll give them the choice."

I turn to ask Freyda what she thinks about this, but she's gone.

"Freyda?" I ask.

I spin around a few times until finally, I spot her moving toward the Hub's podium. She climbs up on the platform and moves toward the microphone.

Overhead, natural light beams down on her, making her look like an angel coming to save the day.

She taps the microphone a few times and clears her throat.

Everyone's attention shifts to her.

"Hey, everyone," she says awkwardly. "I know most of you don't know me, but my name's Freyda. Freyda Mills. I've been by Eve's side ever since she led us to Eden." She pauses, trying to find a few familiar faces in the crowd. "I know a lot of you are confused. Eve's always been nothing but a rock for us. I get that. But I'm here to tell you that Eve's been sick for a while."

A few women say something along the lines of *bullshit*.

Even after witnessing Eve confess to Vrin's murder, some of her hardcore followers refuse to believe she's done anything wrong.

"Is that how you want to live?" Freyda asks.

The Hub goes quiet.

"Always angry? Always pissed off at someone? Look at you." She points at the crowd of angry women and everyone turns to look at them. "You're unhappy. Deep down, you know that. You don't have to live that way."

The women look at each other uncomfortably. They probably didn't expect Freyda to single them out.

"And you have every reason to be angry," she adds.

This seems to confuse the crowd.

"Men slaughtered us in cold blood. They took

advantage of us. Stripped us of our rights."

I look at James, then at the crowd. What the hell is she doing? If she's trying to get these women all riled up again, it's working. The audience nods passionately, some with balled fists and others with aggressive stances.

"I'm angry too," Freyda says. She goes quiet and lowers her head, along with her voice. "But not at men."

No one speaks. Probably because they're too confused by what's going on.

"I'm pissed off at corruption, power, and greed. I'm pissed off at a world in which money triumphed over love, health, and family. Don't you see what happened? We fell apart. We grew distant from one another, and we were miserable. Our system didn't work. People worked themselves to the bone and they were miserable."

The whole crowd starts nodding and goose bumps erupt all over my body.

"Our system and our government put us under a lot of stress. A lot of financial and social stress. People stopped working together and started looking out only for themselves. And on top of that, our boys have always been raised that crying isn't okay. Says who? Males are taught to suppress their emotions. Is it any wonder that many of them develop anger problems as adults? That they suffer silently? We did this. All of us."

Freyda scowls at everyone. I've never seen her so passionate before. It's like she was born to deliver this speech.

"So now, we need to come together. Not just women, not just men, but everyone. I don't care what color of skin you have, what language you speak, what you believe in, what gender you identify as, or what sex you're attracted to. We're all human beings, and we're all the same, despite our differences. It's time to put all of this hateful bullshit behind us and do better. We can't let corruption win. We can all do better."

A heavy silence weighs down on everyone until someone finally says, "She's right."

"Enough's enough," comes another voice.

James pops a brow at me. "You found yourself someone real special, Gabe."

He's right. I have. I'm so proud of Freyda that I want to run up there and throw my arms around her. But I don't. She isn't finished.

"If you're ready to join us in the New World, I'm here to tell you that America is being rebuilt from the ground up. I've seen it for myself. Washington DC is almost back on its feet, and soon, everyone will have a home to go to."

Gasps fill the room as women wrap their arms around their children or their lovers.

"The choice is yours," Freyda says. "You can either stay here, or you can join us in the New World."

The crowd breaks out into excited banter. Freyda comes off the platform with a serious look on her face, obviously still worked up from all that passion. But I'm beaming like a kid unwrapping a gift.

"You were amazing," I say.

She sighs. "Yeah, well, I hope it was enough."

"Are you kidding me?" I say. "That was beyond—"

"Excuse me?" someone says.

We turn sideways to spot a plump woman with short brown hair and rosy cheeks. Her gaze shifts from me to Freyda but seems to stay on me a few seconds longer.

"Can I help you?" I ask.

She locks her fingers in front of her small round belly and clears her throat. "Um, actually, I was hoping you could."

I give her my full attention.

"My name's Mary-Anne," she says. "I was by Eve's side most of her time here. I thought she was doing good... thought she was only trying to help people. But I realize, now... I realize I made a mistake. I... I'm so sorry."

I lean forward. "Sorry? What are you talking about? Did something happen?"

She pouts and inspects her shoes. "Um, yeah, you could say that."

"Lucas!" Freyda exclaims beside me.

In the distance, Lucas comes running toward us with Emily and Abigail, Lucy's other friend.

"Freyda!" he shouts back. "Where's Lucy?"

Freyda gives me a look that says she'll talk to me later. She joins Lucas and Lucy's friends, guiding them away from me and Mary-Anne.

Mary-Anne leans closer to me, so I lower myself even more. With a hand next to her mouth like she's about to reveal some big secret, she says, "Some of these people were brainwashed."

I can't help but smile.

"We know, Mary-Anne. That's what Eve does.

We'll do everything in our power to revert this."

She pulls her face back, adding two additional chins to her face. "You know? How?" She swipes the air. "Never mind. That doesn't matter. How are you gonna fix it? How're you gonna take them out?"

Am I missing something? Take what out? "What are you talking about?"

"The chips," she says next to her wall of a hand again. "The Zytek chips."

"Chips?" I repeat.

She makes her eyes go huge. "Careful. I'm not sure how many more are infected."

Holy shit. Is she saying what I think she's saying? That Eve went so far as to use brainwashing technology? I thought that stuff was a myth. I'd heard about it before, that it was theoretical, and the intent was to create super soldiers. I never imagined it would come to life.

I'm too stunned to say anything.

"They disappear when they touch skin," she says. "So I don't know how it works."

"James," I say, my heart skipping a beat. He takes a step backward and leans into me. "You ever heard of Zytek chips?"

He spins around so fast that a light breeze tickles my beard.

"I've heard of them, but Vrin destroyed those," he says. "All of them."

"Apparently, not all," I say.

His pensive gaze drops to Mary-Anne. Then, as if standing in front of a live android, he watches her, mouth agape, and slowly waves a hand in front of her eyes. "Does she have a—"

I pull his wrist down. "No, not her. Others."

"Several," Mary-Anne whispers, again with the hand gesture.

What she doesn't realize is that everyone here is too preoccupied with talking to each other to give a damn about our conversation.

General James's spine goes erect and with a deeper voice than earlier, he says, "Thank you for the information. But there's no need to worry. We've dealt with this sort of technology before. We have an EMP-style tank that eradicates anything like that in the human body."

"So you're going to put everyone in the tank?" I ask.

He looks at me like I'm an idiot. "Not all at once."

I hold back a smile. General James is one hell of a character. It's like he doesn't catch on to social cues and seems to have a habit of taking things way too literally.

I don't bother responding. It sounds like the man knows how to handle this, so I'll let him take care of it. Until then, we're going to have to treat everyone here like a threat, which is why we've already stripped them all of their weapons.

I thank Mary-Anne for the information with a pat on her shoulder before making my way through the Hub, offering help to anyone who might take it.

CHAPTER 52 – LUCY

My palms get clammy as I watch dozens of rovers rattle down the large metal ramp. Each carries passengers from Elysium—mostly women, but a few men.

The mothers come in looking frazzled, with blankets around their shoulders and small children at their sides.

This place is a lot to take in, but they'll get used to it.

I still can't believe this is happening. Where will I live? Will it be in a real home? One with my own kitchen? My own living room? My own bathroom that isn't the size of a broom closet?

If only you were here to see this, Mom.

I spin in a circle, taking in the underground architecture. I can't believe an entire population lives down here. Every few seconds, someone comes by to shake my hand and introduce themselves.

"Clara," one young woman says, watching me with such intensity I wonder if we've met before. They probably don't get many new faces around here. She looks only a few years older than me, with soft skin and sparkling eyes. When I introduce myself, she sweeps her arm around the room. "This is the Intake Room." She searches the ceiling and I follow her gaze. "It isn't much, but it's big and has everything we need."

Overhead, industrial lights fill the space with a bright white glow. While it can't even compete with Elysium's advanced technology, there's something warm about this place—something that makes me feel like I'm going to like it here.

Around us are a few parked rovers, some of which are currently being worked on by mechanics. As the other rovers roll in, soldiers move forward to help the Elysium citizens step out. They're gentle about it—something I wouldn't expect from soldiers. Many of the men offer their hands to the women in such a gentlemanlike way that I forget they're soldiers.

"You must be Lucy," comes a woman's voice.

I twirl around to find a dark-skinned woman wearing a name tag that reads, *Thompson*.

"I'm Commander Thompson. Freyda said I should expect you. I wanted to let you know that Eve has been contained in our isolation unit. If you'd like to have a few words with her, you're more than welcome—"

"Why would I want to do that?" I ask. I don't mean to sound snippy or to cut off the commander, but I'm still so angry at Eve that I don't know what I'd do if I saw her face.

Unbothered that I cut her off, she parts her lips slightly and continues. "I imagine Eve has hurt you quite a bit. But I sense there's a connection between you two. She wouldn't stop saying your name behind those bars."

I'm too stunned to say anything.

"There's a good chance Eve will remain locked away for a very long time," she adds. "If there's anything you'd like to say to her—anything you need to get off your chest—I'm more than happy to accommodate you."

When I still don't respond, she smiles sweetly at me. "Take your time, Lucy. If and when you decide, let me know."

She goes to turn around.

"Wait," I say. "I... I'll do it. I'll talk to her."

Without a word, Commander Thompson leads me through a series of doors and down a flight of stairs. The air feels damper and cooler as we descend. How far underground have we gone?

She pushes her way through a heavy door, the creaking sound raising the hairs on my arm. It feels like I'm about to be cast in some horror movie. All that's missing down here are spiderwebs and roaches. Fortunately, despite how archaic the place looks, everything is polished and stain free.

As we walk down the prison corridor, several hands poke out from in between bars. As we move closer, they disappear. They must sense the commander coming—either that, or they know to behave the moment anyone comes through.

The commander looks back at me one last time before gesturing toward a cell positioned about halfway down the row. I hesitate, swallow hard, then step toward the bars. In the corner of the room is the back of Eve's blond head. She fidgets with something

on her pillow like she's trying to remove a thread and
fix the zipper.

Her rounded shoulders bounce as she wriggles
whatever she has in her grasp.

Commander Thompson clears her throat and Eve
rotates the upper half of her body, her features wild-
like. Yet the second she sees me, she softens, almost
as if we've gone back in time and she's visiting me at
home, with Mom.

But I'm not a little girl anymore, and Eve isn't the
woman I thought she was.

"Lucy," she breathes, springing toward the bars.

She wraps her fingers around the dark metal and
squishes her face between the gaps. "My sweet Lucy.
Are you all right? Have they hurt you?" She glowers at
Commander Thompson. "I'll make them pay—"

"No one hurt me," I say coldly.

Why is she doing this? Why is she making it so
hard for me to hate her? I can tell she loves me, even
if it's in her own twisted way. But Eve is sick.
Extremely sick. I don't think anything can fix her.

With slanted brows, she pushes her face even
harder between the bars and reaches for me.

I step back as the tips of her fingers graze my
shoulder.

"Lucy, I... I'm so sorry." Her lower lip trembles. "I
know you can never forgive me. I fucked up. I should
have listened to O. I should've stopped. I should've—"

She averts her gaze toward the cement floor and
bangs her forehead against the bars. "I... I'm so sorry."

Tears trickle out of her eyes and drip off the tip of
her nose.

I've seen Eve pretend before. I've seen her fool countless women into believing she was ashamed or saddened by something out of her control. But this... it feels real. I don't think she's faking it, which makes this so much harder.

She looks genuinely sorry. The kind of sorry that tells me she'd do things differently if she could go back in time.

"I wish things could have turned out differently," I say. "You always meant the world to me."

Her bloodshot, sparkling blue eyes roll up at me, pleading.

I reach for her dangling hand and squeeze it. She perks up, wiping away the moisture on her face.

"I'm sorry," she says again, this time her lips trembling so badly it looks like she's about to convulse.

"I hope you find the help you need, Eve," I say. "And I hope you get better. I really do." I withdraw from her touch.

She stands upright, wrapping and rewrapping her fingers around the bars. "I-I will, Lucy. I promise. I'll get better. I'll do whatever they tell me I need to do. Therapy. Anything."

I turn to Commander Thompson and nod as a way of saying, *I'm ready to leave.*

As I walk away, Eve calls after me, sounding frantic. "Lucy? Lucy! I promise! I'll do better! Please. Please. Please." The last word jumps an octave. "Come visit me, okay?" she whispers.

I glance back one last time to watch as she frantically pushes her face against the bars, disfiguring herself. She claws at the air in front of her, desperately trying to see me leave. "I love you, my Lucy. I love you. Please come visit me again!"

My throat swells as Commander Thompson leads me back upstairs. When we return to the Intake Room, she turns to me. "You'll always be welcome to visit her, if you like."

I'm not sure how to respond to that. I feel torn. How is it possible to hate someone so much yet still love them deep down? Eve's a murderer, but I keep rationalizing to myself... convincing my mind that she didn't kill my mom and that my mom happened to be at the wrong place at the wrong time. I see that now. It still hurts, though. More than anything.

But then I remind myself that Eve murdered Vrin in cold blood. That was no accident.

She's evil.

Commander Thompson warms my shoulder with her touch. "You decide whenever you're ready."

"Thank you," I say, meaning it more than anything.

She leaves my side to help newcomers out of the rovers.

"Lucy!" comes Lucas's voice.

He lunges out of the rover without even opening the door. Behind him—and stepping out of the vehicle properly—are Emily and Abigail.

"Are you all right?" he asks, racing toward me. Before I can even respond, he throws his arms around my shoulders and squeezes me tight. "Lucy... I was so scared. I was scared that Eve—"

"She didn't hurt me," I say. "I'm okay."

He kisses my forehead hard and squeezes me

tighter.

"Lucy!" Emily calls out.

Lucas lets me go and I move on to hug Emily and Abigail.

"I almost had my hands on a laptop," Emily starts, and I beam at her.

"Don't even worry about it," I say. "Things got messy."

She laughs, though I can tell it's strained. "Yeah, you think? What the hell happened?"

Physically and emotionally drained, I sigh. "It's a long story."

Abigail nudges me. "One you'll tell us all about in Washington, DC?"

My eyes bulge out at the three of them. "What are you talking about? I thought we were staying here, on this base. Whatever this place is."

They all look more excited than I've ever seen them before.

"Freyda made the announcement," Lucas says. "They're rebuilding America. We should be moving out in a couple of months."

My throat swells so much it hurts. I'm happy, devastated, excited, and relieved—a combination I've never felt before. Lucas must sense I'm on the verge of a breakdown. He makes a come-hither gesture and smirks at me, inviting me into his arms again.

With my face pressed against his chest, I burst out into uncontrollable sobs.

Next to me, Abigail says, "What's up with her? Isn't this a good thing?"

Her voice sounds distant.

"She's been through a lot," Emily says. "Like, a lot. I think it's just coming out."

Emily knows me well. I'm lucky to have her here. And Lucas. I'm lucky to have my amazing friends. That gratitude only makes me cry harder, and Lucas kisses my head again.

Finally, I pull away, wiping my hot tears. "I-I think I need to nap or something."

Emily smirks. "You think?"

I laugh, sniffle, then wipe slobber away from my chin.

"Get your fluffin' hands off o' me," comes Mavis's voice. She shoos one of the soldiers away, telling him she's quite capable of walking on her own. Beside her, Perula climbs out of the rover, wincing painfully with every movement she makes. Mavis grabs a suitcase that's almost her height, pulls it out of the rover's back trunk, and slams it onto the cement floor.

"Mavis!" I shout out. "Perula!" I run toward them.

"Oh," Mavis says, huffing at me. "You think you can disappear and stop talkin' to us and then act like everything's *cool*." The word *cool* doesn't suit her.

"Give her a break," Perula says, approaching us with a wooden cane. "The girl's been busy."

Mavis sticks her nose in the air. "Yeah, too busy for us old hags, apparently."

Without a word, I throw my arms around them both, squeezing them as tight as I can. Perula hugs me back and Mavis stiffens like she's being electrocuted. But she doesn't pull away, and that speaks volumes.

"I missed you guys," I say.

Perula pets my hair back. "Ditto, kid."

Mavis huffs again. "Yeah, yeah. I missed ya too, ya good-for-nothin' monkey's ass."

Perula smacks her sister. "Mavis!"

Mavis makes a childish face, imitating her sister. "She knows I speak from my bloody, beatin' old heart."

They go on to bicker back and forth as I watch more rovers come in, and I wonder who I'll see next. After four or five drop-offs, Nola comes rolling in next with a group of teenagers.

"Nola!" I call out.

"L-Lucy?" she says, standing up in the rover. "Lucy!" She tries to jump out like the teenagers are doing, but gets stuck on the door. Grunting, she opens it by the handle and stumbles out, catching a soldier's arm before falling flat on her face. He helps her up and even offers to take her luggage. Unlike Mavis, she doesn't refuse the help.

"Lucy!" she calls out, leaving her bag with the soldier.

She throws her arms around me, her plump body feeling like a giant pillow. "Oh, Lucy. Are you all right? I'm... I'm so sorry. I should have never—"

I pull back and give her a stern look. "Let's forget the apologies, okay? Eve messed with a lot of our heads. I don't blame you or resent you for anything."

Her mouth tightens and her eyes fill with tears.

"I'm glad you're safe." I hug her again.

She wipes her face as I lead her to my friends, feeling like my family is whole again.

"I call dibs on the first house I see with a garage," Emily says, staring absentmindedly at the back wall.

Nola chuckles. "I don't think it works like that,

honey. I assume we'll go back to using regular currency and owning property the way we once did. And then there's the whole question about the government. We have no idea who will be in charge."

"You think they'll host an election?" Abigail asks.

Lucas bites his bottom lip. "You think? I don't know. But if they do, I hope Freyda becomes a candidate."

I smile at the thought. "President Freyda." It sounds a bit funny, but if anyone can do right by us, it would be her.

"Someone call my name?" Freyda says.

She approaches us with Gabriel at her side and I feel stupid for having referred to her as the president.

"As much as I appreciate the vote of confidence," she says, "we aren't going back to that sort of democracy. If you even want to call it a democracy."

I'm not sure whether to feel relieved or terrified at the prospect of trying out a new form of government. Or, is she saying they'll abolish the government entirely?

Commander Thompson joins our group and places a hand on Freyda's shoulder. "Actually, we will be operating as a council going forward. The council will consist of thirteen individuals, with representation from various racial and ethnic groups, sexual orientations, and gender identities, including nonbinary, two-spirit, and transgender. This will ensure that all voices are heard. And I can assure you that we'll thoroughly vet our council members. We will not tolerate any form of corruption."

"So... no President Freyda, then?" Emily jokes.

Commander Thompson doesn't smile. Instead, she turns to Freyda. "Unfortunately not, but we would like to offer you a seat on the council." She looks at Gabriel. "Both of you."

Gabriel and Freyda stare at each other as if they've been offered a winning lottery ticket.

"Wait... Are you serious?" Freyda asks.

Commander Thompson smiles and raises her chin. "Very."

Gabriel frowns, but it's obvious he's ecstatic about this. "Is this for Washington, DC, or the District of Columbia?"

"States have been abolished, Mr. Rodriguez. This is for all of America."

"One people," Freyda mutters.

"That's right," says Commander Thompson. "What do you say? Do you accept?"

Freyda still seems stunned by the offer. "I-I um," she sputters. "Of course. Of course, we accept."

"Absolutely," Gabriel says.

"Wonderful," Commander Thompson responds. "I'll get the paperwork ready and we'll announce the news this evening, during our celebration."

"Celebration?" I ask.

Commander Thompson's posture loosens like she's getting ready to stop being the commander for the night. "We're rebuilding America, Lucy. Wouldn't you say that calls for a celebration?"

Everyone is looking at me, waiting. For the first time in as long as I can remember, I'm genuinely happy. People are laughing, playing, and hugging each other everywhere I turn. No one seems stressed or uptight the way they did in Elysium or Eden. We're free—all of us.

I wish Mom were here to celebrate with us, but I know she's up there, watching. And if I were to guess what she's thinking, I'd say she's proud of how far I've come. Of how far all of us have come.

"When does the party start?" I say, chuckling.

Everyone laughs along with me, and Lucas pulls me into his arms.

"Party?" Mavis shouts. "Someone said party!"

I shake my head and laugh as Mavis starts dancing funny, smacking her feet on the hard floor.

"Tonight, we celebrate," Commander Thompson says loudly, her voice carrying throughout the Intake Room.

Freyda and I lock eyes.

"And tomorrow," I say, "we rebuild America."

Visit **www.shadeowens.com** for more works by Shade Owens.